Y0-CPC-973

NOV. 2017

Apollo Dreams

Syd Gilmore

Dee Jay Bee Publishing
1170 Del Rio Road
Powell, WY 82435

First Paperback Edition November 2017

This is a work of fiction. Any similarity to real persons, living or dead, is coincidental and not intended by the author.

ISBN 978-1542833981

Cover Design by Tom Martinek
Cover Illustration by Jason Winter
Author Photo © Chuck Novak

ACKNOWLEDGEMENTS

This book would not have been possible without the help and encouragement of several people. First, a big thank you to my sister Cindy; your help was invaluable during both the writing and publication of this book. Despite your own busy schedule, you still found the time to research historical information for me and worked behind the scenes as both secretary and advisor, sometimes under protest. Thanks to my brothers, Bill and Tom, for moral (and technical) support, and to my dad for never giving up on me. Thanks also to Lance, my editor, who caught my mistakes and convinced me it was all worth it.

I reserve my biggest thank you for Tom Martinek, my best friend in the world for over thirty years, for always having my back. No one has ever had a better friend and confidant. There is no one whose opinion I value more, and your complete honesty and unbiased suggestions helped make this a better book. Thanks also for all your help coming up with a brilliant cover design and for finding an artist talented enough to do it justice. You always know exactly what I want.

Syd

To Mom,

for encouraging me to dream

ONE

Countless billions of stars shone through the void, each pinpoint of light reaching out from millions of light years away. Even from inside his ship, through the filter of the viewscreen, Captain Billy Apollo thought they were beautiful. Unfortunately, he didn't have the luxury of appreciating their splendor at the moment; he was too busy defending the planet Fraxis Six, the newest member of the Galactic Federation, from an attack by the notorious gangster known as *The Butcher*, assassin, bodyguard, and right-hand man to the intergalactic terrorist *Mack the Black*, ruler of the Dark Realm.

Captain Apollo leaned forward in his command chair, the centerpiece of the bridge, and watched the enemy's small ship outmaneuver his massive starship.

The U.S.S. *Constellation One* was the finest ship in the fleet, but with a crew compliment of over five hundred lifeforms, it was not designed to maneuver against a tiny, one manned vessel of that size.

The Butcher swung his ship around and fired a volley of proton torpedoes at the *Constellation One*.

"Hard a port!" Captain Apollo commanded. "Mr. Shon-do, lock weapons and fire!"

"Impossible, sir, they are too fast," his alien First Officer replied.

"Very well. We'll have to go after him ship to ship. Mr. Shondo, you're with me. Mr. Sherman, you have the con."

Billy Apollo was the youngest captain in the history of the Galactic Fleet, and *Constellation One* was the newest and largest starship ever built. She was five-hundred meters from bow to stern and two-hundred-fifty meters port to starboard. The atomic engines were the latest technology, tested at more than twice lightspeed, and while that was essential for interstellar travel, it was currently not much use in orbit around Fraxis Six.

Fraxis was the twelfth planet to join the Galactic Federation of Planets, a multi species humanitarian alliance dedicated to peace and exploration.

Earth, Captain Apollo's home world, had been the ninth planet to enter the fold, more than a century ago, after their sister planet, Mars, approached them once they reached maturity.

When it was first discovered that life existed on Mars, two centuries ago, the people of Earth were fearful. It was a shock to discover they were not alone in the universe, forcing people to re-evaluate their belief systems and throwing the planet into chaos. In time, they came to understand their Martian neighbors were not their enemies, but in fact peaceful and benevolent, and eventually they became Earth's most trusted friend and ally.

They learned that millions of years ago, when dinosaurs were still the dominant species on Earth, Mars' oceans receded and the surface of the planet became uninhabitable. The Martian race was forced to move underground, living miles below the surface. For eons they watched their neighboring planet evolve until the human race rose up to dominate the planet and eventually mature into a species technologically advanced enough to venture out into space.

It was then that the Martians revealed themselves, cautiously at first, but eventually sharing their technology and, when it was decided they were ready, invited Earth to join the Federation.

At first, the governments of Earth were reluctant, but finally decided it was in the planets' best interest to accept the invitation, especially when it was revealed there were other malevolent species in the galaxy that did not share the Galactic Fleet's peaceful ideology. Of course, there were still some on Earth who did not trust the Martians or the Galactic Fleet, and never would, but they were few.

Captain Apollo was not among them. In fact, his first officer and trusted friend, Lieutenant Shondo, was a Martian. Far from the stereotype of a "little green man," Martians were more human than not, though there were differences. Their limbs were longer and thinner, with four digits on their hands and feet. In addition, having lived underground for millennia, the pallor of their skin was a pale grey and their over-sized eyes and ears gave them unusually keen sight and a kind of sonar. With the exception of Matt Sherman, his Chief Engineer, there was no other member of his crew he would trust to have his back in a dogfight.

They reached the hanger bay, seven decks below the bridge in the aft section of the ship. The cavernous room was enormous, housing a small fleet of a dozen one-man fighters and four ship-to-shore shuttles.

The *Constellation One* was constructed in space dock orbiting Earth and was incapable of landing, except in case of emergency. The shuttles could each hold twenty-five comfortably and provide ample transportation to and from any planetary body, with enough emergency supplies on board to last a month.

The fighters were more compact, maneuverable, lightning fast, and equipped with state-of-the-art weapons systems, including lasers and proton torpedoes. Captain Apollo and Shondo climbed into Fighter One and Fighter Two, respectively.

Apollo fastened himself into the cockpit of the fighter. "Bridge," he said into his built-in helmet microphone. "Bridge here," Lieutenant Matt Sherman replied.

"Depressurize the hangar bay and open space doors."

"Aye, sir."

With a *whoosh* of air, the deck emptied its artificial atmosphere and the doors opened to the vacuum of space. A moment later, both fighters exited the ship and honed in on their target.

The Butcher's ship was a modified shuttle, about a third of the size of *Constellation's* shuttles, built for attack and speed. The outer hull was overlaid with a stealth material, giving it a black appearance and rendering it virtually invisible to both the naked eye and sensors.

"Shondo, I can't see anything. Can you get a visual?"

"It is difficult, but I am able to make him out. Barely."

"Bless those Martian eyes of yours. I'll follow you in."

"He is entering the planet's atmosphere. He will be easier to see once he breaks through to the stratosphere."

"Copy that. Arm your weapons."

"Already armed, sir."

Captain Apollo followed Shondo into the planet's atmosphere, the skin of their fighters' super-heating and leaving them momentarily blinded by orange flames as they punched their way through. Then, the flames were gone, replaced with a purple sky and pink cotton-like clouds. Immediately in front of them, no longer concealed, was the Butcher's ship. The two fighters closed in.

"Shondo, attack formation delta-one," Captain Apollo said.

"Acknowledged."

The two fighters split away from each other, each flanking the enemy ship from different angles. The moment they opened fire, the Butcher suddenly dove and reversed himself, disappearing from view.

"After him!" the captain yelled.

Both fighters dove and followed. Before they could catch him, he flew into a populated area and opened fire, destroying several structures. Captain Apollo caught up and unloaded a barrage of laser fire into the Butcher's back panel; Shondo hit it with a proton torpedo, causing minor damage through its shields, but enough to cause him to retreat.

"Consider that a message from Mack the Black," a cruel voice said through the com system, as the Butcher's ship headed up toward space. Shondo turned his ship in pursuit.

"Let him go, Shondo," the captain said. "Let's go down and see if we can help clean up the damage. I doubt we've seen the last of him."

"Yes sir."

Shondo's fighter came up alongside Captain Apollo's, and together they descended to the surface of the planet. The ships landed simultaneously next to each other. Through his window, he could see a crowd had gathered.

"Looks like a hero's welcome," Shondo said over the com.

"Or a lynching," Captain Apollo said.

Through the hatch, it sounded like...

"Captain Billy...?"

...someone was calling...

"Billy...?"

...his name.

"BILLY!"

I popped the clothes dryer door open and poked my head out of the opening. "Yeah Mom?" I yelled.

"Come upstairs and get ready for bed, you have school tomorrow," Mom yelled back from upstairs.

"Okay, I'll be right up!"

I pulled my head back inside, turned myself around and climbed out of the door feet first. It was easier getting in than getting out.

It had been a lot easier when I first started pretending the dryer was my spaceship, around two years ago after the first Moon landing. I was seven years old then, and could fit a lot better. My ninth birthday was only a week away and I had grown quite a bit since then. I barely fit inside anymore. I won't have any problems fitting into the new dryer my mom just bought—I helped pick it out and made sure it was big enough—but that won't be delivered for another two weeks. I grabbed my Cub Scout flashlight (it was dark in there!) and ran upstairs.

At the top of the stairs, there were two choices: either you could go straight, out the side door of the house, or you could go right, into the kitchen. I ran through the kitchen into the living room where I found my parents sitting on the couch watching *The Ed Sullivan Show*, a staple of Sunday evening television for over two decades. The same show that introduced American audiences to The Beatles six years earlier, and the world hasn't been the same since. And Mr. Sullivan was still introducing new musical acts to the world.

Just this past year he had on a group of five brothers, a black family from Indiana who called themselves The Jackson Five, and you could just tell they were going to be big. The youngest one, Michael, was only three years older than me and he was already an amazing singer and dancer.

I sat down on the couch between my mom and dad to watch TV with them. Even though my mom had just called me upstairs to get ready for bed, I still had plenty of time. It wasn't even eight-thirty yet; bedtime wasn't 'til nine.

"What'cha watching?" I said, knowing full well what they were watching but asking anyway. On screen was a guy juggling flaming sticks.

"Ed Sullivan," Mom replied. "You just missed the cutest dog act." Mom knew I liked the animal acts; I especially liked chimps, ever since I saw *Planet of the Apes*, but dogs were okay too.

"Are you ready for next Saturday?" my dad said. "What time is the big event?"

He meant my birthday, but he meant something else too. April 11, 1970 is going to be a big day! Not only was it my birthday, but it was also the day Apollo 13 was taking off for the Moon. I just hope it doesn't rain. I'd been praying for nice weather next Saturday since we're planning to have my party in the backyard. Not just here in New Jersey, but at Cape Kennedy in Florida, too. I wanted the launch to go smooth—smoother than the day of my birth at least.

See, I was born dead. When I came out, I was strangled by my umbilical cord. It took a team of doctors six minutes to revive me, and according to my mom, the second she heard me cry she knew I would be all right. My entire head had been one big bruise, with varying shades of blues, blacks, and purples. Mom said I was the most colorful baby in the hospital nursery.

"My party starts around eleven," I said, "but Apollo 13 launches a little after one in the afternoon."

"Excited?" he asked.

"Oh man! I can't wait!" I said, bouncing a little in my seat. How could I not? Of course I was excited! Apollo 13 was launching on my birthday! NASA was giving me the ultimate birthday present.

For me, there was no greater honor than to have an Apollo mission go up on my birthday. Ever since Apollo 11, the world's first lunar mission landed on the Moon two years ago and I heard Neil Armstrong's voice from the surface of Earth's only natural satellite say, *"One small step for man... One giant leap for mankind,"* I was hooked. I fell in love with anything and everything to do with NASA and the space program. I guess you could say I was a space junkie.

So, when I first heard the news that the next Apollo mission was scheduled to launch on the same day I turned nine, I was so proud I announced it to everyone I met. By the end of the day, practically everybody I knew had heard the news, even grumpy Old Man Hughes who lived at the end of our cul-de-sac, the guy who was rumored to unload his shotgun full of rock salt at any kid who got caught cutting through his backyard. I never actually met anyone who had gotten a butt-load of salt, but I did my best to avoid him just the same. That's not to say I never cut through his yard; hopping the fence behind his garage could save a kid a good thirty minutes walking to or from school. I just never got caught. So far, anyway.

My dad finished his can of Budweiser and said, "Grab me another beer from the fridge, would you Sport?"

"Okay Dad," I said, getting up from the couch and going to the kitchen. He always called me Sport, just like the dad on that show *The Courtship of Eddie's Father*, about a cool single dad raising his young son in Southern California. Eddie and I were the same age. I have to admit, I was always a little jealous of Eddie. His dad was young and hip and they always did stuff together. My dad was a little older, definitely not hip, and we never really did anything together.

Don't get me wrong, I love my dad, he's a great guy that would do anything for me, it's just that he worked all the time. He sold insurance and was gone six days a week, from eight in the morning until nine at night. He would come home for supper whenever he could, so we could eat together as a family, but even then, we rarely saw him. His only day off was Sunday, and after church in the morning, he spent the whole day reading the Sunday newspapers and drinking beer. I honestly couldn't remember a single time we even played catch together.

I guess I shouldn't complain though, we had a nice house in a nice neighborhood and we had everything we needed. We even had a color TV and a summer bungalow on the Jersey shore. I just wish we could spend some more time together, that's all.

I had just taken a beer out of the refrigerator when my mom called, "Billy, did you feed Gomer and Oliver?"

"Not yet."

"Why don't you do that while you're in the kitchen, before you forget? There's some lettuce in the crisper drawer." She pronounced it "draw" in her northern New Jersey accent. We also said "cawfee" and "dawg" instead of coffee and dog.

"Okay Mom."

Gomer was the goldfish my big brother Sean had won two summers ago at Seaside Heights, on the Jersey shore; it was named after Gomer Pyle, the goofy redneck mechanic on *The Andy Griffith Show.* Oliver was my turtle, named after *Oliver Twist.* I belonged to the Glee Club at the local Boy's Club and we did a few songs from the musical *Oliver!* It was a big Broadway play and an even bigger movie; it won a bunch of Academy Awards including Best Picture. I know that because I own the soundtrack album and it says so on the cover. My mom bought it for me so I could learn the songs we sing in Glee Club. I even got to sing a couple songs by myself because I'm the only kid in the group who can copy an English accent perfectly. Last year we even got to sing at the Waldorf Astoria Hotel in New York City. It was supposed to be an honor, and I guess it was a pretty big deal because they wrote about us in the newspaper. My mom cut out the article.

I tapped a little fish food into Gomer's bowl, then fed Oliver some turtle food and gave him a little piece of lettuce before returning to the living room with a beer for my dad.

"Why don't you go upstairs now and get ready for bed," Mom said before I had a chance to sit back down and get comfortable. "And don't forget to brush your teeth. I'll be up in a little while to tuck you in."

"Okay Mom," I said. No point in arguing. "'Night Dad."

"Goodnight Sport."

I kissed my dad on his unshaved cheek and turned to go upstairs. I didn't kiss my mom since she would come up to say goodnight later.

I shared my bedroom with my twelve-year-old brother Sean. Besides being brothers, we were best friends too. Ever since I can remember, he called me his "Little Tiger," although lately he's been acting kind of moody.

Take tonight for instance. Just a few months ago, he would have been down in the basement with me playing spaceship (he was Shondo). Now all he wanted to do was lie on his bed listening to records with headphones on. Ever since he formed a band with some friends from school and he started hanging out with that new kid, Tim. I try my best not to annoy him but, since I didn't know from one day to the next what was gonna bother him, I usually failed. Dad says he's just going through puberty and it would pass eventually. I sure wish he would hurry up already.

Our room is pretty big with plenty of space so we each have our own halves decorated the way we want. We both have the same furniture: a single bed, a nightstand, a dresser, and a desk for homework. Other than that, we couldn't be more different. We pretty much like completely different things.

On my side, I have a poster of Captain Kirk and Mr. Spock from

Star Trek, next to one with Will Robinson, Dr. Smith and the Robot from *Lost In Space*; my two favorite TV shows. I watched them both every day after school along with *Batman* and *The Adventures of Superman*. Okay, so, I'm a geek. Sue me. I also have some NASA posters; one of the Apollo 11 Lunar Lander on the Moon, one of a rocket on a launch pad, and my favorite, one of Earth taken from outer space called *Big Blue Marble* hanging over my headboard. My dad gave that one to me last year for my birthday. The guys at NASA were right when they named it—it really does look like a big blue marble!

The comforter on my bed was dark blue with a pattern of shooting stars, planets, and rocket ships. Sitting on top of my pillow is my favorite stuffed animal: Snoopy from *Peanuts*, wearing an official NASA astronaut space suit and plastic helmet. Hanging from my ceiling over my desk is a model of the U.S.S. *Enterprise* that I put together all by myself, although Sean helped me with the painting and decals.

Sean's half of the room was totally opposite from mine. He has posters too, just different kinds, like a psychedelic "peace symbol" that glowed in the dark when you turned on a "black light" that was really purple. He also had a giant black and green *Frankenstein* monster face poster that glowed in the dark too. Then there was a poster for the movie *One Million Years B.C.* featuring a prehistoric lady with big boobs in a skimpy little caveman costume holding a spear.

Above his bed was a Beatles collage poster, and over his desk were four individual pictures of John Lennon, Paul McCartney, George Harrison, and Ringo Starr. Both the poster and the four pictures were included in a two-record set that came in a plain white cover that said *The Beatles* in raised letters, but everyone just called it *The White Album.*

Sitting on top of his nightstand was a record player that Santa left for him last Christmas. It was one of the expensive new ones that came with two speakers called "Stereo," whatever that means. Sean tried explaining it to me once, saying different sounds come out of each speaker, but I couldn't tell the difference. It all sounds the same to me.

"Hi Sean!" I said when I came into the room. He was on top of his bed with his eyes closed and his headphones on listening to music as usual, so I guess he didn't hear me. He had it turned up loud enough so I could hear it even without the headphones. He was listening to one of his favorite albums, *Sgt. Pepper's Lonely Hearts Club Band*, and right now, he was traveling with John Lennon in a boat on a river with tangerine trees and marmalade skies. I didn't really understand what the words meant and once I asked Sean to explain it to me. He told me *Lucy in the Sky with Diamonds* was about LSD. I didn't know what that was, so he told me it was acid, a kind of hippie drug. I told him that LSD stuff must make you pretty confused if the words to that song made any sense when you took it. When Sean said it made you trip, I said that didn't sound like much fun to me, the last time I tripped I skinned my hands and knees. That made him laugh. Sometimes I just don't get him.

Even though we're brothers, we don't look very much alike. At five feet six inches, he was nine inches taller than me, but he was also four years older, so that was normal. It was the other things that were different. He had a good athletic build; I was just skinny. He had long brown wavy hair; I had short blonde straight hair. He had perfect 20/20 vision; I wore brown tortoise-shell "Clark Kent" glasses. He had straight bottom teeth; mine were crooked because I sucked my thumb until I was almost five years old. About the only thing Sean and I had in common were our hazel eyes. He was definitely the better-looking one. He was handsome; I was goofy looking. At least I thought so. He got the looks, but I got the brains, talent, and imagination, so I guess it was a fair trade-off.

Since he didn't hear me when I came in, I walked over and shook Sean's arm to get his attention. He opened his eyes, took off his headphones, and picked up the needle from the record.

"Hey Tiger, what's up? Have fun in your spaceship?"

"Yeah, it was good, 'til Mom made me come upstairs. I wish you would play with me more. It's always better when you play too. Shondo gets to do more."

"I'm sorry, we're learning a couple of new songs, so I'm listening to try and get them down better," Sean said. "Maybe next time, okay."

"Yeah, okay," I said, but I doubted he really meant it. He told me "maybe next time" a lot lately, but he almost never actually did. "Hey Sean?"

"Yeah?"

"I wanted to ask you... do you think Octopus's Garden could play at my party on Saturday?" Octopus's Garden was the name of Sean's band.

"I'll ask the guys, but I don't see why not. Sounds like a good idea. We could use the practice playing in front of a live audience."

"Cool, thanks!" I knew he would do it.

"And I know just the song to play in your honor," he said. "Of course, we have to learn it first. It shouldn't be too hard though.

It's a pretty easy song and we have five days."

"Really? What song?" He had my curiosity up now.

"You'll find out next Saturday."

"Oh, come on. No fair! You can't tell me and then not tell me!"

Sean just smiled at me. "You don't want to ruin the surprise, do you?"

"Ahhhh!" I said in frustration, but I was smiling now too. Sean giggled at me, so I jumped on him. We laughed and rolled around and wrestled until we fell off the bed and then laughed even harder.

"What's going on up there?" Dad yelled from downstairs.

"Nothing!" we both shouted in unison, and laughed again.

"Well knock it off and get ready for bed," he yelled.

We separated from each other and I went to my dresser to get out my *Batman* pajamas.

"Hey Sean," I said, pulling the grey pajama top over my head.

"Yeah?"

"Can I come with you to band practice tomorrow?"

"No."

"Why not? You never let me go with you anymore. I love watching you guys play."

"Nobody wants a noisy little brat hanging around. We're there to practice, not baby-sit you."

"I won't make a sound. You won't even know I'm there."

"I said no!" he scolded. "Now drop it. You can't come. Period."

This is what I meant about him being moody. One minute we're laughing, playing, and having a good time, and the next he's mad and yelling at me.

"Fine," I said, more hurt than anything.

"Besides," he said, softening his tone, "we won't be able to practice your birthday song if you're there."

"Okay," I conceded, feeling a little better.

He got into bed wearing just a T-shirt and underwear; he stopped wearing pajamas about a year ago saying they were for kids. He put his headphones back on and put the record back on from the beginning.

"G'night Sean."

"'Night Tiger."

I got in my own bed, pulled the blankets up and cuddled with Snoopy while I waited for Mom to come up and tuck us in.

TWO

I was sitting at my desk, second from the front in the third row, minding my own business reading a *Star Trek* novel called *Spock Must Die!* I'm one of those nerdy kids that like to read just for the fun of it (sacrilege for a second grader!), which I suppose is the reason it happened in the first place. It was 7:50 Monday morning, still ten minutes before class started, when Butch Anderson, the class bully, snatched the book away from me.

"Hey, what's this?" he said, loud enough for everyone to hear.

"Give it back!" I protested.

"Hey, everyone! McBride's reading *Star Trek*!"

The entire class erupted in spontaneous laughter. Through the noise I heard the usual taunts that I was used to, like "geek" and "nerd," but then someone shouted, "What a space case!" and a new nickname was born. The only kid who didn't join in the taunting and laughing was my best friend, Matt Sherman. I could see in his eyes that he felt bad for me. He was frequently the victim. He was a space junkie like me; he even played spaceship with me during recess. We nerds tend to stick together.

"Come on Butch, give it back," I said in a lame attempt to appeal to his better half.

"Oh, you want it? Here catch!" he said and threw it across the room to Joey Martino, a bully-in-training who followed Butch around like a shadow and did anything he said. Butch, like me, was a year older than most of the class. The difference was my mom held me back a year before I started school; Butch was left back last year because of bad grades.

I got up and moved toward Joey in an attempt to get my book back, when he threw it to another kid. The next thing I knew I was in the middle of a full-blown game of "Keep Away." My poor book flew around the room from person to person with me trying desperately to snatch it from the air. Then Butch had it back in his possession and kept it. By now, I was almost crying in frustration. I held my hand out and pleaded with him, "Please, Butch. Can I just have my book back?"

He looked right at me, an almost evil gleam in his eyes. His lips curled back into the cruelest smile I'd ever seen. Then, without a word, he held my book out to me in both hands. Just as I reached for it, he ripped it in half, not along the spine so I could still read it but across the middle, throwing the ruined pieces in my face and saying, "Read this."

The laughing stopped. Everyone watched in silence as I bent down to pick up the two halves of my book. I couldn't make a sound I was so stunned. Tears were falling from my eyes, but I couldn't stop them. Butch just stood there with a huge self-satisfied grin on his face. Mercifully, the bell rang and everyone took their seats as Mr. McLean came in and put his briefcase on the Teacher's desk up front.

"Good morning!" he said cheerfully, oblivious to the cruel game that had taken place moments before.

"Good morning," the class unenthusiastically answered. He glanced around at the room at all the sullen faces and then looked right at me. I had already wiped the tears away, but I guess he could tell I'd been crying.

"Alright, what's going on?" he asked. No one said anything. "Billy? Is there anything you want to tell me?" I just shook my head. I knew better than to tell on Butch. So did the rest of the class.

"Alright then," he said, shifting his gaze to Butch, who sat there looking as innocent as can be. He was good at that. I'm pretty sure Mr. McLean knew that whatever it was that made the class scared into silence, Butch must've been behind it. But since he didn't see it himself, and nobody was willing to admit what happened, he couldn't do anything about it. "Since you're all such a gloomy bunch today, I think it's time for some calisthenics. Everybody stand up."

Everyone looked at each other wondering what was going on. Gym class wasn't until Friday. We all got up, murmuring nervously, and stood beside our desks. I glanced at Matt, two rows over from mine, but he just shrugged his shoulders, confused like everyone else.

"Okay, fingers up," he said, then demonstrated to the class by holding his hands up about a foot apart and poking his index fingers straight up. The class copied him.

"And... one, two, three, four." He pumped his fingers up and down and in and out, like miniature squat thrusts. "One, two, three, four..." We all laughed and followed his lead, exercising our fingers. After a couple minutes of this, the mood in the room completely changed. Even I forgot about Butch and my destroyed book, laughing at the absurdity of "finger exercises." Mr. McLean was one of those rare teachers that actually made school fun. Most of the time in his class, you didn't even realize you were learning.

"Alright, I think that's enough," he said. "You can sit down. Get out your science notebooks. You won't need your textbooks today."

I sat down with the rest of the class and bent down to search for my notebook. Our desks were the one-piece kind with an opening under the seats to store our books and papers. Mine was a mess. I'm not exactly the most organized kid in the world. I tend to just cram everything inside wherever it would fit. On top of my schoolbooks, I had a bunch of junk and old papers and tests stuffed in there too. My mom said I was a pack rat because I never threw anything out. The drawer in my desk at home was the same way. The thing is though, somehow, I always kind of knew where everything was. After a minute of digging, I found my notebook and put it on top of my desk.

"With less than a week to go, today we're going to talk about Apollo 13," Mr. McLean said, writing "Apollo XIII" on the green slate blackboard. I never understood why they call it a "blackboard" when it's green. Just like I never got "black lights," they're purple! Am I the only one who notices this stuff?

"Can anyone tell me the name of Apollo 13's commander?"

I raised my hand.

"Billy," Mr. McLean said.

"James Lovell," I said. "This is his fourth mission."

"Very good. Now, who can tell me the names of the rest of the flight crew?"

I raised my hand again.

"Anyone else?" he said, looking around the room. Mine was the only hand up. "No? Okay, Billy."

"Command Pilot John Swigert, and Lunar Pilot Fred Haise. Ken Mattingly was supposed to be the Commander, only he got grounded last week on account of he has German measles."

Mr. McLean stared at me for a minute with his mouth open in surprise. "Wow. That was excellent, Billy."

Someone in the back of class muttered, "Space Case" under his breath, causing chuckles. I shrank in my seat embarrassed.

"That's enough of that," Mr. McLean said. "At least someone is paying attention."

"Who cares anymore?" a kid named Bobby White said. "We've already been to the Moon twice now."

"Yeah," another kid, Dennis Smith, agreed. "Its like been there, done that."

"Why don't we go to Mars already?" someone else said. The class started talking at once. Mr. McLean raised his hands trying to restore order.

"Alright, quiet down. Quiet down, people." When everyone settled down, he said, "There's a lot about the Moon we still don't understand. We also don't know what the long-term effects of space travel are yet. One reason for these space flights is to see how the human body reacts to zero gravity. And traveling to Mars isn't like going to the Moon. A trip to Mars would take years to get there. Plus, we don't have the technology to get them home yet. We don't even know what they'll find even if we could send a manned mission. We need to send an unmanned robotic probe first. We're probably decades away from sending anyone to Mars. We need to take things slowly when we're talking about human lives."

"Is it true NASA is building a space station?" Matt Sherman asked.

"That's what I've heard, but it's still about three or four years away," Mr. McLean said. "They're calling the project 'Skylab' and it's supposed to be..."

Before he got to finish his sentence, there was a knock on the door. Mr. McLean crossed the room to answer the door and went out into the hallway to talk to whoever it was. A moment later, he came back into the room followed by the principal, Sister Mary Joseph, and a shy looking girl. She walked into the room with her head down looking at her feet and hiding her face so all we could see was her straight yellow hair.

"Good morning, class," Sister Joseph said.

"Good morning, Sister," the class responded together.

"I'd like to introduce you to the newest member of your class," she said. I noticed the girl trying to hide behind her. "Her family just moved here from Houston, Texas, and I want you all to give her a big Saint Anthony's welcome. Everyone, say hello to Lucy Ross."

"Hi Lucy," we all said together.

Lucy lifted her head for the first time, nervously looked around the room, and barely above a whisper said, "Hi."

What I saw when she lifted her head was the face of an angel. She had big, round blue eyes, a slight turned up nose, full lips with just a hint of a smile, and a cute little dimple in her chin. Her face was framed with shoulder length blonde hair. I thought she was the most beautiful girl I'd ever seen in my life. I could feel my heart pounding in my chest. If anyone asked me before today if I believed in love at first sight, I would have said no, but not now. I sat up straight in my seat and tried to comb my hair with my fingers. I wished I didn't wear glasses.

"Lucy, why don't you take a seat in the second row," Mr. McLean said.

Wait a minute. That was the seat right next to me! That desk was empty because nobody wanted to sit there next to the nerd. I guess they were afraid my geekiness would rub off on them or something. Oh no, here she comes! She looked right at me! And she smiled!

"Hi," she said to me.

"Hi," I said and smiled. I could see her eyes go right to my silver fake front tooth and look away. I slapped my hand over my mouth and must have turned three shades of red from blushing. I hate this stupid tooth! How could I have been so stupid?

My capped tooth was the result of a near fatal bicycle accident that happened a year and a half ago on All Saints Day when I was in the first grade. I remember the day because it was the day after Halloween and it was a Catholic holiday, so we had the day off from school. At Saint Anthony's we got all the Catholic holidays off, and the public schools got all the Jewish holidays off, so I guess it all worked out in the end.

I remember that morning: Sean and I had gone shopping with my mom and she bought us a rubber stamp printing press toy. Sean and I spent hours in the basement putting together a "newspaper." Then Sean went out to ride his bicycle to the corner deli to get some gum. He'd been gone a long time, so I decided to ride my bike to the store to see what was keeping him. I went outside to get my bike, only it wasn't there. Sean had taken my cool bike, and left his behind. My bike was a chopper with monkey bars, a banana seat, and a sissy bar in the back, and it was smaller and lower to the ground and fit my legs.

His was a big, old-fashioned Schwinn. My feet barely touched the pedals, but it was all there was so I took it. If I didn't try to use the seat, I could make it go, but it was wobbly and hard for me to control; it was made for someone bigger. I got it going pretty good, when a tow truck started coming down the hill after going up a minute earlier and turning around at the cul-de-sac, and I decided to race it. Bad idea. I was on the sidewalk and started pedaling as fast as I could...

And that's the last thing I remember until I found myself in the hospital being wheeled down the hall on a bed with doctors and nurses all around me and my mom crying at my side. They said I was awake the whole time, but I don't remember any of it. There's about an hour or so missing from my memory.

Here's what they figured happened: I was going pretty fast when I lost control of the bike. I hit either a tree or a telephone pole, flipped over the handlebars, and landed on my head in the street. They know it was the street from all the blood at the scene, plus they found gravel in my mouth. After I hit my head, I got up and started walking Sean's bike back home. By that time, Sean was coming up the hill behind me and was calling my name, but I didn't stop or turn around because I was in shock.

I made it home and put the bike back in the yard where it belongs, then walked into the kitchen calm as could be as if nothing was wrong and said something like, "Hey Mom, what's for supper?" My mom turned around from the stove, saw me covered head to toe in blood, and called 911.

My mom is one of those people that is totally calm in a crisis and didn't freak out. The next thing I knew, she was standing over me in the hospital asking if I wanted anything. I remember I told her to bring Snoopy and my G.I. Joes.

I also remember the nurses wouldn't let me go to sleep, making me really mad because I was so tired. My mom said later that was because I had such a bad concussion that they were afraid I would slip into a coma and die if I fell asleep. The doctor also told her my concussion was so bad, if I ever got another one I would either die or become a "vegetable," so I'm forbidden to play any kind of contact sports.

They said my nose flattened like a pancake on my face and if I had been any older, it would have broken, but since it was still just soft cartilage, it just bounced back into shape. The only scars from the accident I have now are a little scar under my nose, and my stupid silver fake front tooth. Maybe with this new nickname of "Space Case" they'll stop calling me "Tinsel Tooth," but I doubt it.

"I expect everyone to help Lucy feel at home here," Sister Joseph said. "Now I'll let Mr. McLean continue with his lesson. Miss Ross, if you have any questions or problems, come see me. My door is always open."

"Yes Sister, thank you," Lucy said. She glanced my way, smiled, and looked away again. That's when I realized I'd been staring at her like some love struck idiot, which I was. I wondered if she would wear my I.D. bracelet. Sean told me that when a girl wears your I.D. bracelet, that meant you were going steady. I didn't actually own an I.D. bracelet, but I wondered if she would wear it if I did.

Sister Joseph left the classroom and everyone started whispering to each other.

"Okay, settle down," Mr. McLean said. The whispering abruptly stopped.

"Lucy, why don't you tell us a little about yourself?"

She stood in the aisle next to her desk. I could tell she was nervous.

"Well, like Sister Joseph said, I just moved here with my family from Houston two weeks ago," she said with a cute little Texan twang. "My daddy's company transferred him to their headquarters in New York City. I have two sisters, one younger and one older. I like to climb trees and ride horses, but y'all don't have any horses around here." Some kids snickered when she said "y'all," and she got embarrassed and sat back down.

"Thank you, Lucy," Mr. McLean said. "You're going to need text books and stationary. Does anyone want to show Lucy where the supply room is?"

My hand shot up into the air at warp speed, waving back and forth in a blur.

"Okay Billy. Help Lucy with her books and come right back."

I got to my feet, a huge grin on my face. I didn't even try to hide my hideous metal mouth I was so happy. The rest of the class watched as we walked to the door. I heard Mr. McLean say, "Okay, back to Apollo 13. Who can tell me..." as I shut the door and turned back to face Lucy.

"The supply room is this way," I said grinning and pointing down the hallway. "Follow me."

"Billy, right?" she said. Ugh! I forgot to introduce myself!

"Uh, yeah," I said stupidly, offering my hand. "Billy McBride."

"Pleased to meet you, Billy McBride." She shook my hand. "I'm Lucy Ross."

We walked down the empty hallway in silence, our shoes echoing off the green tiled walls, neither of us knowing what to say to each other. I wasn't very good at small talk and I guess she wasn't either. I was always quiet around new people; it's when I get to know them that you can't shut me up.

The short walk to the supply room seemed longer than it actually was. It felt like it took forever, when in fact it was probably less than two minutes. I knocked on the door and Mrs. Thompson, the school secretary, was already waiting for us.

"Sister Joseph told me you'd be by to get your textbooks, so I already put together everything you'll need." She loaded us up with all the second grade textbooks, plus notebooks, loose-leaf paper, pens and pencils. Between the two of us, we had our hands full. "Do you think you can carry all that?" the secretary said.

"Yes ma'am," Lucy answered, and together we turned to return to class.

"This is a lot more than I thought it would be," Lucy said, as we walked back slowly, careful not to drop anything.

"I know, me too."

"Sorry you volunteered to help me?" she teased.

"No way!" I may have said a little too fast. "I don't mind helping you at all."

"Thank you, Billy. You're a real gentleman."

I felt myself blush. "So, how do you like New Jersey so far?"

"It's alright. Different. And I miss my friends back home."

"Yeah, I guess that's gotta be hard. 'Course I don't really have any friends, so I wouldn't know." Did I really just blurt that out?

"You must have friends. Everybody has friends," she said, sounding a little shocked.

"Yeah, well, there's this one kid Matt. But he's about the only one, besides my brother, and he's been kind of hot and cold lately."

"What about all those kids in class?"

"They just think I'm weird."

"Are you?"

"I guess."

"Well, weird or not, you seem nice. Now you have two friends."

I smiled again, just as we got back to class. "Thanks Lucy."

I knocked on the door and Mr. McLean opened it. He took some of the books from both of us and let us back inside.

Sean walked with his two friends and band mates, Ben Shaw and Jimmy Mason, the three quarters of a mile it took to get to Jimmy's house from school where they would meet up with Tim Bennet, the fourth member of the quartet known as Octopus's Garden. Tim was the only member of the group who didn't attend Saint Anthony's; he was thirteen and in the eighth grade at Mount Clayton Junior High, the local public school. Saint Anthony's went from kindergarten through eighth grade, whereas the public school system ran from kindergarten through sixth grade for elementary school, then seventh through ninth for junior high. Public school also had a more liberal dress code than parochial school, so Tim had the longest hair in the band, reaching almost two inches past his collar in back, and almost to the corners of his mouth in front, making him look more like a Beatle than any of the others. Sean was both impressed and jealous.

Sean wore his hair as long as he was allowed, past his ears and just touching his collar. Longer than that and he was in violation of not only the school's, but also his father's, dress code. His hair length was actually a big deal in the McBride household. Three summers ago, his parents had gotten into an argument over the length of their boys' hair. He remembered his father saying, "No son of mine is going to school with hair over his ears!" His mom had been much more sympathetic, countering with, "But Leo, it's the style." His father lost that argument.

He tried to dress the part of a rock star too, at least when he wasn't in his school uniform of navy blue slacks, white dress shirt, and navy blue tie emblazoned with the school crest. His "street clothes" were pretty mod. He, like Tim, tried to emulate The Beatles as much as possible, especially Ringo, though they changed styles so often it was difficult to keep up with the latest fashion. He usually wore bell-bottom pants, shirts with either stripes, flowers, or tie-dye, love beads around his neck, and five gaudy rings, three on his right hand and two on his left, which he had to remove during school hours.

Sean still felt a little guilty from banishing Billy from band practice today. He knew the little guy just wanted to be with his big brother and feel like he belonged. And most of the time he really didn't mind Billy coming with him wherever he went and trying to copy everything he did. But now he was getting older, he would be thirteen in a couple months, and sometimes he just wanted to do his own thing and hang out with his friends without his little brother tagging along. Especially now that he was a drummer in a rock band.

He'd started drum lessons a couple years ago and he practiced hard until he was good enough to join a band. His dad recognized his talent, and on his teacher's recommendation, bought him a "real" drum kit. He had a red pearl Ludwig kit with a bass drum with the band logo stenciled on the front, a floor tom, two tom-toms, a snare drum, and two cymbals.

They played songs by The Beatles, The Rolling Stones, The Who, The Monkees, Herman's Hermits, and a few others. He loved The Beatles—no, make that worshipped—but so did almost everyone else under the age of thirty, especially girls, which was really the only reason for playing in a band in the first place.

Tim was already at Jimmy's house, waiting by the side of the garage not visible from the street. He wore red bell-bottom pants, a purple T-shirt with lime green peace symbol on the front, and black Converse All-Stars. He casually leaned against the building smoking a cigarette. To Sean, he was the epitome of cool.

"Put that out! Are you crazy?" Jimmy said when he saw Tim smoking. "If my mom catches you we can forget about using my garage to practice. Not to mention I'll probably be grounded for a month!"

"Okay, chill out, man," Tim said, exhaling a cloud of smoke. "She can't even see us from here. Don't be such a square." He defiantly took one more puff before he dropped it on the ground and stepped on it. "Happy now?"

"Look, I just don't want to get in trouble," Jimmy said.

"You worry too much," Tim chided.

"Just forget it, the both of you," Ben interjected. "No harm done, right? Let's just get on with practice, okay."

"Yeah, okay," Tim said.

"Fine," Jimmy agreed.

After Jimmy unlocked the garage door to let the others in, he disappeared inside the house to change out of his school uniform. Ben stripped off his school shirt and tie down to his undershirt, while Sean elected to practice shirtless due to how much he sweat during rehearsal. Playing the drums was definitely a workout. He took his seat on his throne behind the drums just as Jimmy returned wearing jeans and a plain white T-shirt and barefoot.

"Hey guys," Sean said, "I got a gig for us if you're interested. How would you feel about playing my little brother's birthday party this Saturday?"

"Yeah, sure," Ben said.

"Sounds good, man. Billy's a cool little dude," Jimmy said.

"How much does it pay?" Tim said.

"Nothing," Sean said. "It would be like a birthday present."

"Yeah," Ben added. "Besides, it'll give us a chance to play in front of a real audience, even if it is just a bunch of second graders."

"We do need the practice," Jimmy agreed.

"Alright, alright. I just think we should get paid."

"Next time," Ben said.

"Okay, if that's settled, let's practice," Sean said. He waited while the other three picked up their instruments.

"What do you want to do first?" Jimmy said.

"How about, *Eight Days A Week*?" Ben suggested.

"On four," Sean said and raised his sticks. "One, two, three, four!"

The boys played for almost two hours, practicing almost a dozen songs. They were less than perfect, but not bad. Some songs sounded better than others did, but with more practice, they could be really good. Rehearsal was over when Jimmy's mom flashed the overhead light, signaling that dinner was almost ready and Jimmy would have to come inside to eat.

Sean stood up and stretched, grabbing his towel and wiping off the sweat from his face. Tim un-strapped his imitation Hoffner bass, a cheap copy of the same one Paul McCartney played, and rested it in his guitar stand. Ben put his Fender Stratocaster in his guitar case and went in the house to call his mom. Jimmy leaned his own guitar against his amplifier.

Ten minutes later, the *Beep! Beep!* of a car horn sounded outside. "That's my mom. You want a ride Sean?" Ben and Sean lived on the same street.

"No thanks, I'm gonna walk home with Tim," he said, as the four boys walked outside together.

"Okay. See you guys tomorrow," Ben said.

"Yeah," Sean said, "see you at school."

"See you tomorrow," Jimmy said, locking the garage and heading into the house.

"Later," Tim said, as he and Sean began walking along the sidewalk. When they were about a block away, Tim pulled a pack of Marlboros from his pants pocket and put a cigarette between his lips, lighting it with a silver Zippo lighter.

"Can I have one of those?" Sean said.

Tim gave Sean a cigarette, flicked his lighter, and held the flame to the tip. Sean sucked in a lung full of smoke and immediately started choking. It wasn't his first cigarette, both his parents smoked and he had sneaked some of theirs a few times to try it, but he hadn't quite gotten the hang of it yet.

"Take it easy, man," Tim instructed. "Take smaller puffs."

Sean followed his friend's advice. The next puff he didn't cough quite so much.

"That's it," Tim said encouragingly, as though he was an expert, when in fact he had only started smoking a few months ago and was still the victim of coughing fits himself. He took a puff from his own cigarette, inhaled deeply, and exhaled slowly. Sean copied him, and this time, didn't cough at all. "Cool, now you got it."

Sean and Tim walked and smoked together in silence for the next few minutes.

"So, how old is your brother?"

"He'll be nine on Saturday."

"You must really like him if you want us to play his party for free."

"He's okay."

"Man, I can't stand my little brother. I swear, sometimes I wish he would just drop dead. He's always ratting me out and getting me in trouble."

"Billy's not like that."

"Yeah, keep telling yourself that. They're *all* like that." Tim tossed his cigarette butt on the ground and crushed it with the toe of his sneaker, never missing a step. "You smoke grass, right?" he blurted out.

"Of course," Sean lied, stepping on his own cigarette.

"Groovy. One of these days I'll have to introduce you to this guy I know. We can go over his house and party. You'll dig him; he's really a cool cat. And he's always got the best grass."

"Groovy," Sean repeated, swallowing nervously as a lump suddenly formed in the back of his throat. He still had the taste of smoke in his mouth, and that, combined with the sudden fear of smoking marijuana, made him want to throw up. He fought the impulse and held it in, not wanting to look like a square in front of the coolest kid he knew. He couldn't let Tim know he was actually scared to try it.

He knew all The Beatles smoked grass, so he figured it couldn't be that bad, but he'd seen all the hippie burnouts drugged up in the park, and they were all dirty and smelly and he was afraid that could happen to him.

"Hey, are you alright, man? You look kind of pale," Tim said.

"Yeah, I'm fine. Just a little light headed from the cigarette I guess."

"Yeah, they can do that. Especially if you're not used to it. Almost feels like getting high. Almost," Tim said, and gave Sean a knowing nudge with his elbow. They stopped at the bottom of a steep hill.

"Well, this is my street. See you tomorrow at practice," Sean said.

"Right on. See you tomorrow. Maybe I'll bring a joint."

"Cool," Sean said and started up the street. He secretly hoped Tim would forget to bring the joint.

I'd spent the last couple of hours playing in our unfinished basement waiting for supper to be ready, just not in my spaceship. The room was essentially one big open space with no actual rooms, though the basement was broken up into different areas.

The bottom of the stairs emptied out onto the center of the room. Directly in front was a brick chimney connected to the furnace behind it. Immediately to the left was the laundry area, set up with my mom's ironing board, sewing machine, washing machine, and my beloved dryer/spaceship. To the left of the washing machine was a utility sink, and in the corner was an upright freezer.

On the far right opposite wall, behind the furnace, was my dad's workbench where he kept assorted tools, a vice, and old paint cans on the floor underneath. Next to the furnace was the hot water heater. The rest of the basement was empty space.

In the center of the room, I had just put the finishing touches on an elaborate Hot Wheels racecourse, and stood back to admire my handiwork. The starting line was clamped to the top rung of my dad's seven-foot ladder—you needed gravity to achieve the fastest speeds from the miniature hot rods. From there, the orange track fell to a near vertical drop leveling off into a double-loop followed by an S-turn, a right curve into a short straightaway into another S-turn, then a left curve into a long straightaway to the finish line.

I selected my favorite car, a gold-flaked Corvette I got by trading with Brian Chumly at school last year, and climbed the ladder to the top. I set the car in place against the plastic start-bar and poised my index finger over the trigger that raised the checkered flag. I counted to myself, "Five, four, three, two... one!"

I hit the switch; the start-bar released the car—I watched as it dropped down, defied gravity through the twin loops, and navigated the rest of the course without flying off until it cruised through the finish line and off the track, slowing to a stop on the cement basement floor.

I was so startled by the applause that erupted from the stairs I almost fell off the ladder, but caught myself and averted disaster.

"Wow!" Sean said, coming off the bottom step just in time to witness the car flying around the track. "That was awesome! How long did it take you to set all that up?"

"A couple hours," I said, climbing down the ladder to retrieve my car. As I crossed in front of Sean, my nose picked up an all too familiar odor. “You smell like smoke.”

“Shhh. Don’t tell, okay.”

“I don’t want you to smoke.”

“I only tried it. Don’t worry. I didn’t even like it that much. If you don’t tell Mom and Dad, I’ll play Spaceship with you.”

“When?”

“I don’t know, how about Saturday?”

“Saturday’s my birthday.”

“Okay, Sunday then.”

“How about tonight after supper?”

“Not tonight, I’m kind of beat from practice.”

“But I wanna play tonight. You do this all the time. You say you’ll play with me and then when I want to you always have some excuse.”

“I said I’ll play Sunday.”

“But that’s a week away!”

“Sorry. Take it or leave it.”

“Play tonight or I’ll tell that you were smoking.”

“That’s blackmail!”

“Yup,” I said, smugly. I had him this time. He was going to play with me, or else.

“Well, you can forget it now.”

“Oh, come on! Please?”

“You know, it’s funny, I *just* defended you not fifteen minutes ago. My friend Tim said all little brothers were tattletales, and I said, ‘not *my* brother.’ But you know what? He was right.”

“I was only kidding! I’m not really gonna tell on you.”

“I don’t care!” Sean yelled. “I’m not playing Spaceship with you ever again."

I stood there stunned. "But..."

"I don't want to hear it."

"I'm sorry," I pleaded. "I won't tell, I promise!"

"Get out of my way," Sean said, pushing past me and stomping angrily up the stairs.

I don't know how long I stood there staring off into space, trying to figure out what just happened. It could have been a minute or it could have been an hour. Finally, I just walked over to the clothes dryer and climbed inside.

THREE

Hundreds of cheering Fraxens greeted Captain Apollo as he walked through the main street toward the city's central square. He waved to the crowd as he climbed up the steps to the Primary Hall, home of their benevolent sovereign, Empress Lucinda. He stood anxiously awaiting the arrival of the leader of Fraxis Six. It was the first time anyone from the Federation was meeting with the Empress herself.

All negotiations regarding the planet's acceptance to the G.F.P. had been conducted through diplomats and ambassadors. If half of what was rumored about her was true, she was an extraordinary woman. A hush fell over the crowd, as the royal Vizier strode forward to address the masses.

"People of Fraxis," he announced, his voice amplified by a hidden apparatus, "please welcome Her Grace, Lucinda, Empress of Fraxis Six." Jubilant applause erupted from the throng.

Captain Apollo did a double take as she walked through the doors of the hall. She was a vision of beauty the likes of which he'd never seen. She wore all white robes, flowing regally with every graceful step she took. Her fair complexion only enhanced the supple curves of her face, accented with a slight dimple in her chin. Her blonde hair was held in place by a white tiara, a large blue stone embedded in the center, matching the color of her eyes.

Captain Apollo's heart raced as she stood beside him to speak to her people. She raised her arms, signaling silence. Her subjects respectfully complied.

"Citizens of Fraxis," she began. "Today we faced a ruthless enemy. Mack the Black sent one of her minions to attack us to try to test our resolve. It was a blatant attempt to frighten us into submission. I have heard some among you say we brought this upon ourselves when we joined the Galactic Federation of Planets."

A low murmur spread throughout the audience. She raised her arms again and continued, "I tell you this: our very survival depends on our new alliance. Mack the Black did not attack us today because we have joined with the Federation; she attacked us because we did not submit to her. Because she has been unable to conquer us!"

The crowd reacted with loud applause. Empress Lucinda raised her hands for silence.

"If the attack did not come today, then it would come next week, or next month, or next year. Her forces grow stronger every day, and soon we would no longer be able to defend ourselves. But there is strength in numbers and that is why I have chosen to ally ourselves with the Federation. We will not be defeated!"

Another loud cheer rose up.

"With me here is a representative of our new show of strength. I introduce to you Captain Billy Apollo, commander of the starship

Constellation One, currently orbiting our planet. He fought off the first attacker, saving us from untold destruction. He and his people are our allies, our protectors, our heroes! We shall welcome and honor him as a friend of Fraxis!"

Another cheer went up, louder this time. The Empress took Captain Apollo's hand in hers and raised them both in the air to symbolize their two peoples union.

To Captain Apollo she said, "Please join me." She released his hand and turned to return to the Primary Hall. Her Royal Vizier bowed slightly in their direction, signaling he follow him. Captain Apollo followed the Empress into the building, an impressive white marble structure with six giant Roman-style columns lining the front, more aesthetic than structural.

Inside was open and spacious with thirty-foot high ceilings, a long red carpet running the length of the room leading to a raised platform with an ornate throne perched on top. Beautiful embroidered tapestries lined the walls depicting scenes from Fraxis history that Captain Apollo couldn't even begin to guess.

Two elegantly robed figures flanked either side of the throne, each holding a long spear vertically at their sides, points in the air. They were largely ceremonial, but also formidable weapons should the need arise. Lucinda led him down the carpet to the throne. Captain Apollo stood in place at the bottom of the platform as Lucinda took her place on the throne.

"Captain Billy Apollo," she began, "I would like to personally thank you for defending us. You have proven that my planet's recent decision to join your allegiance was the correct one."

"With all due respect, Highness, thanks isn't necessary. We will always support our members. I only wish I'd been able to prevent the damage they caused to your city. I feel personally responsible for allowing the Butcher to get through our defenses."

"Never-the-less, Captain, you are very brave. You will stay and dine with me."

"That's very generous, but I..."

"Please?"

Captain Apollo was about to continue with his protest, when he looked into her gentle, almost pleading eyes.

"Sure," he said, and smiled.

*****

The dining room table was enormous; intricately hand carved from a dark green indigenous hardwood, it was ten feet wide and sixty feet long and could easily seat at least a hundred. The room itself was triple those dimensions with high vaulted ceilings lined on both sides with high arched windows at ten foot intervals.

Empress Lucinda sat in an elegant high backed chair at the head of the table, Captain Apollo flanking her on the right. With the exception of the Royal Server, who stood silently behind Lucinda, they were alone in the room. On the table was a feast featuring some of Fraxis' finest foods.

"Try the Xanderbeast, Captain," Lucinda said, offering a plate of roasted meat. "It's one of my planet's most succulent delicacies."

The captain helped himself.

"Delicious. In fact, everything is excellent. But I hardly think I'm worthy of such a magnificent banquet."

"I disagree, Captain," she said. "Without your aid, we surely would have sustained much heavier damage. We have limited defenses."

"What I mean is we should have been able to protect you from any damage at all. What I can't figure out is why Mack the Black attacked you in the first place. Fraxis Six has limited natural resources."

"You forget, Captain," she said, "that I am to be the guest keynote speaker at the upcoming peace conference on Alpha Centuri. I will be unveiling the plans for a new force field technology developed by our scientists capable of encompassing an entire planet. Imagine a prison moon with no escape."

"If Mack the Black got hold of such a device, she could pervert it into a devastating weapon," Captain Apollo said with growing concern. "Where are these plans, Empress?"

"I had them implanted in my brain. There are no other copies."

"Do you think that's wise?" Captain Apollo said. "If Mack the Black learns you have the plans, your life will be at serious risk."

"Then I guess you'll have to protect me, Captain," she said with a smile and a wink.

Captain Apollo returned the smile.

Just then, a loud alarm bell started ringing outside. The Empress sprang to her feet.

"What is it?" Captain Apollo said, getting to his feet.

"We're under attack!"

I reached over to my nightstand without even lifting my head off the pillow and slammed my fist on my Mickey Mouse alarm clock, silencing the shrill noise of the bells.

I rolled over, groaned loudly, and slowly opened my eyes. I

fumbled for my glasses, found them next to my souvenir clock from Disneyland, and put them on my face, bringing the world into focus. I started wearing glasses last year when it was discovered my mediocre grades were due to the fact that I couldn't see the blackboard. It wouldn't be so bad if I could get a cool pair like the ones John Lennon wears, but I'm stuck with the big brown plastic ones.

I threw off the covers, swung my legs over the side of my bed, and sat up.

"Sean," I said sleepily, "it's six-thirty. Time to get up."

He just groaned and rolled over, burying his head under the pillow. I got out of bed, stumbled to the bathroom, relieved myself, and then made my way down the stairs to the kitchen, still half-asleep. I couldn't believe it was Wednesday already. Only three days left until my birthday and Apollo 13.

Mom was preparing breakfast when I sat down at the table. She insisted on us having a good breakfast to start the day. Today, she was making toaster waffles with Tang and milk for Sean and me; half a grapefruit, coffee, and cigarettes for her and Dad. Like Sean, my dad had a hard time getting started in the morning.

Even this early, with her hair a mess and no makeup on, Mom still managed to look pretty. She was average height, thin but not skinny, and she had a nice face with kind eyes. We were Irish, so she had fair skin and freckles with medium brown hair that had natural red highlights that seemed to shine when the light hit it just right. She wore a white bathrobe over her nightgown and had baby blue slippers on her feet.

"Good morning," she said, pouring me a glass of Tang, the NASA astronauts' official breakfast beverage, so naturally I had to have it too.

"Morning," I grumbled.

"Where's Sean?"

"He's still in bed."

She walked over to the stairs, situated between the kitchen and living room, and shouted, "Sean! Get out of bed and come down and get your breakfast!"

"Five more minutes," came the reply from upstairs.

"Now!" Mom insisted. She was putting a plate of waffles in front of me when Sean sleepwalked into the kitchen and plopped down into the chair next to me, his eyes thin slits. He hadn't bothered to put on his robe, coming down in just his T-shirt and Fruit of the Looms. Dad wandered in a minute later wearing a T-shirt and over-sized striped boxers. Like father, like son. He kissed my mom, poured himself a cup of coffee, lit a cigarette, and sat down at the table. Mom served Sean his waffles, gave Dad half a grapefruit, and finally sat down to enjoy her own breakfast. I tried to avoid eye contact with Sean; every time I glanced up at him, he was glowering at me.

"Eat up," Dad said. "You're going to have to walk to school today. I have an early appointment first thing, so I can't drive you."

Sean and I both groaned. We did not approve.

"Can't you drop us off on your way?" Sean said.

"Sorry, it's in the opposite direction and I have to be there by eight o'clock. Unless you want me to drop you off forty minutes early."

"Nooooo," we both said in unison.

"Can't Mom drive us?" I asked.

"I have to wait for the plumber," Mom said. "He's coming

sometime this morning to install the new faucet, but I don't know exactly when he'll show up."

"It's not that far," Dad said. "And it's a beautiful day."

We ate the rest of our breakfast in silence, resigned to the fact that we wouldn't be getting a ride to school. Most days we walked home from school, but dad usually dropped us off in the mornings. For some reason, walking to school seemed like much more of a chore than walking from school.

I sat as quietly as I could, but Sean had no trouble showing off his anger, aggressively attacking his waffles with a fork and slamming his juice glass down on the table. Mom ignored him, but I guess Dad had had enough of Sean's behavior, because he threw down his napkin and stood up from the table.

"Alright, that's enough!" he shouted. "Knock it off unless you want my belt when I get home tonight." Sean sat still, his eyes on his plate and his face screwed up in an angry grimace. "Do you understand me?"

"Yes," Sean said bitterly.

It was an empty threat and we both knew it; Dad never hit us with his belt. In fact, he never really hit us at all. Still, when he threatened us with his belt, you knew he was really mad.

"I don't know what's gotten into you lately, but it better stop. I'm getting fed up with this attitude of yours. Why can't you be more like your brother? You don't see him making a fuss about walking."

Oh, great. Why did he have to bring me into it?

"Oh that's right, perfect little Billy! Maybe it's because I'm not a total wuss! Why don't you just admit that you love him more than me?"

“Sean!” Mom gasped.

“It’s true! You’re always telling him how *special* he is. When’s the last time you told me *I* was special? You wanna know why he doesn’t have any friends? Because he’s weird. Do you know what they call him? ‘Space Case.’ Because all he does is go around pretending he’s some kind of stupid astronaut. He’s special alright!”

All during Sean’s sudden tirade, I had been shrinking down into my chair. It’s not as if he was lying, but the truth hurt, and each word cut deeper and deeper. And worst of all, he was telling it to Mom and Dad! I didn’t want them to know what a total loser I was and how all the kids hated me.

And how did Sean even know about them calling me “Space Case?” That one only started Monday. Never underestimate the underground kid network and the speed of a new derogatory moniker spreading throughout the school, even to the upper grades.

I couldn’t take any more. I sprung from my chair and ran to the basement, taking the stairs two at a time and right to the refuge of my spaceship, slamming the hatch closed behind me. I could still hear them upstairs arguing, but I couldn’t make out what they were saying. Then it got quiet and the bickering stopped. A few minutes later, I heard a soft knock on the metal door of the dryer.

“Honey?” Mom said in a soothing voice. “Are you okay?”

“Go away,” I said. I didn’t want to talk to anyone, not even Mom.

“Sean doesn’t mean those things.”

“It sure sounds like he means it.”

“He was just angry. I’m sorry he took it out on you.”

“What did I do to him?”

“I don’t know, sweetheart. Why don’t you come out of there?”

I opened the door and looked at my mother. I stopped crying, but my face was still wet. I hated that I cried all the time, but I couldn't help it. Maybe Sean was right. Maybe I was just a wuss.

"Am I really as weird as he says?" I asked.

Mom wiped my face dry with her thumbs and said, "I'm going to tell you a little secret. Everybody's weird."

"Really?"

"Uh-huh."

"Even Sean?"

"Even Sean."

"Even you?"

"Especially me," she said with a laugh. "But you know what? I think you are the sweetest, smartest, most creative little boy I've ever known, and I wouldn't want you to be any other way. You just keep on being you and don't worry about what anybody else thinks. They're all just jealous. And besides, I love you just the way you are."

I grinned at her, reached out, and hugged her as tight as I could.

"Thanks Mom, I love you."

"Sean, slow down," I pleaded. He purposely ignored me and quickened his pace. We were headed for the shortcut behind Old Man Hughes's garage and I was terrified, as usual. I didn't want to get shot in the butt with rock salt.

Jeremiah Hughes was the scariest, most seldom seen man in the neighborhood. Tall and thin with sparse, stringy grey hair, straggly whiskers, and a mouth down-turned in a permanent sneer, he could make your blood run cold with just a look from his one good eye.

Every once in a while you could catch him outside doing yard work: either mowing his lawn, or trimming his bushes, or on his knees puttering around in the flower bed that went around the borders of his house. Mostly, you would just catch him spying on you through one raised slat of his window blinds, his old bloodshot eye staring out.

One time last fall, I had been riding my bike on the sidewalk in front of his house, when my front tire hit a small rock and caused me to temporarily lose control and veer up onto his lawn. Seconds later, Mr. Hughes's front door flew open and the old man appeared, screaming at me to get off his lawn. I pedaled away as fast as I could, never more scared in my life!

Everyone knew the story: one time, back in the 50's, a kid not much older than me got caught hopping the fence behind Mr. Hughes's garage. They say Old Man Hughes got his shotgun and shot him right in the butt with rock salt. The cops wouldn't do anything because they said he was defending his property from trespassers, but the kid couldn't sit down for a month! And now we were headed straight for his yard.

"Sean, pleeeease!"

Sean finally stopped and turned around to face me.

"What?"

"You're walking too fast."

"So quit following me if you can't keep up."

"What if Old Man Hughes catches us?"

"Take the long way and go around if you're so scared."

The long way meant adding another half hour to the walk to school, and it was mostly uphill, whereas the shortcut was mostly level ground.

At the very top of our street was the city power company. To the right was Mr. Hughes's house, on the left was Mr. Sullivan's house, the one with the little black lawn jockey in front that my mom says was an embarrassment to the whole neighborhood. In the center between the two houses was a ten foot high chain-link fence with barbed wire along the top, erected to keep trespassers off the power company grounds.

Behind the fence were three enormous, square red brick buildings generating electricity twenty-four hours a day, seven days a week. Four legged aluminum towers, as wide as a house, stretched a hundred feet high into the air. The towers ran through the city, spaced one hundred-fifty yards apart, along grass fields. Dozens of black electric cables, as big around as my legs, were strung along the tops of the towers, bringing electricity throughout the city. The electrical fields started behind Mr. Hughes's property and passed directly behind the school playground. Cutting through Mr. Hughes's yard and walking through the fields took about twenty minutes to get to school. Twenty-five if you took your time.

The alternative meant you had to walk to the bottom of our hill to the end of the street, then turn right and walk about three blocks around the power company, then right again and back up the hill. It took almost half an hour of walking around the power company, just to get back to the same starting point on the opposite side.

"I don't want to walk all that way by myself," I whined.

"Then shut up and quit being a wuss."

It was obvious Sean wasn't going to listen to me, and I didn't want him to be any madder at me than he already was. Maybe if I showed him that I wasn't afraid—wasn't a *wuss*—Sean would like me again. Or at least not be so mad at me. Even though Sean was being mean to me right now, I knew it was only temporary and it would blow over. Eventually. After all, he was still my big brother and we loved each other, no matter what. Right? I stayed quiet and followed closely behind.

We approached Mr. Hughes's property from the next-door neighbor's side on the right. A row of tall hedges separated their properties, and we sneaked along behind them on the side of the house. So far, there was no sign of the old man. When we made it to the side of his garage, I exhaled a sigh of relief, which startled me a little; I didn't even realize I'd been holding my breath. Now out of sight of the house, I followed Sean around to the back of the garage, past a stack of medium sized terra-cotta planters, an old-fashioned, rusted out, manual push lawn mower, and a long forgotten bald tire, to the opposite corner and a four-foot high chain-link fence that sagged in the center from countless young feet hopping over.

Sean hopped the fence easily, leaving me on the other side to fend for myself. Even at only four feet, it was still too high for me to climb over without help, especially in my school uniform and good shoes. I pulled the old tire over to the base of the fence and stood on it to give myself a boost. I made it over and had to run to catch up with Sean.

"Hey, wait up!" I yelled. I finally caught up to him, but he was walking so fast I had to take two steps for every one of his. "Sean, come on."

He stopped short and spun on me so quickly I had to jump back in surprise. "Why can't you just leave me alone?!" he shouted.

"I just want to tell you I'm really, really sorry, okay."

"Fine. You're sorry. Now leave me alone."

"Won't you forgive me? Please? I hate it when you're mad at me like this."

"Why should I? That was really low, threatening to tell on me like that."

"I didn't mean it. I wouldn't really tell on you. I was just trying to get you to play with me!"

"Yeah, well, that's a pretty dirty way to get me to play."

"I know and I'm sorry. I'll never do it again, I promise."

"And you're not gonna tell Mom and Dad about me smoking?"

"Cross my heart and hope to die."

"Alright, I'll forgive you," he conceded.

"Thank you," I breathed, grinning. It felt like a huge weight was lifted off my shoulders.

"But this is the last time," he warned. "One more time and that's it."

"Don't worry, I'll be good," I promised.

We didn't say anything else the rest of the way to school. We didn't have to. All was right with the world again. I was so happy I was practically skipping.

"That about does it ma'am," the plumber said, wiping his hands on a soiled work rag he pulled from his rear pants pocket. He wore a blue work shirt with the name *Tony* embroidered over the left breast pocket. He'd just finished installing a brand new lever-style faucet on the kitchen sink.

"Just lift the lever," he said demonstrating. The water flowed freely from the tap. "Tilt left for hot, and right for cold. Simple."

"Thank you so much, Tony," she said.

"My pleasure, Mrs. McBride. Is there anything else I can do for you?" he asked, putting his wrenches back in his toolbox.

"No, I think that will be all."

"Alright then, I just need your signature."

He handed Katherine a large metal clipboard with three sheets of paper attached: white, yellow, and pink. She signed her name on the line at the bottom with the "X" next to it and handed it back, shaking his hand and slipping him a five-dollar bill.

"Thank you very much," he said, smiling and pocketing the tip. "You have a nice day now."

After he'd gone, she went to the sink to try out her new faucet. She lifted the lever and let the water flow a moment before filling the water kettle and setting it on the stove and turning on the gas burner to put it on the boil. Satisfied with her newfangled modern gadget, she turned the water off and prepared a single drip filter for a cup of coffee.

Thank goodness he called to confirm she'd be home first, if he hadn't, she would have still been in her housecoat and slippers when he showed up. Her mind was otherwise preoccupied and she'd completely lost track of the time worrying about her boys.

Sean had always been a good boy. He did well in school, made friends easily, respected and listened to his elders and, most of all, loved and protected his little brother. But lately, something had changed. Something was different and she didn't know what. Her husband Leo simply chalked it up to adolescence, but in her heart, she knew it was more than just that. His outburst at the breakfast table that morning confirmed it in her mind. Something was wrong. Call it her mother's intuition.

It started about five or six months ago, right around the same time Sean and his friends formed their band. At first, it was just little things, like falling test scores or talking back at home, along with his newfound moodiness. But then he started acting differently toward Billy.

Ever since last summer, when one of Sean's friends at the shore had gotten a Boston Whaler, a type of small fiberglass outboard boat, he'd been begging for one of his own. They tried to explain to him that a boat was not a toy, and owning one was a big responsibility. Not to mention the expense of renting a slip in a marina and maintaining it. Above all, safety was their biggest concern. They used the excuse that Billy was still too young to go out on a boat alone with Sean. He tried arguing that he wouldn't take Billy out with him, but that would be nearly impossible; Billy wanted to do everything Sean did, and trying to keep him off the boat would be like taking a gambler to Las Vegas and keeping him off the slot machines. As a result, Sean blamed Billy for not getting his boat.

Until recently, he had adored his younger brother, affectionately calling him his "Little Tiger." They were adorable together; there was nothing Sean wouldn't do for him. But not anymore. Oh, Sean occasionally still used the nickname, but now she heard it less and less. The phrase coming from her eldest child's lips these days was more likely, "Mom, get Billy out of here!"

She tried not to be the kind of mother that was too over-bearing. She knew other women who attempted to control every aspect of their children's lives. She always felt it was best to allow her children to make their own choices and pick their own friends.

Her own mother had always picked her friends for her, unfortunately, she never liked any of the girls her mother picked out for her. She suspected the other children felt the same way toward her, as they seldom had anything in common. To make matters worse, her mother was a notoriously poor judge of character.

One of the girls her mother had chosen for her as a playmate liked to saw the heads off her dolls and set them on fire. The last Katherine had heard that girl was in prison now. In fact, Katherine could trace almost every negative thing that happened to her as a child to her mother's direct interference in her life. No, she trusted her boys enough to let them pick their own friends. She wondered now if that was the right decision.

She first met Sean's new friend, Tim Bennet, the longhaired protestant boy from public school that played in her son's band, last December when he came to their neighborhood Christmas party as Sean's guest. She already knew Jimmy Mason and Ben Shaw from Sean's class in school, had known them, in fact, since they were all in Kindergarten together. Nice boys. But she had instantly disliked this "Tim" character. She knew of his family by reputation; they lived on the proverbial "wrong side of the tracks." And they weren't Catholics.

She'd heard his grandmother watched those television evangelist preachers that spread hate and intolerance and shouted about God's wrath while bilking good-hearted and unsuspecting people, who were mostly uneducated and barely scraping by, of every last dime they had, all in the name of Jesus Christ. She automatically distrusted non-Catholics, but especially that breed of "fire and brimstone" Pentecostal. That wasn't the God of love she was raised to believe in. She wondered if Tim wasn't a bad influence on Sean. She was pretty sure he was.

Billy had been troubling her lately too, but for very different reasons. He had always been somewhat introverted, but it seemed to her he was withdrawing into his fantasies more and more. She felt sorry for him, he was such a sensitive little boy. He was already the odd man out; she'd held him back a year before starting Kindergarten because she felt at five years old he wasn't mature enough yet to begin school, so he was a year older than the other children in his class. She knew many of the other children thought he was weird, and maybe he was a little. But she didn't necessarily think that was such a terrible thing. He had the best imagination of any child she'd ever known, and she didn't think that just because he was her son.

And he was smart too. At school, they had given the children a state exam that secretly turned out to be an I.Q. Test. Billy had performed in the top percentile, scoring in the range of genius level. It had been suggested that he be sent away to a school for gifted children, but she quickly decided against that idea. She felt it would be better for him to be around regular children so as not to stigmatize him further. It was for that reason she decided not to tell him, fearing it might go to his head and affect him adversely. Better to let him keep thinking he was of average intelligence.

He was also naturally multi-talented. He was an artist in almost every way; he could sing like an angel, draw elaborate pictures (he'd won a city-wide art competition when he was five years old with his drawing of Batman and Robin in the Batmobile riding through Gorham City), and had a fertile imagination, making up fantasy stories in vivid detail. He loved acting too, putting on little plays in the backyard and recruiting local kids to be in them, sometimes against their will.

His Glee Club teacher, Mrs. Grady, told her she should consider taking him to New York on auditions for film, television, and plays. She had even given her the name of a theatrical agent who specialized in children, but in the end, she decided the life of a "stage mother" was not for her, dragging her child around on audition after audition. It sounded exhausting, and she just didn't have the time. This information, too, she kept from her son. What he didn't know wouldn't hurt him.

On top of all that, he was also very funny. He adored the old comedians such as the Marx Brothers or Abbot & Costello. He never missed one of their movies when they were on television. He had such a wonderful sense of humor, he could always make her laugh. Even when he was misbehaving, which was rare, she could never stay mad at him for very long. He would always do or say something to make her laugh. He was so gifted, in so many ways, she often wished others could see in him what she saw.

That was why when Sean had blurted out this morning that Billy was being bullied at school, it was particularly upsetting to her. She had no clue that anything was wrong. She always believed that if her boys were experiencing any problems they would confide in her.

Apparently, this was not the case. What was especially troubling to her was her inability to spot something amiss. If Billy was having trouble in school, he hid it well. He showed no outward signs that his life outside the home was anything other than happy. He still woke up almost every morning singing, something he'd done since he was four years old, although these days she didn't always recognize the tunes, a combined result of the generation gap and cultural influence of The Beatles.

She didn't really care for their music, and she didn't like them personally, especially that John Lennon person, carrying on with that home wrecker Yoko Ono, the two of them running around like a couple of immoral weirdoes, posing naked on an album cover. Disgusting.

Still, even though she hated to admit it, some of their songs were quite catchy.

By the time the kettle on the stove started to whistle, she'd decided she would have to start keeping a closer eye on both her sons.

I hung around outside the school doors, waiting for Lucy to come out. I don't know why, but I was nervous. I mean, it's not like I was planning to ask her to marry me or anything. I just wanted to invite her to my birthday party. Finally, she stepped through the door. I ran up beside her.

"Hi Lucy," I said, startling her.

"Oh, Billy! Hi. I didn't see you there."

"Sorry." I felt bad for scaring her like that. Maybe I could make it up to her. "Mind if I walk you home? I could carry your books."

"Why thank you," she said, transferring her load into my arms. "That's really nice of you."

"No problem," I said, though the books were heavier than I thought. We had the same homework, but for some reason her load was heavier than mine.

"I'm having a birthday party on Saturday," I said. "I'd really like you to come, if you can make it."

"Well, happy birthday! I'd love to come, thanks."

"Really?" I said, smiling.

"Of course, silly," she said, looking at me curiously. "Why wouldn't I?"

"I dunno. I thought maybe you were busy or something."

"Nope. The only thing I was going to do on Saturday was watch the Moon launch."

"You can watch it at my house. I wouldn't miss it. And we have a color TV."

We were only a block from school when Lucy said, "Well, here we are."

"This is your house?" I said, looking up at the big, three story grey shingled house. It was twice as big as our house and I realized that Lucy's family must be rich. Not that it made any difference to me, but I started to think for the first time that maybe I wasn't good enough for her. I decided to put that thought out of my head. "I didn't realize you lived so close to school."

"Yup. I'll take my books back now."

"Oh yeah," I said, but as I started handing them back I dropped them in a heap on the sidewalk. Lucy giggled as I bent down to pick them up.

"Sorry, I'm such a klutz sometimes. I didn't mean to... hey, what's this?"

I picked up a thick book, not one of our textbooks titled, *An Introduction to Astronomy*. No wonder her books were so heavy. I flipped through the pages. "Cool! I didn't know you were into space too!"

"Yeah, well, I guess it's okay," she said, avoiding my eyes. "I'll see you in school tomorrow, okay. I gotta go now." With that, she disappeared inside the house.

I turned and headed for home with a spring in my step. The next thing I knew I was singing *Good Day Sunshine* by The Beatles.

And it was. It was a *great* day!

FOUR

Captain Apollo ran through the archway of the dining hall in time to see the Butcher's ship make a strafing run through the town square. Dozens of Fraxens ran for cover as multiple explosions erupted all around. Empress Lucinda joined the captain at his side followed by several of her aides.

"He's back," Lucinda said, just as a second ship skimmed across the sky firing its lasers.

"And he has company," Captain Apollo added. He opened his transceiver and said, "Apollo to *Constellation.* We're under attack!"

"This is *Constellation,*" Shondo acknowledged. "We are monitoring your position, Captain. Mr. Sherman is already en route to intercept. He should be within range momentarily."

As if in answer to Shondo's statement, a one-man fighter swooped down from the sky in hot pursuit of the enemy ships.

"We got 'em on the run, Captain!" Lieutenant Sherman bellowed enthusiastically into the com. "I could sure use your help up here though."

"Good work, Matt. I'll be there in just a minute." After a pause, he said, "Shondo, see if you can monitor their long range transmissions. I don't want any surprises if the *Black Widow* is in the vicinity. Meanwhile, I'm going to assist Mr. Sherman."

Black Widow was the name of Mack the Black's starship. She was behind the attack, and the Empress, with the new force field technology plans mnemonically implanted in her brain, was the primary target. It was up to him to keep her safe.

"You need to take shelter, Highness," he said gently, but firmly. "You're in danger out in the open."

"I will," she promised. "You be careful too." She surprised him by kissing him on his cheek. "Now, go get 'em."

Captain Apollo grinned and nodded, then turned and ran to his fighter. Minutes later the tiny but powerful ship ascended into the purple sky. Using his ships sensors, he quickly located his shipmate and sped to catch up.

"Welcome to the party, sir," Mr. Sherman said, as Captain Apollo's ship pulled alongside. The two friends looked at each other from their cockpits. Ahead of them were the two enemy ships.

"You stay on the second ship. I'll try to draw the Butcher's fire," Captain Apollo said. Matt gave his captain the "thumbs up" as Apollo's ship veered off.

Matt Sherman had been Billy Apollo's closest friend at the academy and he knew that the captain had hand picked him for his assignment as Chief Engineer aboard the *Constellation*. He was shorter than the captain, and at least ten pounds heavier, having always struggled with his weight, but was loyal to a fault and would give one hundred and ten percent. And while there may have been some bias in the captain selecting him for his current position due to their close friendship, they both knew it was well deserved. Matt had graduated at the top of his class in engineering and he knew his stuff. He simply was the best man for the job. It was an honor and a privilege to serve under Captain Apollo, and he wouldn't let his friend down.

Matt was also an excellent and accomplished combat pilot. Apollo, Shondo, and he had all trained together and fought side by side in the Battle of Antonius Four, where the Galactic Federation first encountered Mack the Black. Like Fraxis Six, Antonius had recently joined the Federation and Mack the Black was determined to strip the planet of its abundant natural resources. That skirmish had lasted over two weeks, with a loss of seventeen personnel, but in the end, they were victorious and had successfully driven off the invading force.

Now, here they were again, defending the newest member of the Galactic Federation, and although this was merely two fighters, no doubt sent as a warning and a taste of things to come, Mack the Black and her insidious mega-ship *Black Widow* was probably not far behind.

Matt closed the distance between himself and the small fighter in front of him. With the aid of his targeting computer, he took aim and fired, hitting the little ship on the rear quarter panel and causing it to rock against the impact and lose altitude, black smoke pouring from the blast point.

"Take that," Matt said to himself.

The ship in front of him quickly recovered, suddenly banking upwards and turning one-hundred eighty degrees and firing. Matt took evasive action and avoided getting hit by mere inches. He got his bearings and turned to follow his attacker up into the cloud cover.

Meanwhile, Captain Apollo stayed in pursuit of the Butcher. He knew when Shondo and he had vanquished him earlier that he would be back with reinforcements, he just hadn't realized how soon. The second ship that Matt was currently engaging must have already been on its way. Not that it was a problem, they had both seen worse with much greater odds; one on one was practically child's play. Still, he was dealing with the Butcher, a more formidable and cunning adversary than the average opponent. He would have to be careful.

As if in answer to Captain Apollo's musings, the Butcher's ship abruptly dove toward the surface and the city. Captain Apollo immediately adjusted course, staying right on his tail. Just as he was about to fire, the nose of his fighter was struck by some kind of electrical pulse, like a directed bolt of lightning from the vessel in front of him. The instruments in Billy's cockpit erupted in fireworks of electrical arcs as all the ship-wide systems shorted out at once, leaving him powerless and plummeting like a rock from the heavens.

"Well, that's new," Captain Apollo said in a calm, matter-of-fact voice. He prayed the com system built into his helmet still functioned, as he reflexively prepared to eject manually. "Matt, do you read me?"

"Loud and clear. What's up?"

"I've been hit by some kind of new energy weapon. All my electrical systems are dead. I have to eject."

"Are you okay?"

"I'm fine. I'm activating my homing beacon. Your first priority is to protect the Empress. I'm pretty sure she's the Butcher's target."

"What about the second ship?"

"Let it go, that was just a diversion. Preventing the Butcher from getting to the Empress is our primary goal."

"Understood," Matt said.

Captain Apollo pulled the release cord under his seat, simultaneously blowing off the roof of the cockpit and launching him from the plummeting ship. Instantly, a parachute deployed, slowing his descent, giving him a bird's-eye view of Lieutenant Sherman's ship streaking downward to intercept the Butcher. A moment later, the second ship appeared in pursuit of Matt. Captain Billy, now in a slow, controlled descent, drew his hand-held laser pistol from his side, aimed carefully, and fired. With deadly precision, his laser struck the ship's engine, causing an instantaneous and fatal explosion; the ship blew up, expelling fire and debris in every direction. Fortunately, he was a safe distance and didn't get hit with any shrapnel.

"What was that?" Matt shouted in concern.

"A lucky shot," Captain Apollo replied. Below him on the surface, outside the city limits on undeveloped land, he saw his own ship crash to the ground, exploding on impact. The next second all he could see was pink fog as he passed through a thick cloud. Moments later, he emerged from the cloud and saw a giant plume of smoke filling half the town.

"Matt!" the captain shouted. "What happened?"

"I lost him! He released some kind of smoke screen and disappeared off my scope. Whatever else is in that smoke, it's causing my engines to stall. I've got to put down before I crash."

"Alright, get safe," he commanded. "I'll be on the ground myself in a few more seconds. I'll get to you."

"Aye, sir. I'll try to stop the Butcher before he can get to the Empress," Matt said.

Captain Apollo touched down and immediately undid the straps holding him in. He started running in the direction of the city center as fast as he could. He was less than a hundred yards away when he caught sight of the Butcher's ship taking off and heading for open space.

Suddenly, a bell started ringing from the highest steeple in the city. Captain Apollo froze in place when he heard the sound. He knew what it meant. The Empress was gone.

Sister Mary Immaculata stood outside the cafeteria door, Butch Anderson at her side ringing the hand-held brass bell that signaled the end to lunch recess. Butch was her personal student assistant, he had her completely fooled into thinking he was a perfect little angel.

Matt and I froze in place at the sound of the bell, along with every other kid in the playground, like a big game of red-light/green-light. After about a minute, Butch rang the bell a second time, signaling our permission to move again. Everyone in the yard, including Matt and me, grumbled at our disappointment that after-lunch playtime was over, as we all slowly headed back toward the building.

"Man, just when it was getting good!" I said. "I think she rings the bell early."

"I know," Matt agreed. "I'm pretty sure she does that on purpose."

Sister Immaculata (Mack the Black herself!) was dressed in her usual black and white, head to toe, nun's habit, with a long string of Rosary beads strung around her waist like a belt, and a Crucifix on a black cord slung around her neck. Her sixty-two year old wrinkled face wore her usual scowl, as if she was mad at the world. We all called her Mack Truck behind her back, even her "pet" Butch, because of her rain barrel-like shape. She was the meanest teacher in the school. I could never figure out how someone so bad tempered could be a nun. No wonder she was the scourge of the galaxy!

"Maybe we can pick it up tomorrow where we left off," Matt said.

"Yeah, we have to get back to the ship so we can rescue Empress Lucinda from the Butcher," I said and glared right at Butch. I know the boy with the bell had no idea his alter ego was a villain in my space fantasy, but I couldn't help holding him in contempt just the same.

"Right now, I'd say she needs rescuing from the Female Faction," Matt said, pointing to the small group of popular girls who were crowded around Lucy, no doubt filling her in on who was cool and okay to be seen with, and who was a dork, like me, and should be avoided like the plague. I could see from here that her facial expression was a cross between polite attention, and helplessness, as if she would prefer to be anywhere else.

She glanced in my direction and saw me watching her, making eye contact with me and smiling. I smiled back and gave her a little wave. The group of girls surrounding Lucy was moving toward the school a little more quickly than us, so I moved a bit faster in an effort to arrive at the door about the same time she did. Matt walked beside me, seemingly unaware that we had just quickened our pace.

I liked Matt a lot; he was the best friend I ever had, though sometimes he was a little odd, even by my standards. He was a little shorter than me, and a bit on the pudgy side. Whereas I was on the thin side, Matt was simply overweight. He wasn't fat exactly, he just didn't exercise so he was soft in the middle, not that I cared. Don't get me wrong, I cared about my friend and maybe he would be healthier if he lost a few pounds, but I didn't pick my friends based on how much they weighed, unlike the Female Faction. His weight had nothing to do with his being odd though.

I guess it must have started when his mom died, when he was only five. According to my mom, who got it from Matt's father, he took his mom's death really hard. He started to withdraw into himself and wouldn't talk or make friends. Until he moved here and met me, that is. It took a while after he came to this school, when we were in first grade, until he started talking to me, but when he did, it turned out we had a lot of things in common.

Even now, he's still my best friend, even if he does talk to himself sometimes. I play by myself all the time, so I guess that makes us kind of even. I just wish he would stick to one thing at a time. His brain is so hyper he jumps from one subject to the next so fast it makes my head spin. One minute we could be talking about an episode of *Star Trek* or something, and with the next breath, he's asking if I was going to enter the Pinewood Derby in Cub Scouts. It can be a little irritating sometimes, but I learned to go with the flow.

"We're gonna watch the Apollo 13 launch at your house, right?" he said out of left field.

"What?" I said, taken by surprise. "Oh, yeah, of course. Duh."

"Good. I was hoping we could watch it on your TV. You're so lucky! I'm sick of black & white."

We were one of only about a dozen or so households in the neighborhood that owned a color television set. My dad won ours in a church raffle four years ago, making us the first family on the block to have a color TV. When we first got it, people came over almost every night to watch it. Back then, it was a big deal. Even now, most people, like Matt, still didn't own one and had to make due with black & white. It's not like Matt's dad couldn't afford one, he taught college and was a musician, it's just that it wasn't important to him and he hadn't gotten around to it yet. Matt's dad was a bit of a hippie, and even though Max was pretty cool, it almost made me feel sorry for Matt.

We were almost to the door now, and I had timed it perfectly; Lucy was directly in front of me. We smiled at each other just as we were passing in front of Sister Immaculata and her sidekick. As I opened my mouth to say something, Butch nonchalantly stuck out his foot and tripped me, causing me to lurch forward into Lucy, knocking her to the ground. I nearly fell on top of her, but somehow kept my balance.

"McBride!" Mack Truck bellowed.

"But it wasn't my fault," I said defensively.

"He pushed her, Sister," Butch lied. "I saw him."

"Detention!"

"But... but..." I stammered.

"Not another word or I'll send you straight to the principal's office," she said. "Now march."

I helped Lucy to her feet and she, Matt, and I entered the building, smoldering at the injustice I had just been dealt, and headed for the classroom. The Female Faction looked back pointing and giggling at us. "Shut up!" Lucy yelled at them, but that just made them giggle louder.

We were almost to the classroom when Butch made his way over to me.

"Hey, Space Case," he whispered in my ear, now that Mack Truck was out of sight. "Have a nice trip?"

"Shut up," I said.

"Make me," Butch said, punching me in the arm for good measure before slipping past me into the classroom.

"Man, I hate that guy," Matt said.

"Why don't you stick up for yourself?" Lucy said.

Oh great, I thought, embarrassed. *The girl of my dreams thinks I'm a complete wimp.*

"They're bigger than us," Matt said, coming to my defense.

"Yeah," I agreed. "Besides, Mack Truck is already mad at me. I don't want to get suspended for fighting right before my birthday. It's bad enough I got a detention."

"I just hope he doesn't cause any trouble at your party like he did at Tony Meyer's last fall."

"You invited him to your party? Why?" Lucy said, shocked.

"My mom made me. She said it wouldn't be fair to invite the whole class and leave him out."

"What did he do at Tony Myers party?" Lucy asked.

"You know that game, Pin the Tail on the Donkey?" Matt said. Lucy nodded. "They were using real pins. Butch stuck it right in

Tony's back on purpose."

"That's awful!" Lucy said.

"He claimed it was an accident," I said. "But before it happened I heard him tell his buddy Joey he was gonna do it. I tried to warn Tony, but he wouldn't listen."

They entered the classroom and took their seats just as the bell rang. A moment later Mack Truck came in the room and sat down in her chair behind the Teacher's desk she shared with Mr. McLean. There were two classrooms and two teachers for every grade in the school, and the teachers switched rooms after lunch. In my class, Mr. McLean taught Science, English, and Math in the mornings, and Mack Truck taught History, Social Studies, and Religion in the afternoons.

"Alright class, everyone take out your History books and turn to page two-hundred and forty-three."

I bent down and began searching under my desk for my History textbook. I scavenged through the books, notebooks, papers full of old homework assignments, countless drawings, long forgotten tests, a few candy wrappers, my poor destroyed *Star Trek* book, but try as I might I couldn't put my hands on my History book. I was aware that everyone else had their books on their desks and they were all waiting on me.

"Is there a problem, Mr. McBride?" Mac Truck said impatiently.

"I can't find my book," I said without abandoning my search. I was starting to sweat. This was getting embarrassing. It has to be in here somewhere. I know I didn't take it home last night, we didn't have any history homework.

"Why not?" she said, walking toward me. Her feet stopped directly in front of me. My eyes started on her black orthopedic shoes, traveled up her droopy-stocking ankles to her black dress, all the way up to her black and white veiled head, only her angry red face exposed and staring down at me. If this were a cartoon, smoke would be shooting out of her ears.

"No wonder you can't find anything," she said, angrier than I'd ever seen her before. "I've never seen such a filthy rats-nest!"

I turned red from embarrassment as laughter broke out around me. What happened next took me completely by surprise.

"Stand up," she commanded. I stood. Then she over-turned my desk, spilling the entire contents onto the floor. The laughter got even louder. I bent down to pick up my desk.

"Leave it," she said. I stared at her blankly. "Can you find your book now?" I looked at the pile at my feet. Free from the confines of my desk, I saw it lying on the floor. It must have been lodged in the back somewhere. I picked it up.

"Here it is," I said, and bent down again to pick up my desk.

"I said leave it!" she bellowed. I was really confused now.

"But I need my desk for class," I protested. She went and got the trash can beside her desk and brought it over to me.

"You will spend the rest of the day on the floor," she told me. I stared at her in disbelief. Was she serious? Was she really going to make me sit on the floor beside my over-turned desk all afternoon?

"Well? Sit!"

I was flabbergasted. My legs were shaking as I lowered myself to the ground. I could feel my face burning from total humiliation. The laughter was ringing in my ears.

"Now, clean up that mess!" she said, and walked back to the

front of the class. "The rest of you settle down. The show's over." The laughter died down and stopped. "Now, who can tell me where we left off?"

Several hands rose into the air. She called on someone and the history lesson began, but I have no idea what anyone was saying. I slowly picked up the scattered books and papers all around me, crying silently to myself, going through all my things one by one, throwing away anything I didn't need. True to her word, she made me sit on the floor the rest of the day, even after I'd cleaned everything up. She would not allow me to put my desk upright.

I was aware of Lucy watching me, but I couldn't look at her. I couldn't bear to look into her eyes and let her see my face. I'd only known her a few days and then this had to happen. Exposed for the loser I am. She'll never want to be my girlfriend now.

Lucy waited for Billy after school, but he never came out. He must have gone out another door. She knew he wasn't in detention yet, that wasn't until tomorrow. Not that he deserved it. He didn't even do anything wrong, he was tripped! But that nun, the one they called Mack Truck, wouldn't even listen.

Then she went and made Billy sit on the floor all afternoon, just because his desk was messy. What kind of a teacher does that? And a nun no less! Teachers were supposed to help students, not publicly humiliate them. For some reason it seemed like everybody in this school picked on Billy McBride.

Disappointed that she'd missed him, she started toward home. She wanted to tell him how angry she was at how he was treated. She didn't understand why they all treated him so cruelly. Maybe he was a little different, but so what? He was about the sweetest boy she'd ever met. She loved it when he'd offered to carry her books home the other day—the chivalrous gentleman! More than any of the other boys in this place.

He was so cute when they'd gotten to her house, he seemed so sad she lived so close and the walk was over so quickly. And she had to giggle when he dropped her books and then fell all over himself trying to pick them up. She didn't know why she'd been so embarrassed when he found her astronomy book. She should have just admitted she liked outer space. If anyone would have understood, it was Billy. But she didn't want to be labeled a geek again, the way she had been at her old school in Texas. The way Billy was here. Still, she should have told him. He was so excited when he'd seen her book.

She also didn't want him to get the wrong idea. She could tell he liked her, but the idea of a boyfriend was just too repulsive even to think about it. She liked him—maybe even more than liked him—though she would never admit that, even to herself. She wasn't the kind of girlie-girl who liked to play with Barbie, like her two sisters. She would much rather climb trees than kiss a boy, even one as cute as Billy.

Lucy turned off the public sidewalk onto the stone walkway leading to her front door. The house was larger than the one they'd owned in Texas, but had considerably less property. She was used to more open spaces, unlike New Jersey, where the houses were packed in right next to each other.

The backyard was pretty big, long but not wide; probably about twenty-five yards from the back of the house to the end of the property line, but between houses there was only about fifteen feet on both sides. One thing they did have was trees—two in front and six in back—a mix of maple, elm, pine, and apple. The maple tree overlooking their driveway was her favorite to climb, giving her clear views of the backyard, front yard, and side of the house simultaneously.

The house itself was narrow and tall with three stories, a finished basement, and a walk-up attic. The first floor consisted of a large kitchen, dining room, and living room. The second floor housed the Master bedroom, Master bathroom, and family room, with three bedrooms on the third floor, one for each girl. They had just moved to New Jersey less than a month ago and were still unpacking. To Lucy, it didn't feel like a home. At least not yet.

"Mama?" she called out, as she removed her shoes in the front foyer, a habit she'd gotten into in the Lone Star state when they'd had a mudroom. There, where most every surface wasn't paved or cemented over, tracking mud into the house was commonplace. Her father said the people in New York City call the suburbs of New Jersey "the country." That had become a family joke, since where they came from this would be considered a city. It was all a matter of perspective.

"In here Sweetheart," her mother answered from the dining room. Lucy walked in to find her mother unpacking her good china from boxes and putting them away in the mahogany and glass hutch that matched their dining room table and chairs. "How was school today?" Karen Ross asked, while wiping a plate with a dishcloth and placing it carefully in the cabinet.

Lucy pulled out a chair and slumped down into it with a sigh. "I hate it here. People are so mean, even some of the teachers."

Karen put down the plate she had just removed from the box and came around the table to sit beside her daughter. "What's wrong, Honey, did something happen? Was someone mean to you?"

"Not to me, to my friend Billy." Lucy proceeded to tell her all that happened, starting with Butch tripping Billy and his unwarranted detention to the incident with the desk and his subsequent humiliation at the hands of Sister Immaculata. Karen listened with growing shock, especially at the actions of the nun entrusted with the care and well-being of the children in her charge. When Lucy finished her account of the day's events, Karen sat back, taking it all in and deciding on the best course of action. Finally, she said, "What's your friend Billy's last name?"

"McBride, why?"

"I'm going to call his mother and let her know what's going on," she said, standing up and going to the wall mounted rotary dial telephone in the kitchen. She opened a drawer in the counter next to the phone where she kept the phone books, both county and personal, along with the list of her children's classmates' phone numbers. She scanned the list from Lucy's class and found the number for the McBrides.

"Wait," Lucy implored. "Don't tell her I told. I don't want Billy mad at me."

Karen picked up the phone and began dialing. "She ought to know her son's being tormented. I'd want to know if it was happening to my child."

"Please Mama. I know he feels bad enough right now. I could see it in his eyes all afternoon while she made him sit on the floor. It would crush him if his mother found out."

Karen put the phone back in its cradle. "Alright. It's against my better judgment, but I'll keep this between us."

"Thank you, Mama."

"For now. But promise me you'll let me know if anything else like this happens."

"Yes ma'am."

"You said his birthday is this weekend?" Karen said, picking up the receiver again.

"Uh-huh. Saturday," Lucy confirmed, nodding as her mother dialed the phone. "Who are you calling?"

Karen raised her finger, signaling her daughter to wait a moment. "Hello? Is this Mrs. McBride?"

Lucy's eyes went wide as she frantically shook her head.

"This is Karen Ross. That's right, Lucy's mother. He did? Well, isn't that sweet. The reason I'm calling is Lucy told me Billy invited her to his birthday this Saturday. I was wondering if you would like some help. I'm new in town, and... yes, that's right. You would? Wonderful! Okay. Okay. Eleven o'clock? Oh, it's my pleasure I'm sure. All right. See you Saturday. Bye."

She hung up the phone and smiled at Lucy.

"What?" Lucy said expectantly.

"I'm going to help chaperone the party. That will give us a chance to chat. Don't worry, I won't break my promise. There's more than one way to skin a cat. We'll find a way to help your friend Billy without him even knowing."

Lucy wrapped her arms around her mother's waist. "Thank you, Mama. I love you."

It was almost eight-thirty when Leo McBride pulled his 1966 Chevy Impala into the driveway of his modest little home located on a cul-de-sac in a quiet little neighborhood in the suburbs of Mount

Clayton, New Jersey. It was nothing fancy, but it was quite a step up from where he grew up: a tenement apartment in the slums of Paterson, New Jersey, a lower-class city mostly populated by Irish immigrants and Negros. He had been determined to break out of the grip of poverty and provide a better life for his own family.

Thanks to the G.I. Bill, he was able to afford this nice two story, three-bedroom house with a decent sized yard in front and back. It had two bedrooms upstairs, one for Katherine and him, and one for the boys, with a bathroom they all shared. On the first floor was a kitchen, living room and a third bedroom, which he converted into a den/office for himself. They didn't have the luxury of a dining room, but they had added a back porch and used that if they needed the extra space. They also had a spacious basement that he hoped to finish one day and use as a family room.

When the Korean War ended, he retired from the army and married Katherine Jones, his high school sweetheart. He took classes, got his insurance license, and worked hard, saving his money for a down payment. They bought the house when Katherine became pregnant with Sean, who was born in the summer of '57. Billy came four years later in the spring of '61. It was hard to believe that it had been nine years since his youngest boy had come into the world. Where had the time gone?

Insurance was a tough game, but he'd managed to make a good living, putting a roof over his family's heads and food in their bellies. The hours were long and the work was hard, but it was a sacrifice he was willing to make. With the money he made, he even had enough left over to buy a little bungalow on the Jersey shore so his wife and kids could enjoy their summers at the beach.

He personally didn't get to enjoy it much—he had to stay up

north for work—but he drove down on weekends during the summer and spent two full weeks with his family in August when he took his vacation. It was difficult being separated from his family for two months a year, but he didn't mind as long as they were happy. Sure, he missed Katherine and the boys during that time, but truth be told, he enjoyed the peace and quiet. Besides, except in the evenings, he was working all the time anyway.

Sometimes, especially around birthdays, like now, he thought maybe he worked a little too much. He usually put in ten to twelve hour days, six days a week. He felt like he was missing his kids' childhoods. They were growing up right before his eyes, yet he felt, in many ways, like a stranger to them. He had been raised in an Irish household that believed in the old adage, "children should be seen and not heard," along with "spare the rod and spoil the child," but that kind of thinking had gone out of style. He told himself he wouldn't be that kind of parent, that he would be more attentive to their needs and get to know them on a more personal and intimate level. But as the years slipped away, that grew harder and harder. He didn't truly know either of his sons. He loved them both with all his heart, yet they were largely a mystery to him.

It had been so much easier when they were younger. Back then, they were "Daddy's little boys," and he had no problem keeping up with their developing personalities. Sean was always more of the rough and tumble type, always ready to wrestle around and play hard. He was also very protective of his baby brother, right from the beginning. Even at four years old, when Billy was born, Sean would always be there to hold him, or feed him, or check on him in his crib and just watch him sleep. Billy was less than three months old when Sean christened him his "Little Tiger."

But now he was a practically a teenager and everything had changed. He didn't even know him anymore, and worried about what he saw happening to him. He didn't understand any of it: the hair, the clothes, the attitude, the music—oh, the music! He blamed those damned Beatles for corrupting today's youth and especially his sons. He prayed to God they would just go away, but he knew that was never going to happen. His only hope was that it wasn't too late for Billy.

His youngest son had always been different. Whether that was a result of his difficult birth, or his bicycle accident, or both he just didn't know. His birth had been traumatic enough; the time between his coming out not breathing to the time they were able to revive him was the longest six minutes of his life. But that was nothing compared to the emotional stress he went through nearly two years ago after the accident; for twenty-four hours, they didn't know whether he would live or die. Just the thought of losing a child is almost too much to bear. Yet Billy seemed to come out of the experience virtually unscathed.

He was a happy child, waking up almost every day with joy in his heart and a song on his lips. Unlike his older brother, he was much more introspective and artistic. Katherine liked to say he marched to the beat of his own drummer, and that was certainly true; Billy was unique, unlike any other child he'd ever known.

When he was little, everybody loved him, and he was never shy. He could go up to a total stranger on the beach, and within minutes, he would make himself right at home and prattle on, making up his little stories on the spot. No one ever complained or turned him away, he was that irresistible. But as he got older, he grew more introverted. He was perceived as odd, and had trouble making friends with his peers.

Leo tried his best to understand his boy, and he hated to admit it, but even he found it difficult to relate to him at times. As much as he loved him, there was no denying it—Billy was strange. That's why he felt it was so important to try to make more of an effort to get closer to him, and why it broke his heart to have to tell him he was going to miss his birthday party.

But first, he was going to have to explain it to his wife.

He grabbed the six-pack of Budweiser cans from the passenger seat and got out of his car.

"Hi Honey," he said, walking through the kitchen door. He put his beer in the refrigerator, slipped his hands around Katherine's waist, and kissed her neck. "Mmm. Something smells good."

"I'm making cupcakes for Billy's party. How was your day?"

"Tiring," Leo said, loosening his tie. "I spent half the day on the phone, and the other half traveling. At least I managed to write two new policies, and Mike Tucker added a boat onto his auto policy." He sat down, lit a non-filter Camel, a nasty habit he picked up in the war, and said, "Where're the kids?"

"Sean's still at Jimmy's, practicing, and Billy's playing downstairs."

Leo nodded and took a draw of his cigarette. "I have some bad news. I won't be able to make it to the party. I have an appointment in Hoboken Saturday afternoon."

"Leo!" Katherine said, turning from the counter to face him. "How could you? You know how important it is to Billy that you be there."

"I'm sorry. I tried to get out of it, but it's Bill Hamilton and that's the only time he's available."

"I know he's an important client, but it's your son's birthday, for God's sake!"

"I know, and I'll make it up to him. I promise."

"You say that every time you miss a family event like this."

"I said I'm sorry."

"Don't tell me. Tell your son."

The couple stared at each other in silence—Leo apologetic, Katherine reproachful—before she finally turned back around and went back to her baking, signaling the conversation was over as far as she was concerned.

"I'm going to grab a shower," Leo sighed. He snatched up a cupcake from the cooling rack on his way out of the kitchen.

"Honestly, you're as bad as the kids!" Katherine snapped.

She dropped her spoon into the bowl and sat down, lighting a cigarette to calm her nerves. She wasn't mad as much as frustrated. It was typical of Leo to put work ahead of family for things like parties, so she really should have half expected this. But she'd been counting on Leo's help with the party. With twenty-plus eight and nine year olds to wrangle, she wanted a man around. She would have to call Max Sherman and ask if he could help chaperone. Thank goodness Mrs. Ross had called to volunteer to help!

The egg timer bell chimed. Katherine put out her cigarette and checked on her batch of cupcakes. They still needed a few minutes in the oven. She'd spent the better part of the day baking; she had made six-dozen cookies, two-dozen each of chocolate-chip, peanut butter, and oatmeal-raisin, Billy's favorite. She was just now finishing the cupcakes. One more batch and she would have four-dozen, half chocolate and half angel food.

But the birthday cake would be the showstopper. She was keeping it a secret from Billy. She knew he would flip when he saw it and she wanted it to be a surprise. She was making him an Apollo 13 cake, complete with a model rocket ship on top. She still had a lot to do between now and Saturday, which was why she'd baked the cookies and cupcakes today. She had some last minute shopping to do tomorrow, and she still had to assemble the model rocket. It was going to be hectic, but she knew she would get everything done on time. Somehow, she always did. She was determined to make this a birthday to remember!

She checked the cupcakes again, and this time she removed them from the oven.

FIVE

Friday was finally here! Only one more day to go until my Big Day!

Fridays were the best day of the week at Saint Anthony's, because not only it was the last day until the weekend, but also because it was the one day when we didn't have regular classes. We still had Religion class; we always had Religion. But since we had Religion class five days a week, we were spared having to go to Sunday school, unlike the Catholic kids who went to public school.

On Friday mornings, we had Religion, followed by Health, and then Gym. After lunch, our afternoons were split between Music and Art. I loved Friday afternoons. Music and Art were the two things I was best at. They tried to get Matt's dad to teach Music, but he was too busy teaching college, so they found a really old lady who used to play piano for silent movies. She was a little deaf now, but she was nice, and besides teaching us on Fridays, she gave piano lessons at her house. A few kids in my class took lessons from her. Sometimes in her class, she tried to teach us how to read music, which kind of bored me, but mostly we got to sing. That's what I loved. I could sing all day long if they let me.

We never got to sing anything we really wanted to, like The Beatles or The Monkees, she always made us sing show tunes, but I didn't care. I was used to that. When I was little my mom bought me musical soundtracks like *The King and I* and *The Sound of Music*, so that's what I liked. Then, when I joined the Glee Club, we had to learn songs from *Oliver!*, so she bought me that soundtrack. It didn't really matter to me what we sang, as long as I got to sing.

After Music, we had Art class taught by Sister Janet. She was young, pretty, and fun, and unlike the old lady nuns, who dressed in black and white from head to toe and only their faces peeked out from behind a veil that covered their entire head, she wore a modern habit. She wore a light blue dress that stopped above her knees, showing off her legs, and a regular white blouse open at the collar, with a light blue vest that matched her dress. On her head was a short veil, more like a nurse's cap, revealing most of her light brown hair. I really liked her a lot. She was the exact opposite of Mack Truck. She was nice to us kids and she never raised her voice. I wished she was our regular teacher instead of Mack Truck, but at least we got her on Fridays. I'll take what I can get.

It was ten-thirty a.m. when the bell rang signaling the end of Religion class. Easter was only two weeks ago, on March 29, so our lessons were focused on things that happened after the Resurrection. Today we talked about Doubting Thomas and his refusal to believe Jesus really rose from the dead, and the only way he was convinced was to put his fingers through Jesus' wounds in his hands and side. Thomas didn't have faith. I only half paid attention because we learned all this before and would learn it all again and again; they taught the same thing in every grade, year after year, in the weeks following Easter.

I put away my Religion book in my freshly cleaned, perfectly organized, spic 'n span desk and got up with the rest of the class. I waited my turn to grab the plastic bag containing my gym sneakers from the coat closet and walked with the others across the playground to the school auditorium in the basement of the church.

There were four buildings that made up the campus grounds at Saint Anthony's: first was the church where Sunday Mass and other Sacraments, such as Baptisms and Weddings, were held; attached to the church was the rectory where the priests lived—the Pastor, Father O'Malley from Ireland, Father Franklin, Father Edwards, and the youngest priest, Father Scott; the school was next to the rectory in a separate building; and attached but separate from the school, was the convent where the nuns lived. All the nuns taught at the school but none of the priests did.

Besides gym class, the church basement is where they held Boy Scout meetings, pancake breakfasts, school plays, and any other kind of gathering that required a big open space and/or a stage. The school playground doubled as the church parking lot on Sunday mornings.

The gym teachers weren't professionals but "church lady" volunteers, and none of them held any kind of degree in physical education. But the state of New Jersey required every school to have some form of Phys. Ed. class and "free" fit into the school's budget nicely. It didn't matter that the gym teachers didn't really know what they were doing and worked for nothing. So long as we took some kind of gym class, the school fulfilled its legal obligation and the state was happy.

It was nearly a quarter to eleven by the time we made it across the yard to the auditorium for what amounted to an hour of supervised playtime. There were no locker rooms, so we were required to wear our gym clothes underneath our school clothes. Both boys and girls had the same gym uniform: white shorts and T-shirts with Saint Anthony's School silk-screened over the left pocket. Folding chairs lined two walls on opposite sides of the room, boys on one side, and girls on the other.

Matt and I always took chairs next to each other so we could chat while we stripped off our outer uniforms. Every so often, someone forgot to wear their gym clothes under their uniform, not even realizing it until after the entire class got a good look at their "tightie-whities." Charlie Connelly was the unfortunate soul whose memory failed him this morning, and we all got an eyeful of his Fruit of the Looms.

I felt bad laughing along with everyone else, but it *was* kinda funny. I, myself, have forgotten my gym shorts on more than one occasion. At those times, although I was embarrassed, I didn't mind being the butt of the joke. It was my own fault, and besides, it was funny! Since Charlie was laughing too, I knew I would be forgiven.

Usually, when we looked for a couple of open chairs to change into our gym clothes, Matt and I tried to avoid Butch and Joey. Unfortunately, I forgot to pay attention today and the next thing I knew, Butch was in the chair next to mine with Joey on his other side.

"Oh, hey McBride, didn't see you there," Butch said, Joey

snickering at the obvious lie. "I bet you got a real good look at Charlie in his underwear, didn't you. I hear faggots like that kinda thing." Joey laughed outright.

"Shut up," I said, stung by Butch's insulting accusation. I did my best to ignore him. He and Joey whispered and laughed to themselves. I knew it was about me because Joey kept looking over at me and laughing whenever Butch whispered something new in his ear.

I tried not to look at him as he removed his uniform, but when he bent down to tie his sneakers, the tail of his gym shirt rode up in the back, exposing his bare skin. Out of the corner of my eye, I saw purple, which caused me to turn my head and stare, wide eyed. What little I could see was covered with red welts and dark bruises. Stealing a glance at the backs of his thighs peeking out from the hem of his shorts, I saw the telltale edges of purple marks there as well. I looked up, shocked and horrified, and locked eyes with Butch. He glanced down at his bruised legs to see what I was looking at. He must have realized immediately what I'd seen because he momentarily flashed a look of panic on his face and pulled at his shorts to try to cover himself and quickly tucked in his shirt. In an instant, his eyes flickered back to their usual threatening stare.

"What are you lookin' at?!"

"N-n-nothing," I managed to stammer.

"Quit looking at my legs, faggot!"

Once again, his audience of one laughed. Butch just continued to glare at me, almost daring me to say something. I finished getting ready and tucked my uniform pants and shirt under the chair. I put my shoes on the seat so I could easily identify which chair was mine when class was over.

Fortunately, one of the gym ladies blew her whistle, signaling the start of class. I joined the line next to Matt, getting as far away from Butch as I could. She blew the whistle again and we began our regimen of calisthenics; twenty-five each of jumping jacks, pushups, and sit-ups.

I tried to ignore Butch as best I could, but every time I looked at him, he was staring at me. Sometimes he looked like he was afraid, sometimes he looked like he was mad, and sometimes he looked like he was a little of both. But whichever way he looked, he never took his eyes off me. The rest of the period was consumed with a rowdy game of kick-ball, and when we finished, I put my clothes back on as fast as I could and ran back to the main school building for lunch before Butch could get me. Now all I had to do was avoid him for the rest of my life.

As soon as lunch was over, I ran out into the playground to put as much distance between Butch and me as possible. Matt and Lucy both made comments while we were eating that I was acting weird, even for me. I brushed it off as nervous jitters about my birthday. They seemed to accept that answer, but then Lucy wanted to know what happened to me yesterday afternoon and why I hadn't come out the door I usually exit from. I told her my mom picked me up, which was true, but I didn't tell her I left by the front door by the office because I was too ashamed to face her after the overturned desk incident.

Soon after I fled the cafeteria, the rest of the kids started filling the playground, making it easier to avoid being seen. I wasn't exactly hiding, but I was at the far end near the church. From where I was, close to the back fence where the wild honeysuckles grew, I could see the entire playground. The air was sweet with the fragrance of honey, and any other time I might be picking the tiny white flowers and licking the sweet nectar from the pistils, but right now, my eyes were squinted trying to scan for any sign of my nemesis. If only I had Mr. Spock's *Tricorder*!

"Thought you could sneak away from me, McBride?" said a voice behind my right ear. I turned my head already knowing who the voice belonged to. He must've snuck along the outside of the fence through the electric fields and come through the hole in the fence!

"Hey Butch. I wasn't sneaking. I was just picking some honeysuckles," I lied, then picked a few to demonstrate. "See?"

"Save it. Tell me what you were looking at in gym today."

"Nothing Butch, honest. I didn't see anything."

Butch grabbed my shirt collar and threw me back against the fence so fast that I didn't even have time to react. He moved in so close that our noses were almost touching. He looked directly into my eyes with a look that was so mean I could almost picture red heat-beams, like Superman's, boring through my skull. At that moment, I wish I had some "Butch Kryptonite" in my pocket.

"You're lying," he insisted. "Tell me what you saw or I swear I'll knock out your other tooth!"

I knew he wasn't kidding. For a second the image of me with two silver front teeth flashed through my head. "It was nothing, really. I just saw a little bruise, that's all." I was afraid to tell him I saw welts on his back too. He only caught me looking at the backs of his legs.

"Did you tell anyone?"

"No! I swear!"

"You better not. Ever."

"I didn't. I won't. I promise!"

"Because it's nobody's business. It was an accident. I slipped and fell down the stairs on my back."

"Yeah. Right. It was an accident. I won't say anything to anyone."

"Good," he said, then released my collar and stepped back. His expression changed then, as though an idea had just occurred to him. "You like that new girl, don't you? That skinny little Texas tom-boy."

"Lucy? Yeah, she's my friend."

"Looks to me like she's more than just a friend. I seen the way you look at her."

"She's just a friend," I insisted. He was right, I wished she was more than that, but she wasn't.

"Yeah, well, if you tell anyone... *anyone*... about what you saw, I'm not just gonna come after you. I'm gonna get her too."

"Leave her alone! I told you, I'm not gonna tell!" I yelled.

"I know you're not. 'Cause if you do, you and your girlfriend are both dead. You got that?"

No sooner had the words come out of his mouth, than a tall shadow fell over both of us. It was the silhouette of a man standing directly behind Butch, his back to the sun; although he was facing me, I couldn't make out who it was. I saw a look of panic on Butch's face as the man spoke, "Something wrong?"

Butch spun around, facing the priest.

"No Father." It was Father Scott, affectionately known to the students as Scotty.

Scotty stared disapprovingly at Butch, then said, "Go on then.

Get out of here."

Butch ran away from him so fast you'd think he was running a race and someone just fired the starting pistol.

"Was he bothering you?" Scotty asked me, genuine concern in his voice.

"No. We were just talking," I said. I hated lying to a priest, but I was thinking of Butch's threat about Lucy. I didn't care what he did to me, but I wouldn't let anything happen to her if I could help it.

"That's not how it looked from where I was standing," he said. "Walk with me."

I don't know if my face betrayed my surprise at his request or not, but if it did, he didn't say anything. He started walking slowly back toward the church; I joined him at his side. I stared up at him as we walked. He didn't speak so neither did I. He seemed like he was lost in thought and I didn't want to disturb him.

Scotty, like Sister Janet, was young and cool, fresh out of the Seminary—that's what they call priest school. He wore his wavy black hair long, almost down to his collar, but he kept it neat. He had a handsome yet gentle face, with compassionate soft brown eyes and a trusting smile, his upper lip hidden under a mustache. I don't know how old he was, but he looked around the same age, or younger, as the photographs of The Beatles that Sean displayed on the wall above his desk. In fact, it looked to me like he bore a striking resemblance to George Harrison, who, by coincidence, was my favorite Beatle.

I remember the first time we were introduced to Father Scott. It was the beginning of last year when Sister Joseph brought him around to all the classrooms so we could meet the newest priest assigned to our parish. I remember the look on Sister Joseph's face when she presented him to us as "Father Scott" and he told the class, "Call me Scotty." I could tell just by her expression and the way her nose wrinkled, like she caught a whiff of some foul odor, that she did not approve of his encouraging us to refer to him with anything as vulgar and informal as a nickname, but she didn't dare contradict him. He was, after all, a priest, and she was merely a nun. In the hierarchy of the church, he outranked her, even if she was old enough to be his mother.

We walked together as far as the steps leading up the small hill to the church, on about twenty feet of higher ground than the convent or the school. He climbed about a dozen steps and sat, signaling with his hands for me to do the same. I sat next to him, still looking up at him. Finally, he broke the silence.

"I've been watching you, Billy."

What? I didn't know what to say. Did I do something wrong? Was I in trouble? I'm sure he could tell just how shocked I was to learn that he was keeping me in his sights by the way my mouth was hanging open.

"I can see that you're not like the other children," he went on. "And that's not a bad thing. I also see how some of the others treat you because you're different. Like Butch." He paused then, turned, and looked into my eyes. I think he was waiting for me to say something. When I didn't, he said, "I want you to know you can come to me if something is troubling you, okay."

I nodded, but still didn't say anything.

"If it helps, you can think of it like confession. I took a vow never to reveal what someone tells me in confidence."

I nodded again and thought about it for a minute. I decided to trust him. A little.

"What if you knew something about someone that they wanted to keep a secret, but you knew that keeping that secret was going to get them hurt? And they made you swear never to tell or they would hurt someone you cared about?"

"I'd say that was a heavy burden for someone to bear. Can you give me a hint what kind of secret we're talking about?"

"See, the thing is, I don't know for sure that I'm right. He says it's an accident, but if it is then why is he so scared that someone might find out? But what if I'm wrong and it's just what he says it is?"

"I see. How long have you known your friend's secret?"

I didn't consider Butch a friend, but I didn't say that. "I just found out today."

"But you're not sure it's what you suspect."

"Right. I hope I'm wrong."

"You're a good boy, Billy. Remember to trust in God."

I smiled up at him just as the bell rang ending recess. He smiled back, mussed my hair and said, "You'd better get going. We'll talk again."

I stood and started down the steps.

"Oh, and Billy?" he called. When I got down to the asphalt, I turned and looked back at my new friend. "Happy birthday."

Besides me, there were three other kids in detention. A sixth grader named Freddie Weaver who got caught drawing obscene pictures in his notebook, and two eighth graders, Nancy Palmer and Marsha Walsh, who got caught passing notes in class. Unfortunately for Miss Walsh, her name was the same as a character on the hit television show *The Brady Bunch*, and she was teased by the other students with a refrain of "Marsha! Marsha! Marsha!" whenever they passed her in the hall. I always felt bad for her. It was no fun being teased. As far as I could tell, I was the only one in detention who was actually innocent of the crime for which I was incarcerated.

The worst thing about detention with Mack Truck is not being able to do anything. You couldn't talk; you couldn't turn around; you weren't even allowed to do your homework. You just had to sit there looking straight ahead, hands folded on the desk, completely still and silent for one whole hour with nothing to do but stare at the walls and think about stuff.

The rest of the afternoon had gone by without incident. I knew Butch was watching me, but after lunch, he mostly left me alone. He hit me in the neck with a couple of spitballs during Art class, but that was normal. At least he didn't threaten me anymore today.

Matt and Lucy saw me sitting with Scotty and asked me about it, but I said we were just talking. I didn't say anything to either one of them about Butch's bruises, or that I suspected someone at home might be causing them. I kept it to myself for two reasons: first, I couldn't take a chance that Butch meant what he said and go after Lucy; and second, I didn't know that I was right. Maybe he was telling the truth and really just fell down the stairs. I wouldn't want to start any bad rumors. But what if I'm right? No matter how much I don't like Butch, no one deserves to get beat like that. If it is true, maybe that's why he's so mean.

I didn't want to think about Butch anymore, it either made me scared or depressed, and I was tired of feeling both of those. I looked around the room to try to focus on something else. Freddie

Weaver was drawing something in a notebook on his lap, no doubt another dirty picture. The two eighth grade girls were passing notes. Then something in the front of the room caught my eye.

Mack Truck was sitting behind her desk in front of class when I saw her hands drop to her lap. I knew what that meant: the old sneak the candy in the hankie trick. Sure enough, she surreptitiously opened the top desk drawer, fished out a piece of hard candy in a plastic wrapper, and dropped it in her lap. Then she casually lowered her hands to her lap again and very slowly unwrapped the candy, the cellophane wrapper crinkling very loudly as she did it. It seemed like the slower she did it, the louder and more obvious it became. Every ten seconds or so she would abruptly stop unwrapping the candy and look up with her eyes and scan the room back and forth, and then lower her eyes back to her lap and continue when she decided the coast was clear. I couldn't believe she actually thought no one in the classroom knew exactly what she was doing. She wasn't fooling anyone.

It was difficult not to laugh, too difficult for Freddie and the girls apparently. I could hear them snickering, which, of course, caused me to snicker as well. Once she got the candy unwrapped, she put it in a handkerchief and brought it up to her face, pretended to yawn and popped the candy into her mouth. She repeated this ritual several times a day, but somehow it was even more comical in detention with only a few of us in the room. Detention may be boring, but at least it wasn't completely without entertainment!

The hour finally passed, and at precisely four o'clock, she released us into the world. I was walking home today and decided to risk the fields and cutting through Old Man Hughes's yard. Once outside, I stopped to inhale deeply, taking in the air of freedom. The sun was shining and everything was in bloom; it was a glorious spring afternoon and the weekend was finally here, and in eight hours, I would turn nine years old!

Jimmy's Mom turned the lights on and off, signaling the end of band practice for the day. The boys finished the song they were rehearsing for Billy's birthday party, and whooped in approval of their performance.

"Man, that was the best yet!" Ben exclaimed.

"Yeah, we definitely got it down," Tim agreed.

"What time should we come over to set up?" Jimmy said.

"The party's gonna start around eleven," Sean said. "We should get set up by noon. We'll probably start playing around one o'clock."

"Cool," Ben said. "Jimmy, are you sure your brother is gonna help us move the equipment?"

"Yeah, don't worry about it."

"I can't believe it, our first gig!" Ben said.

"Don't get too excited," Tim said. "We're not even getting paid."

"Will you knock it off about getting paid," Jimmy said. "We're doing this as a birthday present for Billy."

"Alright, alright, I'm just sayin'. Geez, don't bite my head off man."

Jimmy's Mom opened the connecting door and poked her head inside. "Jimmy, tell your friends goodnight. Dinner's on the table."

"Okay Mom."

"How did we sound, Mrs. Mason?" Ben said.

"Don't you boys know any nice songs?" was all she said and

ducked back into the house. The boys looked at one another and laughed.

"I'll take that as a compliment," Tim said.

The boys said their goodbyes for the day and promised to meet back in the morning to pack up and move the equipment. Jimmy went back into his house, Ben went his own way, and Sean and Tim headed off in the opposite direction.

"You're sure it's okay that I'm coming over for dinner?" Sean said.

"I told you, don't sweat it, man," Tim said, putting a cigarette in his mouth and lighting it. He offered one to Sean.

"Won't they smell smoke?" Sean said, taking the cigarette. "The other day my little brother smelled it on me and threatened to tell my parents."

"What did I tell you about little brothers? You can't trust any of 'em."

"Yeah, you were right. But what about your grandmother? Won't she smell...?"

"We're not going to my house."

Sean blinked. "We're not? But you said..."

"We're going to my friend Joker's pad."

"Joker? What kind of name it that? What about dinner? I told my parents..."

"Will you chill out? You worry too much. Joker's cool, you'll dig him."

"I gotta be home by ten."

"No sweat," Tim assured him.

"Is it far?" Sean asked, trying to keep his unease out of his voice.

"Nah, it's just a few more blocks. You know those garden apartments over on Monroe Street?" Sean nodded. "He lives in the basement apartment. He's the Super."

That didn't do much to reassure Sean. The Monroe Gardens weren't exactly a slum, but they were close. The phrase "lower middle class" came to mind. They arrived a few minutes later, and Tim led him around back and down a set of concrete stairs. From inside, they heard the sound of George Harrison's guitar gently weeping. Tim knocked twice quickly and twice slowly, like Morse code dot-dot, dash-dash, obviously a secret knock. The music volume immediately lowered and a moment later, the door swung open.

The first thing that hit Sean was the smell, a combination of incense, body odor, and a skunky smell Sean couldn't identify. The man who answered the door looked like some kind of crazed hippie, with long straight greasy hair, a manic smile, and wild, staring eyes that seemed to look right into you, sinister and paranoid, yet somehow friendly and trusting at the same time. He was barefoot, clad only in a pair of dirty blue striped bellbottom pants that looked like they'd been slept in for a week and went unwashed for at least twice that long. Around his neck dangled a set of dog tags, jingling as they bounced against his naked chest. He reminded Sean of that Time magazine cover photo of Charles Manson, the cult leader and mastermind behind those mass murders in California a couple years ago.

The man known only as Joker, a nickname given to him in Vietnam because of his permanent too wide grin, looked at Sean, eyeing him up and down and frowning, before he shifted his gaze over to Tim, his expression instantly changing to one of friendly recognition.

"Timmy!" Joker said, beaming in delight. "Come on in, little dude!" He opened the door wide so the boys could enter.

The room was dark, except for the flickering light of the silent black and white television and a candle burning on the filthy chrome and glass coffee table. The windows were closed and the curtains drawn, giving off a gloomy feeling, like a cave. The walls reminded Sean of his own room, with posters of The Beatles, Jimi Hendrix, Jim Morrison, and The Who. Against the wall was a worn and dirty sofa, full of holes and cigarette burns.

"Who's your friend?" Joker said, looking Sean over.

"This is Sean McBride. I told you about him, remember? He's the drummer in my band."

"Oh right!" Joker said. "Pleased to meet you, Ringo! Call me Joker."

"Hi," Sean said timidly, shaking hands.

"Have a seat, boys. Help yourselves to a bong rip."

"You're reading my mind," Tim said. To Sean he confided, "Joker's always got the best grass."

Sean followed Tim to the couch and sat. On the coffee table in front of them, beside a short, fat candle with excess wax dripping over the sides, was a tall hand-blown glass water pipe and a plastic baggie half-full of green marijuana next to it. Tim removed a quarter-sized nugget from the bag and crushed it up on the table. With his thumb and index finger, he picked up a pinch, stuffed it into the large bowl of the pipe, and lifted it to his lips. He deftly struck a match and held it to the bowl, igniting the freshly packed herb. The water chamber bubbled and the bong filled with white smoke;

Tim took it all into his lungs. He lowered the pipe and exhaled a voluminous cloud of smoke into the air, choking as the last of it exited his body.

"You gotta cough to get off," Joker said, flashing a toothy smile.

Tim's coughing tapered off and he grinned back at Joker. "Man, that's some tasty grass," he said, handing the still smoking pipe to Sean.

"Uh, no thanks."

"Hey man," Joker said, suddenly upset. "I thought you said he was cool!"

"He is," Tim insisted. "What are you trying to do, make me look bad?" he said to Sean. "Take it."

Sean took the bong.

"Here, let me give you some fresh green," Joker said, taking another pinch from the table and topping off the bowl. "Now, just take a big hit."

Sean reluctantly raised the open stem to his mouth, allowing it to cover his lips completely. Tim struck a match and held the flame just above the bowl. "Go slow. Just suck it in."

Sean did as Tim instructed. He could feel his lungs expanding. The taste was weird; now he knew where that skunky odor he smelled before came from. He took in as much as he could and then suddenly, unexpectedly began choking. It was a deep hacking cough, twice as bad as any cigarette. He felt Tim patting him on the back as the second wave of coughing took hold.

"Easy man," Tim said, laughing. "You'll be okay. Let it out."

Sean stopped coughing and sat back, lethargically sinking back into the couch. He felt dizzy; his head was spinning and his whole body was more relaxed than it had ever been. He felt good. He could feel his face grinning ear to ear. He closed his eyes and listened to the music; it was like hearing it for the first time. His mouth was bone dry and he smacked his lips together. "Hey, man, got anything to drink?"

"You got cotton mouth? Timmy, show him where the Coke is," Joker said.

"Follow me," Tim said, standing.

Sean stood and followed Tim, meandering through the living room into the kitchen, passing through a curtain of colorful plastic beads in lieu of a door. He involuntarily shut his eyes when Tim switched on the overhead light, blinking through the sudden brightness.

The room was in desperate need of cleaning. A black iron skillet with a pool of solidified grease in the bottom sat on the stovetop, a pile of dirty dishes in the sink. Tim opened the refrigerator. Inside was a half-gallon carton of milk, half a stick of butter covered in toast crumbs, a bottle of ketchup, a pickle jar with one pickle remaining, a casserole dish that looked like it was once macaroni & cheese but now resembled a science experiment with its grey-green fungus, and four cans of Coca-Cola. He grabbed two cans of soda, handed one to Sean, and quickly shut the door. He turned off the light and they returned to the gloom of the living room, just as Joker was licking the thin adhesive strip on the paper of an expertly rolled marijuana cigarette.

"Are you ever gonna clean your kitchen?" Tim said, cracking open his soda and taking a sip. "Some of that stuff in there looks like it's gonna get up and walk away."

"Be my guest, smart ass," Joker said, not unkindly. "Hey, do me a favor while you're up. Turn off the stereo and turn up the TV.

Laugh-In is on."

Tim did as he was asked, then re-took his place on the sofa next to Sean, who'd sat down while he was attending to the entertainment center. They sat there for several minutes in stoned silence, drinking their sodas and enjoying their intense high, staring blankly at the television as the sexy, young "giggle girl," Goldie Hawn, danced in a bikini on a psychedelic stage to generic electric guitar rock music, her body painted with flowers and hip slogans. The camera froze on her upper-thigh, zooming in on a close-up of the words *Sock It To Me!* The next image on the screen was tall weeds parting in the middle by comedian Arte Johnson in a WWII Nazi costume poking his head through and saying in a phony German accent, "Ver-r-r-ry interesting... but stupid" to canned laughter.

"Man, that Arte Johnson is so funny," Tim said, laughing. "I love when he comes out as that old pervert and the old lady on the park bench hits him with her purse."

Joker laughed in agreement. "Yeah, but what I like best are the go-go dancers. Man, those chicks are gorgeous!"

"I know! I can't believe they get away with that on TV," Tim smiled lecherously.

"Down boy," Joker laughed.

"I love *Laugh-In*!" Tim proclaimed.

"Me too," Joker agreed. "What about you, Sean?"

Sean just sat there grinning and giggling.

"Earth to Sean," Tim said, giggling himself. Sean looked at him, laughing and nodding.

"How about some more grass?" Joker said, lighting the joint he'd just rolled. Sean just nodded even more, taking the joint when passed and smoking enthusiastically. He sat with them the rest of the evening getting stoned and watching TV with a stupid grin on his face. He was hooked.

SIX

I awoke to the smell of frying bacon drifting in from the kitchen downstairs. If there was ever an aroma more pleasant, I couldn't think of it. I glanced over to the nightstand beside my bed and Mickey's hands told me it was seven twenty-three. I sat up in bed and stretched. The day had finally arrived. I was now officially nine years old!

I hopped out of bed and slid the hand-knitted slippers my Nana made me last Christmas on my feet. Every year she gave a pair of slippers to everyone on her Christmas list. Whenever we visited her throughout the rest of the year, she would always be knitting a new pair for someone for next Christmas. It seemed that all Nana ever did, day after day, year after year, was knit slippers. And by the time next Christmas rolled around, the soles of the previous years slippers had worn out and began to unravel, just in time for a new pair.

Sean snored away, dead to the world, as I put on my bathrobe and bounded down the stairs to the kitchen. Mom had her back to me cooking breakfast when I came into the room. Besides bacon, she was busy preparing all my favorites: blueberry pancakes, scrambled eggs, and homemade hot cocoa with real whipped cream on top. It was a feast fit for a king.

"Morning Mommy!" I said with a grin.

"Good morning, Birthday Boy! Sit down and I'll pour you some Tang."

I sat down in my usual seat at the table and stared dumbfounded at the sight before me. I had been asking for a walkie-talkie set all year, but Dad always said they were too expensive, while Mom said I was still too young to take care of them properly. So, I was both surprised and disappointed when I found only one walkie-talkie with a blue ribbon and bow tied around it siting on the table in front of me.

"Do you like it?" Mom said.

I was confused. I looked at her, puzzlement on my face, and said, "Where's the other one?"

"What do you mean?"

"There's supposed to be two."

"We could only afford one."

"But it's no good without the other one."

"I'm sorry. We tried."

"That's okay," I said offering her a weak smile and trying not to sound too disappointed. They did try, after all, and half a walkie-talkie was better than none. Wasn't it? Maybe I could pick up the signal from a police car or a truck passing through the neighborhood.

"Maybe we can get you another one for Christmas," she offered.

"Yeah," I said unenthusiastically. "That'd be great."

She put a plate of bacon, eggs, and pancakes in front of me and left the kitchen. I started on my breakfast, feeling slightly dejected, when I heard my mother's voice coming through the radio transceiver in front of me as she sang, "*Happy birthday to you...*"

I spun around in my chair just as she turned the corner into the kitchen holding the matching radio to her mouth and singing. I jumped up, grinning broadly and hugged her tightly around the waist.

"Surprise!" she shouted, laughing. "I had you going, didn't I?"

"Oh man! You sure did!" I agreed, also laughing. "That was great!"

"Happy birthday, Sweetheart."

"Thanks Mommy, you're the best!"

"You're welcome, but make sure you thank your father too. He's the one who picked them out for you."

"I will," I promised.

"Will what?" Dad said as if on cue, entering the kitchen. He kissed my mom, and then went straight for the coffee. I got up and hugged him just as he was pouring himself a cup.

"Thank you, Daddy," I said, my arms around his waist and my head pressed against his stomach. "I love my present."

"Whoa there, Sport," he said, somehow managing not to spill his coffee. "Happy birthday. I'm glad you like it."

"I do! They're perfect." I kissed his cheek when he sat down at the table. "I wish you could make it to my party."

"I know, I do too. I'm sorry. If I could have gotten out of it, I would have, but Mr. Hamilton is a very important man and one of my biggest accounts. I couldn't just say no."

"It's okay, I understand," I said, even though I didn't.

"I'll make it up to you, I promise. We'll do something special, just you and me."

"Yeah, okay."

He wolfed down a bowl of Corn Flakes, finished his coffee, put his cup in the sink, and kissed my mom again.

"I'll try and be home for supper," he said, straightening his tie. Then he kissed me on top of my head, said, "Happy birthday, Sport," and was out the door.

I sighed and continued eating my breakfast.

"He went to three different stores before he found the right walkie-talkies. He said if he was going to get them for you then they were going to be the best, not some cheap toy."

"He said that?"

"Mmm-hmm. Your father loves you more than you can possibly imagine. He just has a hard time showing it."

"I know he does, but why does he have to work all the time?"

"He works hard so we can have nice things. You're lucky. Think of all the boys and girls who don't get presents on their birthday."

I smiled and nodded, suddenly feeling selfish.

"Now finish your breakfast and go play for a few hours. I'll call you when it's time for your party."

The rockets of *Constellation One's* main propulsion system ignited, propelling the starship out of orbit of Fraxis Six. The onboard inertial dampeners kicked in, countering the G-force effect as the ship gained speed. Within moments, it was free of the planets gravitational forces.

"We are free and clear to navigate," Mr. Shondo informed the captain.

"Galactic Fleet, this is *Constellation One*," Captain Apollo said into the com. "Empress Lucinda of Fraxis Six has been kidnapped by the Butcher. We believe Mack the Black is behind the attack. We are currently in pursuit along their last known trajectory."

"Acknowledged, *Constellation*. Your orders are to rescue the Empress and neutralize Mack the Black if possible."

"Confirmed. That's just what I wanted to hear. *Constellation* out." Captain Apollo turned to face Shondo. "Do we know where he's headed?"

"His current course will take him near the vicinity of the Antonius system. Several known associates of Mack the Black have been spotted leaving the moon orbiting the third planet. I believe that is his destination."

"Good work, Shondo. Helm, plot a course for Antonius-Three."

"Aye, sir, course laid in," the pilot confirmed.

"Engage." Captain Apollo got up from his chair and walked toward the door. "Inform me when we reach Antonius," he said, and exited the bridge.

Billy Apollo walked along the corridor to the ships galley where preparations for a party in honor of Empress Lucinda and the recent induction of Fraxis Six into the Galactic Federation were being finalized. There were delicacies prepared from every member world of the Federation, including Fraxis Six. The crew had worked long and hard in the weeks leading up to the celebration, only to have their plans interrupted by Mack the Black. He vowed to himself that he would make her pay.

And above all else, he would rescue the Empress. Not because he was ordered to. Not because she was the ruler of the newest planet in the Federation. Not because she was beautiful. But because he was falling in love with her. He would go to the ends of the galaxy to...

"Billy?"

...to rescue...

"Come on, Billy."

...her.

"Billy, answer me!"

I felt around for my walkie-talkie, found it, and pressed the button. "Yeah Mom?"

"Come upstairs and get ready for your party. Your guests will be arriving in less than an hour."

"Okay, be right there!"

I climbed out of the dryer, taking the walkie-talkie with me, and ran upstairs. My mom was still in the kitchen, only now she was wearing her best dress with her imitation pearl necklace and earrings. I know they were imitation because I asked her once if they were real. They're not. Her hair was done up in her usual beehive hairdo and she put her makeup on in that way she has where it looks like she's not wearing any. She wore a flower apron over her dress and was decorating something I couldn't see.

"Wow! You look great!" I said as I rounded the corner of the top landing and came into the kitchen. "Is that my cake?"

"Thank you, and yes, but don't look, it's not finished yet."

I tried to look anyway, but she shielded it with her body and pushed me away. "Get out of here!" she scolded, but I could tell she was just playing. I stopped trying to sneak a look at the cake and took a cookie instead. "Go on now, go upstairs and get ready. And brush your teeth."

"Aw Mom, do I have to?" I whined. "It's my birthday."

"I'm sure all the Apollo astronauts brush their teeth on their birthdays."

"Fine," I said. Leave it to Mom to bring up a point I couldn't argue.

I trudged up the stairs and opened the door to my room to find Sean in the middle of a full-blown tantrum, ripping posters off his walls, specifically his Beatles posters. His sheets and blankets were strewn around the room; his stereo was on its side; Beatles records were scattered haphazardly around the room; and the contents of his dresser drawers were thrown everywhere. He'd pulled down the four Beatles portraits, and was in the process of ripping up the picture of Paul McCartney, when I walked into the room.

"I hate you!" Sean screamed at the pieces of the photograph in his hands. "Why?!"

"Sean?" I said, confused and frightened by his meltdown. "What's wrong?"

Sean turned to face me, suddenly realizing I was in the room. "Get out of here! Leave me alone!"

"This is my room too!" I said, standing my ground. "And why aren't you dressed yet? I thought you were going to Jimmy's to get your band equipment?"

"I'm not going to your stupid party and neither is the band!"

"What do you mean you're not going? What's going on?"

Sean ignored me and continued on his tirade, throwing anything within reach.

"Sean, stop it! You're scaring me! I'm gonna tell Mom!"

I hated playing the Mom card, but I didn't see any other choice.

Sean finally stopped.

"You want to know what's wrong? Here!" he said, and threw a newspaper at me. It hit me in the chest and landed at my feet. I picked it up and read today's headline:

PAUL QUITS BEATLES!

I actually felt the color drain from my face. My legs got shaky and I fell backward onto my bed. I was in shock. How could this happen?! It can't be true! I felt like I was in the *Twilight Zone*. I read the headline again. It hadn't magically changed while I tried to wish it away. I looked up at Sean, the same pain in my eyes that were in his.

"Happy birthday," he said, his voice dripping with sarcasm.

Katherine was putting the finishing touches on the rocket cake when Billy came running down the stairs crying, ran through the kitchen onto the back porch and out the back door, letting it slam behind him. She looked out the window above the sink overlooking the backyard, and saw him sitting on the tree stump ten yards from the house with his head in his hands. She could hear his loud sobs from here.

"Sean Michael McBride!" she yelled up the stairwell, using his full name to let him know she meant business. "Get down here NOW!"

Sean took his sweet time coming down. He entered the kitchen wearing the same T-shirt he'd slept in and yesterday's dirty bell-bottom jeans. He stood defiantly in the archway between the kitchen and the living room.

"What."

"Don't you take that tone with me, young man. Why is your brother outside crying?"

"Why don't you go ask him?"

"I'm asking you. A few minutes ago he was fine."

"I told him I'm not going to his stupid party, okay."

"What do you mean you're not going?" she said, losing her patience. "You most certainly are. You promised him your band was going to play."

"Yeah, well, the gig is cancelled."

"You are going to the party, and your band will play or after today there won't be a band! Do I make myself clear?"

"Who cares? Bands are stupid anyway."

Now she knew something was wrong. His band meant everything to him. "Okay, Sean," she said, much more sympathetically, "tell me what's going on. Something happened, didn't it?"

Sean suddenly dropped his angry posture and plopped himself down unceremoniously onto the nearest kitchen chair. His shoulders slumped forward and he looked up at her with a dejected expression. "The Beatles broke up," he said with the sad resignation of genuine sorrow in his voice, a tear rolling down his cheek. "It's all over. Paul quit yesterday."

Oh no, she thought. *So that's it. Why did they have to pick today of all days to announce the news?*

"Oh Honey. I'm so sorry. I know how much they meant to you. Both of you. But that's no excuse for taking it out on your brother, especially today. You know he's probably just as broken up about it as you are. He needs his big brother right now to let him know everything will be okay. Now, I want you to go outside and tell him you're sorry and you wouldn't dream of missing his party. And then you're going to call your friends and tell them you'll be right over to pack up your equipment and get it over here."

"But Mom..."

"No buts. Do it. We'll talk about this later."

"Yes ma'am."

"And before you leave, go upstairs and put on some clean clothes. Phew! And take a shower!"

By noon, about half the kids I invited had already shown up. Mostly boys, but a few girls too. The weather had cooperated and my guests were enjoying the party activities that had been set up in the backyard. A few were on the permanent swing set, some others were taking turns playing horseshoes, but most were inside the rented Moon-House, an inflated plastic box with a rubber "Moon surface" floor that kids could bounce around on. I heard my dad complain that it was a little expensive, but I thought it was worth whatever it cost judging by its popularity among my friends. Everyone was having a good time.

Well, almost everyone.

I sat by myself on our tree stump, the remains of an elm tree felled by Hurricane Ginny that had swept through in October of 1963 when I was only two. I was too little to remember it, but my dad still talks about how lucky we were it didn't fall on the house.

Today wasn't going the way I planned. In fact, it was turning out to be one of the worst days I ever had. The specter of The Beatles breaking up hung in the air like an ominous dark cloud over everything. No one was saying too much about it, as if by not acknowledging it might make it not true. But it was true and everyone knew it. I still couldn't believe it. More than anything, it signaled the end of something special that could never be recaptured. It felt like the end of an era; an end to the 60's, even though, technically, they ended four months ago. The dream was over.

Happy birthday indeed.

"Hey there, Mr. Grumpy Pants."

I looked up from what I was doing; using a lens of my glasses to focus the rays of the sun into a tight beam to fry an ant. "Hey Luce."

She sat down next to me, cross-legged on the grass, covering her skinny knees with her three-quarter length yellow flowered party dress.

"I like your dress," I said, but she made a face.

"I hate dresses," she said. "They make me look too girlie, but my mother made me wear it."

"I think you look nice."

"Thanks, I guess," she said, blushing. "So, how come you're sitting here all by yourself? It's your party."

"I dunno."

"Come on, get up! Have some fun! Go jump in the Moon-House! It's a gas, you should try it. Look, even Matt's enjoying it."

I looked over at the inflated plastic and rubber structure. Sure enough, there was Matt, grinning, and laughing, and jumping around. I smiled to myself. It was good to see Matt letting loose and having fun instead of moping around. Like I was doing right now. I turned my attention back to the ground between my feet and refocused my Death Ray. "I don't feel like it."

"Look, I know how you feel. I love The Beatles too. Everyone does. But you can't let it ruin your birthday, okay. I mean, just because they're not gonna be together anymore, it's not like the end of the world, right? Just forget about it, at least for today. Besides, you have the Moon launch to look forward to in an hour. Apollo 13! It's all you talked about since I met you! So what do you say? Come on and play. Okay? For me? Please?"

And then she leaned forward and kissed me on the cheek.

For the second time today I felt my face change color, only this time, instead of being drained, I knew I was turning several shades of red. I looked at her with a dopey smile and stuttered, "O...o...okay."

She hopped to her feet, grabbed my arm, and pulled me up. We ran together, hand-in-hand to the Moon-House. We took off our shoes, climbed through the vertical flap, and joined the others inside laughing and jumping. For the first time since breakfast today, I was happy.

Katherine, Karen Ross, and Max Sherman enjoyed a complete panoramic view of the yard from the back porch. They sipped fresh coffee while they watched the children play. Katherine was glad she had help, especially Max, to chaperone the yard-full of unruly second graders. She'd heard the stories about Butch Anderson and his pal Joey, but so far, they've mostly behaved themselves. The worst thing that happened was a minor accident involving a boy landing the wrong way in the Moon-House, in which Butch's fist may or may not have been involved. The accident caused some tears, more humiliation than actual injury, and the boy was off and playing again after some root beer and a cupcake. Butch's reputation was the primary reason Katherine had wanted a man present. Fortunately, Max was available and only too happy to help out.

Max was only twenty-nine and already a widower. A talented musician and artist, having mastered several instruments and dabbling in watercolor and sculpture, he made his living as a Professor of Music at Rutgers University in Newark. He was a true bohemian and looked the part; tall and thin, with semi-long tight, curly black hair; an all-black wardrobe—black bellbottoms, black turtle-neck sweater, black Beatle Boots; a silver peace symbol necklace, silver Timex watch on his right wrist, and a silver wedding band on the third finger of his right hand.

He was charming, intelligent, and a devoted father. He was a family friend the way all parents become friendly with the parents of their children's playmates. His son Matt and Billy were best friends—probably the best friend either boy had ever had—so naturally they had gotten to know Max.

Katherine truly liked and admired him, while Leo merely tolerated him for Billy's sake. He didn't care for Max's lifestyle, though in truth, it was his perceived lifestyle and not his actual lifestyle that Leo disapproved of, for Leo knew little of Max's private life. He judged him by his appearance, and in that, Leo and Max were polar opposites. Leo considered Max to be a "hippie," regardless that he was a well-respected professor. Leo was civil to him, but his opinion was formed and his mind made up about the man. Try as she might, Katherine could not change his mind—he was a stubborn Irishman. When she told him Max was going to help chaperone, he resisted the idea until she reminded him if he hadn't decided to work on his son's birthday, she wouldn't have had to call him. That seemed to put an end to the discussion.

Today was the first time either she or Max was meeting Karen Ross. They had both heard about Lucy, their sons' newest classmate, and were glad to have the opportunity to meet her mother so soon after joining the Saint Anthony's fraternity of parents.

Like Katherine, she dressed conservatively, wearing a knee length Spring dress and a simple gold cross necklace; her shoulder length blond hair held back with a white plastic band. Petite and pretty, her five-foot two-inch frame barely came to Max's chest, even in heels.

She related to them, in her pronounced Texan twang, of her husband's recent transfer to New York and the move from the rural outskirts of Houston to the far more congested suburbs of northern New Jersey. As with any drastic move of this sort, it would take some getting used to. And while the place was different, she found the people to be fundamentally the same.

"To be honest, I didn't really know what to expect," she was saying. "I'd heard stories about New York City, and how rude everyone is. But y'all are so nice. I guess it just goes to prove you can't believe everything you hear."

"There are bad parts of the city, that's for sure, but it's really not as bad as people make out," Max said. "Mind you, Mount Clayton isn't New York, but New Yorkers can be pretty nice too. In their own way."

"I haven't actually been to the city itself yet," she confessed. "Frank promised to take the girls and me one Sunday for dinner and a Broadway show, once we get all settled in. I can't believe how much unpacking there is."

"It took me a year until I unpacked my last box," Max said. "You really don't realize how much you have until you move."

"How long have you and Matt lived here?" She inquired.

"It'll be two years this July."

Just then, the front doorbell rang.

"Excuse me a minute," Katherine said, removing herself from the conversation. She walked through the house to the front door and opened it. She was pleasantly surprised when she saw the tall, slender black woman and her young son standing on the front steps.

"Carol! I'm so glad you could make it," Katherine said, opening the door for her guests. The two women kissed cheeks in greeting.

"I didn't think we would. We had plans to go to James's mother's, but he had an emergency appendectomy, so here we are."

"And look at you!" Katherine said, turning her attention to the boy. "You're getting so big and handsome."

"What do you say Sammy?" his mother prodded.

"Thank you, Mrs. McBride," the shy boy said. He presented a brightly wrapped package to her. "I got this for Billy."

"You did? Well, thank you."

"He picked it out himself," Carol said. Sammy beamed proudly.

"Come with me," Katherine said to Sammy, "you can put it with the rest of Billy's gifts."

She led them through the living room to the kitchen where there were about a dozen and a half wrapped presents of various shapes and sizes on a long wooden cabinet against the far wall. Sammy added his to the pile.

Katherine offered Carol a cup of coffee, which she politely accepted. Carol was dressed in the latest casual fashion, a pair of white bellbottom slacks and a lime green top, perfectly accentuating her mocha skin. Her diamond encrusted wedding band and green hoop earrings, the same shade as her blouse, were her only jewelry. Her hair was coiffed in a medium length afro, the overall effect being that she was an attractive, modern woman.

She and her husband James, a resident surgeon at Passaic General Hospital, met the McBrides four years ago on a weekend Thanksgiving cruise when their mischievous little boys went missing for several hours, turning the entire ship upside down searching for them. It turned out to be a false alarm when the two playmates were found in the McBride's cabin, coloring peacefully in Billy's coloring books. After that parental bonding experience, the McBrides and the Washingtons spent the rest of the cruise together, and remained fast friends ever since. Katherine and Carol stayed in touch by phone, and they usually all got together at least three times a year for Thanksgiving and the boys' birthdays.

She sipped her coffee and followed Katherine onto the back porch, where they found Max and Karen engaged in conversation.

"Mark my words," Max was telling Karen, "they will go down in history with the likes of Mozart and Beethoven. Today is a sad day for music."

"Well, I don't see it," Karen said dismissively. "I'll take Elvis any day."

"Max, Karen, I'd like you to meet my good friends, Carol and Sammy Washington."

Carol smiled and said, "How do you do." Sammy hid behind his mom, one eye peeking out from around her back.

Max smiled broadly, taking her hand and kissing it, causing Carol to blush. Karen seemed somewhat taken aback, though she quickly recovered and smiled politely. Carol noticed Karen's reaction, no doubt shocked to see a black woman and her son as invited guests to a "white" party, but she let it go. She was used to it. Civil rights had come a long way in recent years, but there was still a long way to go.

"We were just discussing the tragic news today of The Beatles demise. What are your thoughts on the subject?" Max asked her.

"Max is a professor of music," Katherine informed her.

"I like a lot of their songs, but to be honest, I'm more of a Gladys Knight and the Pips kind of gal."

"Ah, Motown!" Max said. "Some of the freshest music around comes out of there. I love the Motown sound!"

"Sammy, Honey, why don't you go outside and find Billy. He'll be thrilled to see you," Katherine said.

Sammy looked up at his mom. "Go on," she encouraged. With a smile, he bolted out the back door.

Lucy, Matt, and I were taking turns throwing horseshoes when I spotted my friend Sammy coming down the back steps. I dropped the over-sized red rubber horseshoe in my hand and ran over to greet him.

"Sammy!" I shouted.

"Billy!" Sammy shouted back, closing the distance between us. We both collided with each other and embraced in a hug. Sammy's grin was a big as mine.

"How come you're here? My mom said you couldn't come."

"We were supposed to go to my grandma's but my daddy had to go to the hospital."

"Yeah, my dad had to work too. But I'm glad you made it."

"Me too."

"Come on, I want you to meet my friends," I said and brought Sammy over to meet Matt and Lucy.

"Hey guys," I said. "This is my friend Sammy. He lives over in Passaic. Sammy, these are my best friends at school, Matt and Lucy." When you're a kid, last names aren't necessary.

My three friends exchanged "hellos." After that, we all just stood there looking at each other. Finally, Lucy said, "So, how do you guys know each other?"

"We met on a cruise ship when we were five," I told them. Then, turning to Sammy I said, "Remember?" He just nodded and laughed. I guess it was pretty funny now, but it wasn't so funny at the time. At least not for our parents.

We were on a "Cruise to Nowhere," a cruise over Thanksgiving weekend that left New York on Wednesday, sailed out into the Atlantic Ocean, then made a big U-turn and returned to the harbor on Sunday. The two things I remember most about it were our waiter and Sammy.

It was a Greek Ocean liner and Oleg (pronounced Olay), our waiter, was new and barely spoke English. I remember Sean and I ordered Coke to drink and he kept bringing us hot chocolate; he thought we were saying "cocoa." Then he tried to bring us chocolate milk. The poor guy was getting really frustrated, and so were we. All we wanted was a Coke! I mean, how hard is that?

Finally, someone said "Coca-Cola" and then it registered. Oleg's eyes got wide and his mouth opened in a grin of understanding. "Ah! Coca-Cola!" he exclaimed. We'd finally managed to bridge the communication gap, because two minutes later Sean and I each had a big, frosty glass of Coke in front of us. It never tasted so good! Ever since then, whenever I order a Coke in a restaurant, I always ask for Coca-Cola.

The other thing I remember about that cruise is how Sammy and I met and ended up good friends. Like I said, I was five, and I guess my parents wanted to do something that they thought I would be bored doing, so they dropped me off at the ships playroom. It was a big room with lots of toys and games to play with, a place where you could leave your kid for a couple hours while a lady that works for the ship babysits them. The place reminded me a lot of Kindergarten.

When my parents dropped me off, Sammy and a couple other kids were already there. I started playing with Sammy, the only kid there the same age as me, and we hit it off right away. I started getting bored, and so was Sammy, so I suggested we go back to my cabin where I had some coloring books. Sammy thought that was a good idea, so off we went.

We didn't bother to tell the lady that worked there we were leaving; she was busy changing one of the little kid's diaper. Looking back on it now, I guess we should have said something because of all the panic we caused, but we weren't thinking. Come on, we were only five!

So, anyway, we went to my family's cabin and got out my crayons and coloring books and started coloring; I chose *Lost In Space* and Sammy picked *Batman and Robin*. So there we were, just laying on the carpet coloring away for who knows how long, a couple hours at least, just two new best friends as happy as can be without a care in the world, when all of a sudden the door bursts open and there are my mom and dad with Sammy's mom and dad, and the captain of the ship and maybe a half dozen other people all excited and yelling, “We found them! We found them!” Both our parents were so happy they came running in and scooped us up in their arms and started hugging and kissing us to death.

Apparently, when the lady in the playroom realized we were missing, they found our parents and started searching for us everywhere. After a couple hours of searching and they couldn’t find us, they were afraid we went overboard. Both our parents were terrified something happened to us. Then I guess someone asked if anyone checked the cabins. They didn’t bother to check there because we were only five and how could we possibly know which cabin was ours and how to get there from the playroom?

But I knew.

They were all so relieved that they found us alive and unharmed that we didn’t even get in any trouble. And after that, we all had Thanksgiving dinner together and my parents and Sammy’s parents became good friends and spent the whole rest of the cruise hanging out together. And Sammy and I are still good friends, only we don’t get to see each other that much because we live far apart.

I told Lucy and Matt the story of how we met, and they thought it was pretty cool too. The four of us split up into teams, Sammy and me against Matt and Lucy, for a game of horseshoes. Sammy and I were kicking some serious butt, when Matt said, “Hey, what time is it?” None of us was wearing a watch, so I looked back at the house, saw the group of adults on the porch through the screened windows, and shouted, “Hey Mom! Do you know what time it is?” Max looked at his watch and shouted back, “Five after one!”

We all looked at each other and shouted in one voice, “Apollo 13!”

We ran to the house and threw open the door, sprinting onto the porch, and one after the other with me in the lead, raced through the house to the living room and planted ourselves in front of the television. I switched it on, and after a couple seconds of warming up, the image of Cape Kennedy in Florida appeared.

We sat on the floor directly in front of the twenty-six inch color console TV. On the screen was the Apollo 13 rocket, a white vapor cloud emanating from the ship. In the left hand corner of the screen, it displayed the current time: *April 11, 1970 1:09:42 PM*. In the right corner, it showed the countdown: T-Minus 04:08 and counting.

"Oh my God, this is so exciting!" Lucy said.

"This looks so awesome in color," Matt said. "Later can we watch...?"

"Shhh!" I scolded. He shushed. We all listened to the announcer on the television:

"...couldn't ask for a more beautiful day here at Cape Kennedy. Ladies and gentlemen, we are moments away from this, our third lunar mission, taking off into space. In the capsule, our three astronauts, Commander James Lovell, Command Module Pilot John Swigert and Lunar Module Pilot Fred Haise are strapped in and waiting to make history. We take you now live to Mission Control in Houston."

"Apollo 13, you are go for launch," a voice said.

"Roger, Houston, we are T-Minus ten... nine... eight... seven... six... five... four... three... engine start... two... one. Liftoff."

An explosion of flames shot out of the main thrusters. The rocket began to lift from the main platform, slowly at first, then gaining momentum. In seconds, it cleared the rigging and ascended into the sky.

"Ladies and gentlemen, we have a perfect liftoff," the announcer told us.

All four of us applauded, and whooped, and hollered. I ran out the front door and looked up at the sky, trying desperately to catch a glimpse of the rocket leaving the atmosphere, but of course, I couldn't; New Jersey is a thousand miles away from Florida. But I pretended I could.

As I was looking up, I heard the sound of an amplified guitar tuning up from the direction of the driveway. I ran back inside to alert my friends.

"Hey guys, my brother's band is getting ready to play out in the garage!" I said. We all ran back out through the front door and around the house where we found everyone from the backyard migrating over to the driveway. Octopus's Garden was set up inside the garage and preparing to start. Ben Shaw, the group's lead singer, stepped up to the microphone.

"Okay everyone, gather 'round. We're Octopus's Garden and we're here today to help celebrate Billy McBride's birthday. Where are you Billy?" I raised my hand and everyone turned to look at me. "Happy Birthday, Billy!" Ben said. Some kids clapped; I blushed. "As most of you probably already know, The Beatles broke up yesterday..." A few people booed. One girl yelled out, "I hate you Paul!" Ben continued, "...But that doesn't mean you're gonna stop listening to their music, right? And we're not gonna stop playing it! This one's for you, Billy!" He turned to his band mates and said, "Ready? One, two, three, four!"

Sean started with a short double-beat drum solo, and they

broke out into a loud, fast, hard rocking song. Then Ben screamed the song *Birthday* by The Beatles into the mike.

They were really good. In fact, I was surprised how good they were—for a bunch of sixth graders, anyway. The last time Sean had let me come to one of their practices—which seemed like ages ago—they still needed a lot of work. I guess that just goes to show what practice can do.

I looked all around me, watching the kids in my class watching my brother's band. I was really proud of Sean at that moment. Everyone loved them; some danced, some sang along, most just tapped their feet and nodded their heads. I, of course, sang along. Even my mom was getting into it I think. She wasn't covering her ears at least. Matt's dad was bopping along with the kids.

They played song after song, mostly Beatles, with a couple of Monkees and Rolling Stones songs thrown in. My favorite was when they did *All You Need Is Love*. I remember when The Beatles first played it live on TV everywhere in the world at the same time. They used a satellite orbiting Earth to bounce the signal everywhere at once; it was the very first world-wide live satellite TV broadcast in history, and The Beatles used it to spread the message of love. Mom and Dad couldn't care less, but Sean and I were glued to the TV for it. And Octopus's Garden did a great job playing it.

They played for over half an hour. When they finished the last song, everyone clapped and cheered. They were a definite hit.

"Thank you, everyone!" Tim said over the applause. All four guys in the band were sweating and grinning from ear to ear. "Thank you very much! Happy Birthday Billy!"

When the applause stopped, my mom shouted from the back of the crowd, "Okay everyone, cake and ice cream in the backyard!"

A cheer rang out even louder than for the band and all the kids headed back into the yard. A few stragglers stayed behind, Sammy and me among them. I walked into the garage where Sean was putting away his sticks. He had a towel wrapped around his neck and his hair was dripping with sweat.

"Thanks Sean. You guys were really great," I said.

"You're welcome, Tiger. Happy birthday. Sorry if I was a jerk to you before. I was kind of in shock. I guess I overreacted. I didn't mean to take it out on you."

"Aw, that's okay, I understand. I can't believe they broke up either."

"Yeah, well, I'm still sorry."

Sammy walked over and stood by my side. "Hi Sean."

"Sammy! My man!" Sean said. "I saw you rockin' out there. Haven't seen you since last Thanksgiving. How you doin?"

"Good," he said. Sammy was a man of few words. In fact, sometimes it was like pulling teeth just to get him to talk.

Max walked up behind us and put a hand on Sammy's and my shoulders causing Sammy to jump.

"You know, you boys are really quite good," he said to Sean, loud enough for the others to hear.

"Thanks Mr. Sherman," Sean replied, as the other members of the band gathered around to join the conversation. "We practice as often as we can."

"I can tell. Keep it up. Which one of you is the leader?"

"Well," Sean began, "We really don't..."

"I am," Tim interrupted, stepping forward.

Max noticed the other three were a little surprised by that. Sean told me they didn't have a leader.

"I see," Max said. "And you are?"

"Tim Andrews," he said, offering his hand. Max shook hands.

"Well, Tim, I was going to suggest you boys might want to enter the Battle of the Bands at Mount Clayton High. It's next month, Saturday, May sixteenth. I'm one of the judges."

Their faces all lit up at the same time as they exchanged shocked and excited glances with one another.

"But," he added, "you have to have at least one original song. Think you can be ready in time?"

"Sure," Tim said, although his voice lacked confidence. "No sweat."

"You guys are sure to win!" I interjected, adding my two cents. "Especially with Matt's dad as the judge."

"One of the judges. There are three. But don't think I'm going to give you a free pass. You're going to have to earn it. I don't play favorites. Understand?"

"Yes sir," all four band mates said in unison.

"Alright then, we'll talk more later. Now, I'm going to get some ice cream before it's all gone," Max said and left the garage.

"Since when did you become the leader?" Ben said. Sean and Jimmy nodded in agreement.

"Since I'm the oldest. Look, what's the difference? We have to come up with a song if we're gonna enter the contest."

"Oh, just like that," Jimmy said, sarcastically.

"Yeah, just like that. Come on, we got a whole month. How hard can it be?"

"Billy!" I heard my mom yell from the yard. "Hurry up! Everybody's waiting for you to sing *Happy Birthday* and cut the cake."

"Coming!" I yelled back and ran to the yard with Sammy right behind.

Everyone was already gathered around a large table in the backyard when we arrived. The adults must've set it up while Octopus's Garden was playing, because it wasn't there before. We joined Matt and Lucy, who had gone back into the yard when Sammy and I were talking to Sean and the guys with Max. I noticed some of the kids looking at Sammy and whispering to each other. I'm pretty sure I even heard the word *nigger*, which really made me angry. I think Sammy heard it too; he tried not to react but I could tell it made him uncomfortable. I wasn't sure who said it, but I had a pretty good idea.

The back door opened and my mom came out carrying my cake. She started singing *Happy Birthday*, and after she sang the first "Happy" by herself, the whole chorus of kids joined in. She carefully set the cake down on the table in front of me. I was all smiles; someone snapped a picture.

The cake was a true masterpiece. Mom had really outdone herself this time. The base was an extra-long rectangle with green frosting sprinkled with dyed green coconut flakes for grass; in the center was a square with grey frosting for the cement launch pad; on top of the launch pad was a foot tall exact replica model of the Apollo 13 rocket. Nine candles were set in a circle around the rocket, with the words "Happy Birthday Astronaut Billy" written in red on the green "grass." I inhaled deeply, made a wish (I *wish* The Beatles get back together), and blew out the candles to generous applause.

"Thanks Mom," I said, giving her a big hug. "This is the best cake ever." And I meant it.

She bent down to give me a kiss.

"Alright, who wants cake?" she said. Shouts of, "Me! Me!" and, "I do! I do!" greeted her in reply as she cut the cake. She gave the first piece to me.

An hour later, Sammy, Matt, Lucy, and I were having a blast bouncing around in the Moon-House. We were the only ones in there. I hoped it was because everyone was too full of cake and ice cream and soda, at least that's what I wanted to believe, but I knew in my heart the real reason—Sammy. I hated that people were so narrow-minded. Racism is stupid! Sammy is one of the best kids I know. I know he knew what was going on, but he ignored them. *Good for him*, I thought. *He's smarter than the rest of them combined!*

When we first met on that ship and started playing together, I didn't see a black kid, I just saw another kid my age. My parents raised us to believe that people are all the same, it doesn't matter what color their skin is. I remember two years ago, my mom and Sammy's mom cried on the phone together for over an hour on the day Martin Luther King was assassinated.

"Okay everyone, gather 'round," I heard my mom yell even through the plastic walls of the Moon-House. The four of us all stopped jumping around to listen. She was over by the tree on the side of the house and something bright and colorful was hanging from the branches. "Mister Sherman brought a surprise!"

"Oh yeah!" Matt said. "I forgot!"

"What is it?" I said.

"You'll see," Matt said grinning.

I was the first one out of the Moon-House, the other three hot on my heels. We ran to the tree where the rest of the kids were already gathered. I could see now what was hanging from the tree:

a multi-colored papier-mâché donkey.

"What's that?" I said, looking at the strange form in the tree.

"It's a piñata," Max said.

"A what?" I'd never heard of it before.

"A piñata. It's from Mexico," Max explained.

"What's it for?"

"Come here and I'll show you."

I walked over to Max, who produced a black handkerchief from his pocket and proceeded to tie it around my head, blindfolding me.

"Okay, can you see anything?" Max said. I couldn't and shook my head. "Now, take this stick." He handed me what felt like a broom handle. Then he spun me around and around until I became a little dizzy and lost all sense of direction. "Okay, now try to hit it."

I raised the stick and swung, slicing into empty air. I heard the kids laughing. I swung again, and again hit nothing. I didn't know it, but each time I swung, Max was pulling a string, raising the donkey up out of the way. After a few more swings, I connected. The kids cheered. I whacked it a few more times before Max took the stick and blindfold off and said, "Okay, who's next?"

One after another, kids lined up to take a shot. The paper beast was well constructed and took several good hits, but still remained intact. Then Butch stepped up. He grinned and I saw him wink at his friend Joey. Joey snickered; something was up. I told Sammy to stand back. I should have taken my own advice.

Max blindfolded Butch, but forgot to spin him around. Butch raised the stick and swung it directly at me, knocking me hard on the head. There was a flash of bright white and then I saw stars. I heard the other kids gasp at once as I burst into tears and grasped the side of my head. Joey laughed in hysterics. Butch tried to hit me again, but Max grabbed the stick before he could take another swing.

My mom rushed over to my side, moved my hand out of the way and examined my head. There was blood on my hands and a gash on my side temple. Max was holding Butch by the collar while my mom led me into the house.

That night, I laid in bed wide-awake, thinking over the day and the way my party, which was going so well, ended in disaster. Thanks Butch.

After Butch hit me on the head, the party was pretty much over. Max put Butch and Joey in his car and took them home while my mom patched me up inside with first-aid cream and a Band-Aid. When she was finally convinced I didn't have another concussion, she let me go back outside, but the fun mood was gone. Never-the-less, I put the blindfold on Sammy so he could get his turn, and let him have his shot at the piñata. He must've had a lot of pent up rage inside, because my shy, quiet little friend hit that thing like he was trying to kill it. It broke open and hundreds of little candies sprinkled to the ground. Everyone else dove for it, but I just watched. I didn't feel much like fighting for candy. Sammy ended up giving me some of his.

When we were done with the piñata, it was time to open presents. I got the usual stuff; a couple of Hot Wheels cars, a slinky, an Etch-A-Sketch, some clothes. Lucy got me a pocketknife, explaining that all the boys in Texas have one. Matt got me a model *Klingon Battle Cruiser* from *Star Trek*. But the best gift came from

Sammy—a telescope so I can watch the Apollo astronauts on the Moon. Once all the presents were open, my mom handed out party favors and everyone went home.

Sean was already asleep in his bed, headphones still on his ears. The record he'd been listening to had finished long ago. I was about to get out of bed and turn off his stereo when the door opened.

"Hey Sport," my dad said coming into the room and sitting beside me on the bed. "Sorry I missed your birthday. You okay? Mom told me what happened. How's your head?"

"It's alright," I said, touching the lump on the side of my head. "It's just a bump. I'll live."

"Yeah, you're tough," he said, smiling. "Oh, hey, I got you something."

I sat up in bed as Dad produced a small gift-wrapped box. I took it and quickly tore it open revealing an official Apollo 13 mission patch from NASA.

"You can ask Mom to sew it on your jacket."

"Thanks Dad. I love it." I reached up and hugged him. He needed a shave.

"So, besides a whack on the 'ol noggin, how was your day?"

I told my dad all about the party; all my friends from school, how everyone loved the Moon-House and the games, Sean's band, the cake, all the presents, even about The Beatles breaking up and the fight with Sean this morning.

Finally I told him about Sammy and how some of the kids acted around him and how that made me feel. He said some people hate what they fear and don't understand. He told me how we could show others by our example and maybe they can learn to be more tolerant of people who are different then they are.

Then he kissed me on the forehead and said goodnight. He got up, went over to Sean, turned off his stereo and took off his headphones, then kissed him too. Sean mumbled something and rolled over.

"Hey Dad?" I said, just as he was about to leave.

"Yeah Sport?"

I was about to tell him about the bruises on Butch's back and legs; about to tell him how I was tormented and bullied by him almost every day while most of the teachers stood by and did nothing; about to tell him how I was terrified to go to school out of fear of what he would do to me.

But then I remembered what Butch said he would do to Lucy if I told, so I changed my mind at the last second. Instead, I simply said, "I love you."

"I love you too, Sport," he said, and shut the door.

SEVEN

"Apollo to Shondo. Come in Shondo."

"Shondo here, Captain. What is your status?"

"I'm on the Antonius moon surface."

"Instruments read minimal atmosphere. Are you wearing your gravity boots sir?"

"Affirmative."

"Be careful Captain. Sensors indicate the Butcher's ship is in your vicinity."

"Copy that. I am proceeding with caution. I'll keep you apprised of the situation."

"Understood. Shondo out."

Sean put down the walkie-talkie, Billy's birthday present from Mom and Dad, and walked over to the window. Separating two slats of the Venetian blinds, he peered out and looked down onto the backyard, the remains of the party still evident; their mom had not yet found the motivation to start cleaning up. Paper plates, cups, and napkins littered the lawn, even though there were ample trash receptacles set up throughout. Somehow, kids' trash just never seems to make in into the garbage cans, apparently a universal phenomenon no scientist had yet been able to figure out.

Billy was inside the Moon-House pretending he was Captain Apollo walking around the surface of an alien moon somewhere light-years away. On his feet were the Moon Boots Sean had given him for his birthday. They completed a set of astronaut toys he already owned: a space helmet, a water pistol ray-gun that sprayed a fine mist of water, a claw-grip arm extension for picking up "moon rocks," and now Moon Boots, a pair of thick, hollow plastic strap-on "boots" that attached to the wearer's shoes and left a tread-mark impression on loose soil, just like the Apollo astronauts left on the surface of the Moon.

You weren't supposed to wear anything on your feet inside the Moon-House—only socks allowed—for fear of puncturing the rubber floor, but Billy was ignoring the rules. The Moon-House rental company was coming to pick it up later this afternoon and he wanted to take one last trip to the Moon before they had to leave for Sunday Mass.

Sean turned away from the window and put a record on the stereo. He started cleaning up the mess he'd left from his tantrum yesterday as a British boy's choir sang, *"You can't always get what you want..."*

Boy, ain't that the truth!

Captain Apollo treaded carefully on the lunar surface. He had traced the Butcher and his apprentice to this moon, apparently in an effort to hide the kidnapped Empress. Up ahead in the distance, near a large outcropping of rocks—more than a hill but not quite a mountain—he could see the Butcher's ship: dark and ominous, its shape foreboding like a giant insect.

He made his way to the rock outcropping. As he got closer to the ship, he could tell it was unoccupied—at the bottom of the extended gangway, he saw several tracks leading away into the nearby maze of canyons. One of the sets of tracks was small, obviously belonging to the Empress. The other two sets were much larger, clumsier, possibly in pursuit. Since there were no tracks leading back, he deduced they were still somewhere within the towering rock formations. Cautiously, he followed the tracks. It could be a trap.

The narrow walls of the canyon stretched high into the darkened skies. The footprints he'd been following split up and overlapped. A chase had occurred here, the trail crisscrossing in several directions, lost in the maze and backtracking, then trying a new direction. He wished Shondo was with him and not back on the ship. Martians were natural trackers.

Making his way slowly forward, he heard a noise nearby. It sounded like some kind of scuffle. He drew his weapon and moved in the direction of the disturbance. As the sound grew louder, he knew he was close. Then he heard the Empress cry out, "Help!"

Captain Apollo ran toward the cries of distress. He came around a giant boulder and saw the Empress struggling to break free from the Butcher's apprentice, an alien called Joemar. The Empress wore purple armor—she must have put it on while he was engaged in the dogfight back on Fraxis—in her hand was a gleaming dagger that Joemar was trying to wrest free from her. She was stronger than he realized, as Joemar struggled to restrain and disarm her simultaneously. Just as Joemar finally managed to knock the weapon from her hand, Billy stepped into view, his ray gun aimed at Joemar's head.

"Freeze!"

Joemar and Lucinda both stopped their fighting and stared at him. Lucinda grinned while Joemar looked stunned. Then their expressions reversed: Lucinda reflected sudden horror, while Joemar smiled wickedly. The Empress managed to shout, "Look out!" but it was too late. Captain Apollo turned around just in time to see the Butcher standing behind him, a murderous gleam in his eyes as he swung on him. The last thing Billy Apollo saw was the metal staff connecting with his head.

Saint Anthony's church was built in the early 1900's with high vaulted ceilings and beautiful stained-glass windows depicting the Stations of the Cross. There were one hundred hand-carved mahogany pews, each twenty-five feet long—fifty on the left side and fifty on the right. The altar in front was raised three steps above the main floor and nearly as wide as the building itself.

To the left was the tabernacle, the vessel that held the consecrated Eucharist. To the right was the lectern where the priest read from the Bible and delivered his weekly sermon. In the center was an ornate wooden table, the altar itself, where the priest transformed bread and wine into the Body and Blood of Christ through the Sacrament of Eucharist. Directly behind and above the altar was a giant crucifix.

Behind the altar, out of sight, was the sacristy, where the priest donned his robes and the altar boys changed into their cassocks. It was also where the communion wafers and altar wine was kept. It was a well-known "secret" that the altar boys sneaked a little wine before Mass; some of the priests did as well. It was not unusual for an altar boy to nod off to sleep during Mass.

My family sat in a pew in the middle on the right side of the church. Sunday Mass was nearly concluded and I was fidgeting in my seat. Let's face it, the better part of an hour was a long time for a nine-year-old boy to sit still, but especially for one who had been diagnosed as hyper-kinetic, like me.

The doctor wanted to put me on some kind of medication to calm me down, but my mom wouldn't hear of it. She told the doctor, "You're not going to drug my son!" She said she was afraid it would stifle my imagination and creativity, and she wouldn't stand for that. She'd seen the dull look in the eyes of other kids that were "doped up," as she called it. So what if I had a little extra energy? She loved me just the way I was, thank you very much!

Father O'Malley, middle aged with a thick Irish brogue, said the final blessing, concluding the Mass. The organist, a fat lady perched high above the congregation in the rear balcony, played a depressing tune as the priest and altar boys left the altar and retired into the sacristy. Those in attendance slowly filed out the back, past the Baptismal Font, dipping our fingers in the Holy Water and blessing ourselves with the sign of the cross as we exited the building.

Once outside in the fresh air, families and friends gathered in little cliques, chatting and generally catching up from the past week. For many, this was the only time they saw each other. I heard my name mentioned a couple times, along with Butch's, and I caught a few stares at the bandage on my forehead. My parents were talking with Lucy's parents and Matt's dad.

This was my family's weekly Sunday ritual: ten o'clock Mass, followed by five or ten minutes outside chatting afterward. Then a trip to the bakery where Mom would buy a dozen fresh baked Kaiser rolls with poppy seeds, and a half-dozen "crumb buns," individual coffee cakes with large, sweet crumbs on top and dusted with powdered sugar—a family favorite. Then home again for a delicious lunch of Italian cold cuts and cheeses on the just purchased hard rolls. Mmmm!

For most of the family, the ritual ended there, but not for me! Every Sunday on WPIX channel 11, a local New York City station, they showed an Abbot & Costello movie followed by a Johnny Weismueller *Tarzan* movie. This week was two of my favorites: *Abbot & Costello Meet Frankenstein* and *Tarzan Goes to New York*. I couldn't wait to get home to watch them.

Sean had stepped away from Mom and Dad, talking to Jimmy and Ben, while I stood in my own chat group with Matt and Lucy. I saw Butch and Joey off to the side, Butch glaring at me, punching his fist into his hand, and pointing at me. I tried to look away.

"Oh, just ignore him," Lucy said when she caught me looking at them.

"Easy for you to say, he's not out to get you." *Not yet anyway*, I thought.

"Yeah. What did you do to get him so mad at you?" Matt said. I shrugged my shoulders, feigning ignorance.

"Probably nothing," Lucy said. "Bullies like him don't even need an excuse. They're just mean."

"I just wish they would pick on someone else," I said.

"Fight back. Then they'll leave you alone."

"That's what my dad says too," Matt said.

"He's right," Lucy said. "He only does it because you let him."

"I don't like fighting," I said. "I'm afraid I'll hurt someone and then I'll feel worse. Besides, Jesus said to turn the other cheek."

"Suit yourself," she said. "But I bet Jesus didn't have to put up with bullies like Butch Anderson and Joey Martino."

"I don't want to talk about them anymore," I said. "What are you guys doing later?"

"Today?" Matt said.

"Yeah. This afternoon around three. After Tarzan."

"I can't. My dad's giving me my weekly piano lesson."

"How about after?"

"There is no after. My piano lessons last all day."

"Whoa. Are you any good?"

"Yeah," he said, and didn't elaborate.

"I'm not doing anything," Lucy said. "What's up?"

"Do you want to see something really cool?" I said, trying to sound mysterious.

"Like what?"

"If I told you it would ruin the surprise."

"Sure, I'm always up for a little adventure."

"Billy," my dad called. "Say goodbye to your friends. It's time to go."

"I'll call you later," I told Lucy. "Bye Matt."

"See ya'," Matt said, as I headed off with my family.

"Billy, where are we going?"

"We're almost there. It's just up ahead."

I led Lucy through the woods with only a general idea of where we were going. Even though I'd been in these woods a million times with Sean, I always followed his lead and never really paid attention to landmarks. Sean knew the way. This was the first time I'd actually been here by myself. Only I wasn't by myself, was I? Lucy was with me. For some reason I was both nervous and excited, but don't ask me to explain why. It was a weird feeling, but I kind of liked it. Like when she kissed me on the cheek yesterday at my party. It was only a peck on the cheek, but it made me feel all happy inside. Not like my mom's kisses. I couldn't let her know I was lost. I didn't realize there were so many crisscrossing trails when I was here last weekend with Sean. That's when we first discovered it....

"I'm bored," Sean said lying on his bed tossing a baseball straight up into the air and catching it, over and over.

"Me too," I said, also on my bed, but I was reading the novel *Planet of the Apes* by Pierre Boulle. The book was way different from the movie. In the book, the apes lived in cities, and drove cars, and flew airplanes and the astronaut was treated like an honored guest. I liked the movie better.

"Want to go exploring?"

"Sure!" I said. I snapped the book closed and put my sneakers on. I loved doing anything with my big brother.

As I said before, we lived on a hill that dead-ended in a cul-de-sac where the city had a power station at the top. The enormous towers with their thick power cables buzzed loudly overhead day and night. A ten-foot high chain link fence at the end of the block surrounded the station, a big wide gap in the fence on the opposite side from Old Man Hughes's house. All the kids in the neighborhood knew where the gap in the fence was, though apparently no one at the power station did because they never bothered to fix it. Either that or they just didn't care.

There were five other kids that lived on our street besides Sean and me, all of them either younger or older than me. There was Michael and John Owen, fourteen and fifteen respectively, Sarah Wilson, a homely, overweight sixteen-year- old girl with acne who sometimes babysat for us, Ben Shaw, Sean's band mate and best friend since they were in diapers, and little Donnie Foster, an adorable four year old who never tired of asking "Why?" to everything.

"I have to go home now Donnie."

"Why?"

"Because my mom is calling."

"Why?"

"Because it's supper time."

"Why?"

You get the idea. He was a cute kid, but it got really annoying really quickly. And so, there were no other kids my age in the neighborhood for me to play with, and the older ones didn't want me around. Thank God for Sean.

We cut through the hole in the power station fence, sneaked along the perimeter to the other side, and climbed over. We could go around, but like walking to school, that would take an extra half-hour. Besides, it was risky—even riskier than cutting through Mr. Hughes's yard—because of the possibility of getting caught by one of the power station employees and calling the cops on us, which was what made it fun, though so far that never happened. I liked to pretend we were spies like James Bond sneaking through an enemy compound. When we got to the other side, we crossed the street and walked down the steep hill to the railroad tracks behind the dairy and followed them for about a mile to the edge of the woods.

The woods were thick with tall trees, their trunks a light grey—almost white—with specks of black. They seemed to stretch forever in every direction. The rocky ground was covered with small bushes, leaves, moss, and sticks and you had to be careful not to step in any poison ivy. There were at least a dozen foot paths and bike trails. It was easy to get lost. Sean, always the Boy Scout, carried a compass whenever we ventured in, and he seemed to know where we were going. If he didn't, he faked it really well. It was obvious from all the trails that lots of other people, probably kids like us, hiked in these woods, but we never met anyone else when we went out exploring.

We'd been hiking for at least half an hour when Sean suddenly stopped. He narrowed his eyes and peered at something ahead of us.

"What is it?" I whispered.

"Shhh."

We waited. The sounds of the forest resonated all around us in the stillness: birds sang, small animals scurried in the underbrush and through the trees, insects chirped, an owl hooted somewhere, water flowed in a nearby brook or stream, but no people sounds.

"Okay," Sean whispered, "this way."

Slowly, cautiously, we moved through the trees off the path toward an outcropping of large rocks. I was both scared and exhilarated. I could feel my heart pounding in my chest. I reached out and grabbed Sean's arm, clinging onto him for safety. Closer we crept. When we reached the boulders, Sean circled around them, examining the area. I stood back and watched nervously, warning Sean to be careful. After a few minutes, Sean squatted down, sat, twisted, and then disappeared.

"Sean!" I yelled, panicked.

"This is so cool!" I heard his muffled voice, but I couldn't see him. Sean popped his head up through a hole in the ground hidden from where I was standing. "It's okay. C'mere, you gotta check this out!" His head vanished again.

I walked around the rocks to where my brother's head had been a moment before. Now I could see the hole. I eased myself through and joined Sean in the hidden lair. Someone had built an underground fort. The room was six or seven feet square and almost five feet deep, covered with two sheets of four-foot by eight-foot plywood. I could stand comfortably, but Sean had to duck. It was a little claustrophobic, but still cool. The earthen walls reminded me of the underground tunnels on the TV show *Hogan's Heroes*, about the allied resistance in a German POW camp in World War II.

On the outside, the plywood had been carefully camouflaged with bushes, leaves, and sticks, effectively hiding it from the footpath. It was only by pure luck and Sean's keen sense, that he was able to see something was amiss. The rock formation seemed too symmetrical, he said, the land was too flat and too square to be natural. One thing he had learned earning his survival Merit Badge: there are no right angles in nature.

Below ground it was dark. The narrow opening didn't allow in very much light, but it didn't take long for our eyes to become accustomed to the gloom. There were three metal milk crates, stolen from the dairy, apparently used to sit on. On one wall was a shelf about three feet long, a foot high and about eight inches deep, two well-used votive candles on either end. A box of "strike anywhere" blue-tip wooden matches sat on the shelf. Sean lit the candles.

"That's a little better," he said. The candles provided enough light to see our surroundings, though still gloomy. The flickering flames cast dancing shadows on Sean's face. The ground was littered with cigarette butts and crushed soda and beer cans.

"Who do you suppose built this place?" I wondered.

"I don't know, but this would make a great make-out spot."

"A what?"

"Never mind. I'll tell you when you get older."

"We should go."

"What's the matter? Scared?"

"Yes," I admitted. "What if whoever built this place comes back?"

"Then we tell them 'cool fort.' But I wouldn't worry too much. It doesn't look like anybody's been here for a while. There's rust on those cans."

"I don't care. Can we go pleeease?"

"Fine, scaredy-cat."

Sean blew out the candles while I scampered out of the hole. That place was giving me the creeps. Sean joined me outside a moment later.

"We should mark the trail so we can find it again," Sean said. "Look around for a tree branch or something." After a couple minutes of scanning our surroundings, I picked up a relatively straight branch about two-feet long. "How's this?"

"Perfect."

Sean took the branch, reached into his back pocket and brought out his Scout knife, unfolded it, and carved a large "X" in the wood. Satisfied, he brought it out to the trail and drove it into the ground.

"There," he said. Consulting his compass and getting his bearings, he said, more to himself than to me, "Okay, the railroad tracks are due north. The 'X' on the stick points due south, and the fort is twenty-five feet to the west. Now all we gotta do is put a notch in a tree about every twenty yards or so on our way out...."

I thought I had picked the right trail off the railroad tracks, but now I wasn't so sure. I hadn't seen one of Sean's marks in a while. I might have accidentally taken a wrong turn or gone onto a different path by mistake. I was getting worried.

"Billy, my feet are tired," Lucy complained. "Can we take a break?"

"Yeah okay."

We found a nearby log and sat next to each other, an awkward silence between us.

"So," Lucy finally said.

"Yeah?"

"What are we doing out here? I have to be back by six o'clock for supper. It's probably around four-thirty now."

"I know, I'm sorry. Me and Sean found this really cool place. I thought I could find it again on my own. We marked the trail and everything."

"Can't you just tell me what it is?"

"It would be cooler if I showed you."

"So mysterious," she said, giving me a playful nudge with her elbow. "I'll give you another half hour, but that's it. If we don't find it by then we head home, okay?"

"Okay," I agreed.

Back on the path, I looked all around desperately trying to spot any sign of Sean's marks. Finally, after almost twenty minutes since we took our break, I spied one. The tree was about fifteen feet from where I stood, through a patch of trees. This was it! I'd finally found the right path. I was on the wrong one all along.

"See this notch?" I said. "Look for more like these along this path." Once we were on the correct route, I had no trouble following the trees. Then I spotted it—the stick Sean had driven into the ground, "X" marking the spot to the fort.

"There it is!"

I was excited now. My heart was pounding again, but this time I wasn't scared. I was with Lucy. Suddenly, I was glad Matt couldn't make it. I was glad we were alone. This was our fort. I wanted to go down there with her and... what? I didn't know, but I'd figure it out when we got there. I grabbed her hand and pulled her along. "Come on!"

As we reached the stick marker, I saw the rocks. I started toward them then suddenly froze.

"What is it?" Lucy said.

"Shhh. I think I heard something."

I was nervous now. A moment ago, just for a second, I could have sworn I heard voices. I listened harder. Nothing. We inched closer. Still nothing.

"Billy, I'm scared."

"Me too."

I held her hand tighter. She squeezed back. Together we moved closer to the rocks. One of us stepped on a twig. It snapped.

"It was probably nothing," I said, trying to reassure her. And myself. I led her around to the mouth of the fort. I peered into the dark hole...

Suddenly a tall figure sprang from the hole, long arms reaching for us, a horrible dark, hairy face with wild red eyes and long black tangled hair, screaming, *"AHHHHHHHHHH!!!"*

Lucy and I both screamed at the top of our lungs. We stood frozen in terror for a moment, our eyes wide, hearts racing, and adrenalin coursing through our veins. We turned together and fled, running aimlessly, just trying to get away from the monster that tried to grab us. We ran and ran and ran until we couldn't run anymore.

"Oh my God!" Tim said, between fits of hysterical laughter. He removed the cheap latex and fake-fur gorilla mask from his head. "You should have seen their faces!" More laughter. "I wouldn't be surprised if they both wet their pants."

Sean laughed along with Tim.

"Your brother screamed like a little girl!" Tim said, still laughing.

"Wait. That was Billy?" Sean said. He stopped laughing.

"Yeah man," Tim said, his own laughter subsiding now. "Him and his little girlfriend. It's cool though. It was just a prank."

"Yeah. Yeah, I guess."

"Besides," Tim said, lighting the tip of a freshly rolled joint and handing it to Sean, "you didn't want him to catch us down here, did you? He'd probably run right home and narc us out to your parents."

"He better not," Sean said, exhaling a cloud of smoke.

Tim took a big draw off the joint. "Better safe than sorry." He coughed, handing it back to Sean.

They continued passing it back and forth between them until it was too small to handle. Tim snuffed it out and put it in the plastic sandwich baggie with the rest of his marijuana. He sat back on the milk crate and leaned against the dirt wall. Sean followed suit, resting against the wall. They were both too stoned to move.

"Do you think he recognized you?" Sean asked.

"No way, they were way too scared." Tim laughed again, remembering the moment.

"But what if they did?"

"How? I was wearing a Halloween mask?"

"I don't know. Maybe they recognized your hair or your voice. Maybe your clothes."

"Who cares? It's not like they know you're down here too."

"I suppose so."

"Don't be so paranoid, man," Tim said, lighting a cigarette. He held the pack out to Sean, offering him one. Sean took one and lit it; he smoked like a pro now. "How did your brother even know about this place?"

"He was with me when I found it."

"I bet he was planning on bringing her down here and getting himself a little nookie," Tim said, giggling.

Now it was Sean's turn to laugh. "Billy? Please! He's only nine!"

"Hey man, it's never too early to start," Tim said, wagging his eyebrows up and down.

"I doubt he even knows what it is!" Sean laughed at the absurdity of it. He knew Billy didn't know anything about the facts of life.

Heck, Sean was twelve and barely knew anything himself. His father had not yet given him *The Talk* and didn't think he ever would. In his family, you didn't speak about such things. His knowledge of sex education was confined to what he picked up in the schoolyard or gleaned from looking at *Playboy*, and he doubted the veracity of that. Some of the stuff he'd heard seemed highly improbable at best, and totally gross if true.

"I'm just busting your chops, man," Tim said, snubbing out his cigarette on the floor. "So, what do you think of Joker? Cool dude, right?"

"Huh? Oh, yeah. He's okay, I guess."

"Yeah, Joker's the Man. He likes you."

"He does?"

"Yup. Says he thinks you're cool. He wants you to help him with some stuff. Interested?"

"I don't know. I'm not really..."

"Don't worry. It's cool. You trust me, don't you?"

"Well, yeah, but..."

"Good, then it's settled. Meet me in the park after school tomorrow and we'll go over his house." Tim looked at his watch. "We better get going. My grandmother will kill me if I'm late for dinner again."

Lucy and I walked together in silence. Neither of us had spoken to the other since the incident in the woods. We were both too embarrassed to say anything. Whatever moment I thought we shared back there was ruined when that jerk in the mask, whoever he was, jumped out of the hole and scared us half to death. I thought he seemed familiar, but I don't know where I might have seen him before. He could have been anybody, but there was something in the way he moved. He didn't go to Saint Anthony's; I knew that much for sure. The hair that was sticking out of the mask—his real hair, not the fake gorilla hair—was too long for the dress code. But it all happened so fast.

We were getting close to Lucy's house now. I knew I should probably say something while I still had the chance, but I didn't know what. I looked over at her. She walked with her head down, eyes on her feet. She was pouting. Her hair, still damp and stringy from sweat—we ran pretty far pretty fast—hung limply down the sides of her face. *She's so cute*, I thought to myself. I wanted to hold her hand, but I didn't dare.

"Hey Luce?" I said tentatively, not sure what to say.

"Yeah?" Her voice was soft, almost a whisper.

"Are you mad at me?"

"No." Still a whisper.

"I'm sorry about what happened."

"I know. It wasn't your fault."

"It feels like it was."

"You didn't know anyone was down there."

I stopped walking. She stopped a few paces after I did and turned back to look at me. "What?"

"I hope you don't think I'm a sissy for how I acted back there," I said, my head hung in shame. "Please don't tell anyone."

"Of course not. Is that what you're afraid of?"

I nodded.

"You were scared. We both were."

"I screamed."

"We both screamed."

"But you're a girl."

"Oh, gimme a break. Anybody would have."

"You really think so?"

"Of course. But don't worry, your secret's safe with me."

I let out a sigh of relief and smiled. "Thanks."

She smiled back and then kissed me on the cheek for the second time in two days. "Y'all are really cute sometimes, you know that, Billy McBride?" She took me by the hand and we started walking back toward her house. "Of course, if you tell anyone I said that I'll have to kill you."

Sean took his time walking home. Dinner wasn't until six and he still had plenty of time left. At least he thought he did—he left his watch at home. He'd stopped at the stream in the woods and zoned out watching the water cascade around a rock for a while and he sort of lost track of time. Besides, he was still really stoned and he didn't want to go home high as a kite. This was only the second time he'd smoked grass and he wasn't used to the sensation yet. But he liked it.

It was hard to describe exactly. He was sort of light headed, but not dizzy. Colors seemed brighter somehow. In fact, all his senses seemed heightened. When he listened to music, it seemed like he heard things—subtle things—that he could swear he'd never heard before, even though he'd heard it a million times. And everything was funny. Hysterically funny. It didn't seem to matter what it was, Sean found himself laughing at it.

He thought back to Friday night when he got high for the first time at Joker's house when they were watching *Rowan and Martin's Laugh-In*. He couldn't remember when he'd laughed so hard.

They weren't allowed to watch it at home. Mom thought it was vulgar and was going to corrupt them. Just like they couldn't watch the news because she didn't want them to hear about what was going on in Vietnam or all the protests against the war. She took overprotection to a whole other level.

Another effect of the drug was it gave you a voracious appetite. Joker called it the "blind screaming munchies." Everything looked delicious and nothing seemed to be able to satiate it, no matter how much you ate.

There were negative effects as well. For one, it seemed to sap all the moisture from your mouth, something Tim described as "cotton mouth," which was not alleviated by the intake of fluids. You could drink a gallon of water and your mouth was still just as dry, only now you had to pee constantly. It also took away your desire to do anything except sit where you were and veg out. All motivation is lost and you really couldn't care less. And it made your eyes bloodshot and dilated your pupils, a dead giveaway that you were stoned. Visine helped a little for the red-eye, but only time could take care of your pupils. But probably the worst effect of all, at least as far as Sean was concerned, was the irrational feeling of paranoia it gave him. It seemed like he was afraid of his own shadow. Is this normal? Am I going to die? Is that a cop? Will my parents know I'm high? Will Billy? What was that? These were the questions that ran through his head.

Today the thing that troubled him the most was how badly Tim had frightened Billy. Even though Sean couldn't see him from where he was when Tim jumped out of the hole wearing that ridiculous mask, he'd heard the blood curdling screams from both Billy and Lucy. When he found out it was his little brother, he felt awful about it. The humor of the situation left him immediately, replaced with an overwhelming sense of guilt. Even if it hadn't been Billy, Sean thought it was still a mean trick to pull on a couple of little kids. Even though they didn't know who was outside before the prank, they could tell they were just kids by the sound of their voices. But Tim wanted to scare them away—he said it would be funny. Sean thought it was just cruel.

To make matters worse, now Sean was afraid either Billy or Lucy had recognized Tim, even with the mask on.

They had both seen him at the party yesterday. Maybe somehow they could tell it was him. In fact, the more he thought about it the more he convinced himself that Billy had recognized him. Of course he did. Billy was a smart kid. He had to have seen through Tim's disguise. And if he knew that Tim was in the fort, then it follows that he would have figured out that Sean had been down there too. He would have smelled the marijuana and known that Sean was smoking and he would have gone home and told their parents. In fact, he was sure that was exactly what must've happened: Billy knew he was in the hole getting high with Tim and now his parents were waiting for him to get home so they could bust him and call the cops and take him to jail! Dammit Billy! Why couldn't he mind his own business? Tim was right about him all along. Why did he have to be such a tattletale? Sean would get him for this!

It was nearly six o'clock and Sean was still not home. This was the second time in less than a week he would be late for supper. Mom had prepared our traditional Sunday dinner: spaghetti and meatballs with Italian sausage, garlic bread, and freshly grated parmesan cheese (the real stuff imported from Italy, not the cheap powder stuff in a can).

Dad's brother, my Uncle Mike, married a Sicilian girl named Mary Franzetti, now Mary McBride—Aunt Mary to me. Aunt Mary's mom, Mrs. Franz, taught my mom how to cook. My mom's red sauce was about as authentic as you can get. And we're not even Italian!

This part of New Jersey was populated with mostly Irish and Italians, so practically everyone knew how to cook Italian food, with varying degrees of success. Mom was an excellent cook and I know she took great pride in the quality of her food. Her spaghetti and meatballs was about the best in town. In fact, the only thing better than my mom's Italian cooking was from a local pizzeria called Mario's. I bet the pizza in the New York/New Jersey area is the best in the whole country—the whole world even! At least I think so.

Dad and I were already sitting at the table, and Mom was just setting a big bowl of pasta down, when Sean walked through the kitchen door. It was ten-minutes past six. Dad made a big show of looking up at the kitchen clock over the table.

"You're late," he said, not even trying to hide the irritation in his voice.

"I know, I'm sorry. I lost track of time."

"Wash your hands before you sit down," Mom said, putting the meatballs and sausage on the table. Sean went to the sink and did as he was told.

"Where were you?" Dad demanded.

"I was at the park with a friend."

"What friend?"

"Tim, from my band."

"I don't like that boy," Mom interjected.

"Ma," Sean protested, "Tim's okay."

"What were you doing?"

"Nothing."

"You did nothing for four hours?"

"No, we were trying to write a song so we can enter the Battle of the Bands."

"Were you smoking?"

"What? No!" Sean looked at me. I answered with a look that said, *Don't look at me! I didn't say anything!* At least I hope that's what it said. Hard to tell with looks.

"You better not," Dad warned. "If I catch you smoking you'll be grounded for a month."

"Yes sir."

"You hear me?" Wow. Dad was really mad. He only says, 'You hear me?' when he's mad.

"Yes sir," Sean said, louder this time.

"Leo," Mom said, "let the boy be. Can't we just have a nice quiet Sunday dinner?" Mom was always the peacemaker.

"Fine," Dad said. "Let's say Grace. In the name of the Father..."

We all made the Sign of the Cross as Dad led us in the blessing.

After supper, I followed Sean upstairs to our bedroom. I could see he was still upset from his confrontation with Dad and I didn't want to make it any worse. He went to his record collection and started looking for something to play while I sat on his bed, and waited while he rifled through his records. I was still shaken and wanted to warn him about the fort.

"Hey Sean, guess what."

"What," he said, flipping through records. He sounded mad.

"I went back to the underground fort in the woods today."

Sean froze and turned to look at me.

"Only it wasn't empty," I continued.

"Listen, Billy, I..."

"Some big kids were in there. One of them jumped out at me. I was never so scared in my life!"

"Do you know who it was?"

"Uh-uh. He was wearing some kind of mask. Gorilla, I think. I don't think you should go back there. They might try to get you like they did me."

"Like you care."

"What's that supposed to mean?" I said.

"Why did you tell Mom and Dad about me smoking?"

"But I didn't."

"Yeah, right. Liar."

"I promise I didn't! Cross my heart and hope to die!" To me, that was the equivalent to swearing on a stack of Bibles.

"Yeah? Then how did he know?" Sean was starting to lose his temper. So was I. I don't like being accused of lying when I'm not.

"I don't know," I said, raising my voice defensively. "Maybe he figured it out!"

"Or maybe you're nothing but a little tattle-tale!"

"I am not!"

"I don't care, we're through. You told on me for the last time. I said I would give you one more chance, and you blew it. As far as I'm concerned, we're not brothers anymore. And I'm never playing your stupid game again, so don't even ask."

"Why are you being so mean to me? What did I ever do to you?"

"You were born!" Sean shouted. "If it wasn't for you I could've had a boat!"

"It's not my fault if Mom and Dad won't let you get your stupid boat."

"Yes, it is! You're so hyper you can't be trusted to sit still without worrying about you falling in and drowning. I get punished because you're too much of a baby to go out on the water without a grownup around."

"You know, it's bad enough you blame me for telling on you when I didn't, but sometimes you act like everything I do is about you."

"You don't even know what it's like to be related to you. Practically every day at school someone asks me if that weird little kid is my brother. Sometimes I wish I could just say I don't know you. My life would be so much easier if you weren't around. I hate you!"

"I...I'm sorry, I..." I could feel my lower lip trembling. It felt like I'd been punched in the gut.

"Just get out of here. I don't want to see your face anymore!"

I turned without saying another word and left the room, silently closing the door behind me. I walked down the stairs, past the living room where my parents were watching *60 Minutes.* I walked through the kitchen and down the basement stairs into the laundry room. I felt numb. I stood in front of the dryer in stunned silence, trying to grasp what had just happened, the realization finally sinking in - *my brother hated me.* I opened the door and climbed inside, closing the door behind me.

And there, alone in the dark, inside my spaceship—my sanctuary—I cried like I had never cried before.

EIGHT

Captain Apollo groaned as he opened his eyes in the dimness. He sat up on the bare metal slab attached to the wall that he was laying on. He was dizzy and his head hurt. He touched his forehead and winced in pain when his finger found the goose-egg sized lump. Slowly, his eyes became accustomed to the gloom. He was in some kind of cell.

The room was tiny, about eight feet by twelve feet with no windows, three solid walls with the fourth completely open. He knew without trying that it was protected by a force field, if he attempted to walk through it, he'd be repelled back, or worse, disintegrated. He surveyed his surroundings, looking for any means of escape. Nothing.

"You're awake," he heard a soft feminine voice say. He got off his bunk and walked to the open wall. In a similar cage across from him was Empress Lucinda. She no longer wore the purple armor he'd seen her in on the surface of the Antonius moon. She was clothed in a white one-piece jumpsuit, tailored to fit her snugly under her armor. On her head, she still wore the white tiara with the blue stone in the center.

"How long have I been out?" he managed to say.

"A couple hours. How did you find me?"

"My First Officer was able to pick up the Butcher's ion signature. We tracked him here."

"They knew you were coming."

"That's impossible. We blocked their sensors. They shouldn't have been able to detect us following them."

"I heard them talking before they captured you. They were in contact with someone who gave them your exact coordinates. They were after you, not me. You were set up and I was the bait."

"But that doesn't make any sense. Why would anyone want to kidnap me?"

"I don't know, but one thing is certain. If we don't figure out a way out of here, neither one of us is going to make it out alive."

"I can't argue with that. Any ideas?"

"Unfortunately, no."

"Wait a second. What kind of stone is that in your tiara?"

"It's a *Sagari*. The rarest and most powerful substance on my planet. It's our greatest natural resource. It's what our force field technology is based on. A tiny piece no bigger than a grain of sand can provide enough energy to power a city for a year."

"Or deflect a plasma field."

"I don't follow."

"Think of how you can take a glass lens and use it to focus the sun's rays into a concentrated beam to start a fire. If you took your Sagari stone and angled it into the force field..."

"I could focus the beam and use it to disrupt the field."

"Exactly."

"Captain, you're a genius!"

Lucinda removed the tiara from her head, turned it over in her hands, and examined it looking for a way to extract the stone from its setting.

"Can you remove the stone?"

"I think so. It would be a lot easier if I had some tools."

She looked around her sparse room for anything she might be able to use to pry the gem loose. Her eyes settled on the metal slab protruding from the wall. Using the corner of the bed, she managed to catch the edge of the setting. Carefully pushing down on the arm of the tiara, while simultaneously applying pressure to the stone with her thumb, the Sagari popped out like a kernel of corn bursting open in hot oil. With the rock now free from the headdress, she bent the arms inward toward themselves, forming rudimentary forceps. She wedged the stone between the pincers, effectively creating a handle for the priceless gem.

"There," she said, proudly holding up her handiwork.

"Perfect. Now, ease the leading edge of the stone into the force field."

She moved to the far end of the open wall to the source of the energy barrier, holding the gem perpendicular to the field.

"Careful," Billy said. "We may only get one shot at this."

Lucinda inched the stone slowly and steadily forward until it penetrated the field of energy. Suddenly, a flash of blue light filled the room, simultaneously creating a narrow beam of intense force that struck the ceiling between the cells, burning a hole where it touched. Gently turning the stone, she guided the focused beam across the ceiling and down the far wall, leaving a black smoking trail behind, and aimed it at the force field enclosing Captain Apollo's cell.

The field momentarily flashed a blinding blue; sparks erupted from both sides of the wall as the field shorted out. Lucinda withdrew the stone as Captain Apollo rushed out of his cell and crossed the corridor to hers, hitting the control panel and deactivating the force field. She fled her cage to join him, just as a door at the end of the hallway opened and Joemar stepped through.

"Hey!" he shouted in surprise, finding the prisoners out of their holding cells. Before he could reach for his sidearm, Captain Apollo rushed him, slamming him into the wall. Lucinda moved in quickly, kicking him in the face as he fell to the ground, unconscious.

Captain Apollo bent down and disarmed his opponent. He dragged Joemar into the cell previously occupied by Lucinda and reactivated the force field.

"That should hold him for a while," he said. "Come on, let's get out of here."

They both left the brig, stepping through the open door into an anteroom containing their personal effects. Lucinda donned her armor while Captain Apollo consulted the ship's computer.

"Where are we?" Lucinda asked, looking over his shoulder at the screen.

"We're still on the moon," he said. He brought up the ships internal schematics, studying the layout of the vessel.

"The exit is this way," he said, pointing at the computer screen. He grabbed his space helmet. "Come on."

They left the anteroom and stealthily made their way through the small ship, moving together as one. They came to the main airlock and opened the inner door, entering the tiny room. Captain Apollo attached his helmet before pressurizing the air. When the cycle was complete, he opened the outer door, and together, they bolted down the ramp and ran for the rock canyons ahead.

They entered the mountainous formations, zigzagging their way through the cavernous maze of rock. When he was sure they weren't being followed, he opened his communication device.

"Apollo to Shondo, come in. Shondo, come in."

No answer.

"Shondo! This is Captain Billy Apollo, please respond."

Still nothing.

"That's peculiar. He's not answering."

"Did you say Shondo?"

"Yes, he's my First Officer."

"Shondo was the name of the Butcher's contact. He's the one who gave him your coordinates."

"I don't believe it. Shondo would never betray..."

"Believe it Captain. I know what I heard."

"But Shondo. It doesn't seem possible. Why?"

"I don't know, but we have to get out of here quick. I think I saw a cave up ahead."

They ran about twenty yards when they came upon a small opening just large enough for them to fit through in the base of the rock. Just as Captain Apollo was about to go through the opening, the head and arms of a giant, hairy beast with glowing red eyes and sharp teeth lunged forward, grabbing him with its razor-sharp talons!

"AHHHHHHHHHH!!!"

I sprang upright in my bed, screaming. My hair was matted to my head soaked with sweat. I was trembling uncontrollably.

"What the...?" Sean said, just as the door burst open and Mom turned on the light. She rushed to my side.

"Baby, what's wrong?" she said, wiping the wet hair from my forehead. "Did you have a nightmare?"

Dad entered the room then, looking sleepy and annoyed from being woken up. I hugged Mom tight around the neck.

"There was this monster and... it had big teeth and claws... it grabbed me!"

"No more horror movies for you," Dad said.

"There, there now," Mom said, laying me down on my pillow and kissing me. "It was just a dream."

"It was scary."

"I know, but it can't hurt you now. Go back to sleep."

She tucked me back in, kissed me goodnight and got up to leave. Dad was already halfway to their bedroom when she turned off the light.

"Goodnight," she said as she shut the door.

"Nice one, dork," Sean said. "Way to wake up the whole house."

"I'm sorry. I couldn't help it. I got scared."

"You're such a wimp, I swear. No wonder everyone picks on you at school."

"Shut up."

"Make me," Sean taunted, but I refused to say anything else. "Yeah, that's what I thought."

Sean rolled over, and within minutes, he was fast asleep, snoring away while I lay awake in my bed, staring up into the darkness.

"Rise and shine," Mom said, flipping on the overhead light.

I blinked open my sleepy eyes and sat up, groggily swinging my legs over the side of the bed. Glancing at the nightstand through half-closed eyes, Mickey's hands told me it was six thirty-four.

Sean groaned loudly and pulled the pillow tightly over his head. "Come on sleepy head, up and at 'em," Mom said, yanking the covers off of him. "Time to get up. It's a school day."

"Five more minutes," Sean's muffled voice said from underneath his pillow.

"Now!" she commanded, stripping his pillow away. Sean sat up, defeated, while I dropped my feet to the floor and trudged off to the bathroom. "I want you both showered, dressed, and downstairs for breakfast in twenty minutes," I heard her say before she left our room and went back downstair

Nineteen minutes later, we both bounded down the stairs into the kitchen. Dad was already almost finished with his over-easy eggs and toast. He nursed his cup of black coffee while Mom got up to bring over a skillet with already scrambled eggs and divided it up between two plates, one for each of us. A communal plate of buttered toast was already on the table. She poured two glasses of Tang and set one in front of each of us.

I finished my breakfast, put my plate in the sink, and tore off a little corner of toast for Oliver the turtle. I held the toast over his bowl just above his head. He looked at it for a second, stretched out his colorful neck, and quick as a wink, snatched it from my fingers. I laughed and scratched the top of his shell with the tip of my finger. "You like that, don't you boy?" I said, as if talking to a puppy. To round out his diet, I opened his turtle food and picked out a few choice looking flies.

"Wash your hands," Mom insisted. I did. The man at the pet store told me to always wash my hands after handling my turtle. I didn't think tickling his back was "handling" him, but I washed my hands anyway to make Mom happy.

A half hour later, Sean and I were pulling up in front of school in Dad's car. "Have a good day," he told us as we climbed out of the backseat. We still had a good fifteen minutes of playground time before the bell rang. When we got through the main gate, we split up, Sean going off to find his friends while I looked for mine. I quickly spotted Matt and Lucy and went to join them. We exchanged Monday morning greetings; neither Lucy nor I mentioned our misadventure yesterday in the woods.

"Well, if it isn't the *Three Musketeers*," Butch said, coming up behind us, Joey by his side. "You got me in trouble, McBride."

"I didn't do anything," I said defensively.

"You hit him in the head with a stick," Lucy said.

"Yeah, well, your mom told my mom I did it on purpose."

"You did do it on purpose," Matt chimed in.

"Shut up, fatboy, you're next," Joey threatened. Matt shrank back.

"Just so you know, I'm gonna get you McBride. You too Sherman," Butch promised. "When you least expect it." Then he punched me in the head, right on the exact same Band-Aid covered spot where he hit me with the stick.

"Ow!" I said, wincing in pain. My hand involuntarily shot up to cover the lump on my head.

"Leave him alone!" Lucy said, pushing Butch with both hands in his chest.

Butch looked at Joey with shocked amusement, both of them

bursting out in laughter.

"Are you gonna let a girl fight for you now, McBride?" Butch taunted.

"She's no girl, that's a boy in a dress," Joey laughed.

"Take that back," I demanded. Picking on me is one thing but picking on Lucy is a whole different ball game.

"What are you gonna do about it, faggot?" Butch said, balling up his fists and stepping toe-to-toe, his nose just inches from my face.

"Why don't you guys just get out of here and leave us alone?" Matt said.

Joey noticed Father Scott heading purposefully in our direction and nudged Butch with his elbow. "Dead meat," Butch said, staring into my eyes with a look that could kill.

"Is there a problem here?" Father Scott said, hands on his hips, looking pointedly at Butch and Joey.

"No Father," the bullies said together.

"There better not be," he said to both. Then to Butch: "Don't you have a bell to ring?"

"Y-yes Father," he stammered.

"Go on then," he said, "or I'll ring your bell."

Butch and Joey took off running.

"Was he bothering you again?" he said to Billy.

"We were just playing," I lied. I don't know why I was covering for him.

"It didn't look that way to me," he said. "What happened to your head?"

I touched the bump. "It was an accident," I said. "At my birthday party."

"I can't help you if you don't let me," he said, gently placing his hand on my shoulder. "If you want to talk, you know where to find me."

"Yes sir," I said, averting my eyes. He sighed and started away just as the bell rang.

I was staring out the window during math class - my least favorite - daydreaming and wishing I were anywhere else. It was a beautiful day outside. The trees were budding and spring was in full bloom. I remembered that last year around this time it snowed on Easter Sunday, unusual for this time of year, but not unheard of. This year Easter came early, at the end of March, but it didn't snow.

I looked up at the clock again; still two hours to go until lunch. Butch promised to get me when I least expected it and I had no doubt he would. I tried to think about anything else, but it wasn't working so well.

I looked around the classroom. Mr. McLean was writing fraction problems on the board with his back turned to us. Some kids were writing in their notebooks, some just looking bored, like me. I looked at Lucy, beside me to the left, and we smiled at each other.

The desk directly behind her was empty—Mary Ellen Crawford was absent today. I looked over at Butch in the last seat in the far right row. We made eye contact and he smiled his evil grin and punched his hand into his fist. I turned around. Why me?

Mr. McLean finished writing and turned back around to face the class. There were five problems on the board.

"Okay," he said, "can I get five volunteers to come up and solve the problems on the board?" No one volunteered. "Oh, come on. Nobody?" Nope. "Alright then, let's see..." *Don't pick me. Don't pick me.* “How about Sam Reynolds, Henry Michaels, Mary Wilson, Judy Smalls, and...” *Don’t pick me. Don’t pick me.* “Billy McBride.” Damn!

I got up with my fellow students and went up to the blackboard. Butch got up too, even though his name wasn’t called. While we went to the front of the room, he went to the pencil sharpener. I tried to concentrate on the problem in front of me. 2¾ + 3⅝ =? All I could think about was the grinding sound of the pencil sharpener. It finally stopped and Butch went to go sit down.

Finally, I could focus on the problem on the board. After several minutes, I found the common denominator, did my conversions, and reasoned out the solution: 6⅜. Mr. McLean proclaimed the answer correct. I smiled at my own cleverness and went back to my desk.

Neither Mr. McLean nor I had noticed that Butch didn’t return to his own seat. He was now sitting in the desk directly behind Lucy, vacated by the absent Mary Ellen Crawford. As I turned to sit, Butch held his freshly sharpened pencil, point up, on my desk chair.

“Billy don’t!” Lucy yelled, but it was too late. I was already on my way down. I sat on the pencil, impaled by four inches of number two wood and graphite.

The shock and pain was instantaneous. It was like getting hit in the solar-plexus, that part of your gut when the air in your lungs gets forced out and you can’t breathe, only the exact opposite; my lungs tightened and I sucked in air, but the effect was the same: I couldn’t breathe.

I think I screamed, but I’m not sure. I know I sprang up off my chair and looked down at the bloody pencil, still clutched in

Butch's fist. Butch was laughing hysterically. So was Joey and a few others, but I doubt they knew I'd been stabbed. Lucy turned and punched Butch, but that only made him laugh harder.

Mr. McLean came rushing over, shock and anger written on his face. He looked at the blood-covered pencil; looked at the seat of my desk with several drops of blood on the wood; looked at the seat of my pants, a dark growing stain, black against the dark blue fabric.

For a moment, I don't think it registered what had just happened. Then his eyes narrowed and he focused on Butch. He snatched the pencil from his hand, pulled him off the desk by his collar, and said in a tone of voice seething with outrage, "Do. Not. *Move!*"

"Lucy," he said calmer. "Take Billy to the nurse's office. Tell Sister Joseph what happened." Butch tried to shrink away from Mr. McLean, fear gripping him.

"Yes sir," Lucy said and guided me toward the door. I was still struggling to breathe. I was in shock and it hurt to walk, taking baby steps. It felt like a red-hot poker was lodged inside my butt. The walk to the nurse's office was a blur. I know Lucy was talking, but I couldn't tell what she was saying. My brain was in a fog of pain, still trying to process the idea that I had been brutally assaulted. We made it to the front office and Lucy filled them in on what had happened. I was escorted into the nurse's office where I laid face down on the paper-covered green-leather lounge/bed and promptly passed out.

"Ohhh," I groaned, consciousness slowly coming back to me. I was disoriented. It took me a minute to remember where I was. The pain in my nether region brought me back. I rolled onto my back and tried to sit up. I felt a stabbing pain shoot up my back as I settled down, leaning on my elbows for support. A moment later, the nurse, Mrs. Connelly, came into the office.

"You're awake," she said, crossing the room to the lounge/bed and placing her palm against my forehead. "How do you feel?"

"Like I sat on a pencil," I said. How did she think I felt? "How long was I asleep?"

"Not long. Your mother is on her way to take you to your family doctor."

Ever since the Thanksgiving cruise, our family doctor has been Dr. Washington. It was weird though, because even though he was my doctor, I still thought of him as Sammy's dad. I liked him a lot; he was really friendly and had a way of making you feel good even when you felt bad. He was one of the few doctors left who still made house calls. I remember once when I was sick he came over to see how I was feeling. My mom didn't ask him to come over, he just did. After he checked me over, he asked if there was anything I wanted. I said, "Bellbottoms." He just smiled and left my room.

I should probably mention that at that time there was a big battle going on in our household over bellbottom pants. Sean and I wanted them; Dad said "No way." It was just like when he wouldn't let us grow our hair past our ears. Like a lot of adults, he didn't like the changes going on all around with young people. He hated long hair, he hated mod clothes, he hated rock & roll, and he especially hated The Beatles. He blamed them for everything he didn't like. So when we wanted bellbottoms, it was like they represented everything he hated about the 60's, so he put his foot down. Even Mom couldn't talk him out of it this time.

So when I told Dr. Washington I wanted bellbottoms, I could see my dad's face turn red—a sure sign he was getting angry. But I was sick, so he cut me some slack. Besides, it's not like he was going to magically produce a pair of pants. Or so we thought. When Dr. Washington left, I thought that was the end of it, but a few minutes later he returned... with a pair of brand new blue and white striped bellbottoms in my size!

"These were in my car," he explained. "I bought them for Sammy. He's exactly your size."

"Oh, James, no," my mom protested. "Those are Sammy's. We couldn't."

"I have three more pairs for him. Please, I insist."

"Can I keep them?" I said, excited at the prospect.

Mom and Dad looked at each other and I saw my dad roll his eyes. "I guess so," he said reluctantly, losing another battle in the youth culture war. I was so happy I jumped out of bed and hugged Dr. Washington. "Thank you! Thank you!" I gushed.

"You're welcome, but you have to promise me to get well. I don't want to have to come back here," he told me with a wink and a smile.

After that, the floodgates were opened and from that day forth, all our pants were bellbottoms. Even our Sunday best were "flairs"; a cut of pants somewhere in between straight legs and full-blown bellbottoms. All thanks to Sammy's dad.

Mom showed up at school about five minutes later. As soon as she came into the front office, she rushed over to me. She looked almost frantic.

"Oh my God, are you alright?" she said, looking me up and down as if she could determine my well being by giving me a once over.

"I'm fine," I insisted. I hated being fussed over.

"I don't think there was any major damage," the nurse said. "Judging by the puncture mark on his pants and the blood stain, I'd say the wound is in the soft muscle tissue. He was extremely lucky."

Lucky? I didn't feel lucky!

"I would have him checked by your physician as soon as possible."

"I'm taking him right over," Mom said. "I've already called his office." Then to me she said, "Honey, go wait for me in the car. I need to talk to Sister Joseph."

I got to my feet and walked out of the nurse's office into the front office's main reception area where Mrs. Thompson, the school secretary, sat behind her desk outside the principal's office. As I passed through, I saw Butch sitting on the long wooden bench outside Sister Joseph's door, looking more scared than I've ever seen him. He caught me looking at him and his face changed into a scowl. I hurried out the door.

The pain in my backside had subsided to a dull throb now, but I still wasn't very comfortable sitting up yet, so I got in the back seat of my mom's station wagon and lay down on my stomach. A few minutes later, my mom got in the car and we were on our way to the doctor.

Dr. Washington's office was in a little house on the corner of a main street in Passaic. I don't think anybody lived there, he just used it for an office. He was a popular guy, there were always at least four or five people there. Probably because he was the only doctor for miles. My mom said she didn't know how he stayed in business because he was so kind and generous he took care of many people for free.

The waiting room was packed. When we walked in the door, every head turned to stare at us. As usual, we were the only white people in the office, which I always thought was a shame since he was such a good doctor. I guess I'll never understand prejudice.

There was a woman with a crying baby and a little boy about three years old who was running in circles, completely ignoring his mother's demands to sit down, an older man with sad eyes holding a handkerchief under his nose and sniffling, and a middle age lady with a big cast on her foot. My mom told the nurse we were here and told us to have a seat. I decided to stand.

The little boy came up to me and said, "Hi. What's your name?"

"Billy," I said. "What's yours?"

"Kevin. Want to play with me?"

So, I got down on my knees and played with him on the floor, rolling a ball that Sammy's dad kept in a little toy box in the corner. The boy's mom smiled at me. I guess she was grateful that I gotten him to quit running around. About twenty minutes later, Sammy's dad opened the door to the waiting room and escorted an old black lady around my Nana's age to the front door.

"Take those twice a day and call me if it doesn't clear up in a week," he told her.

"I will, Doctor," she said, her eyes twinkling affectionately. He had that effect on people. After she left, he closed the door and turned back to his waiting patients. Surveying the room, he fixed his eyes on me.

"Billy," he said, "Come on back." To the rest of the room he said, "My apologies, this is an emergency. I'll be with the rest of you shortly." No one seemed to mind.

He led me to the examination room and gave me one of those white hospital gowns that are open in the back and told me to put it on. I went into the bathroom and did as he said. I came back into the room feeling embarrassed with my naked butt hanging out for all to see.

"Stabbed by a pencil?" he said, raising his eyebrows. I nodded, looking at my feet. I felt ashamed, I didn't know why, I just did. "Well, that's a first for me. Let's see what kind of damage we're talking about here. Hop up on the table face down."

I hesitated and looked over at my mom, then the doctor. He picked up on my shyness. "Uh, would you mind stepping outside, Katherine?"

"There's nothing I haven't seen before," she said, as if it was the most unreasonable request in the world.

"Please Mom?" I begged.

She sighed and rolled her eyes. "Fine," she said and went into the next room. When she was gone, I said, "Hey Doc?"

"Yes Billy?"

"Don't tell Sammy about this, okay?"

He laughed and said, "I won't. Now, hop up on the table for me."

I got up on the table and lay down on my stomach. He pulled his stool over and sat at the end of the table. "This might sting a little," he said. I felt a wet cloth; it was cold at first, and then, as predicted, it stung. I let out a small *yelp!* The rest of the examination was over before I knew it. He put a Band-Aid on the wound and told me to put my pants back on.

When I came back out of the bathroom, he and my mom were

discussing my injury. He told her to keep an eye on it for infection, but otherwise, I would be all right. She thanked him, and half an hour later, we were home.

I went right to my room and got into bed, face down. Apparently getting stabbed in the butt warranted ice cream because my mom came upstairs with the biggest sundae I'd ever seen that didn't come from Dairy Queen. I switched on the radio to WABC AM, the rock station, and dug into my sundae. I don't recommend getting stabbed in the butt, but I have to admit, the fringe benefits aren't too bad.

The scientists, engineers, and technicians at NASA's Mission Control Command Center in Houston, Texas were all busily monitoring Apollo 13's progress. The space agency's third lunar mission was, by this time, becoming routine. Boring even. It was thirteen-thirteen hundred hours, central daylight savings time, when astronaut Swigert's voice interrupted the silence.

"Hey, we've got a problem here."

The capsule communicator immediately responded:

"This is Houston; say again, please."

"Houston, we've had a problem. We've had a main B bus undervolt. And we had a pretty large bang associated with the caution and warning here. We got a Main bus A undervolt now too... Main B is reading zip right now."

The Mission Control crew was scrambling.

"We'd like you to attempt to reconnect fuel cell one to Main A and fuel cell three to main B," Cap Com instructed.

"Okay Houston... I tried to reset, and fuel cells one and three are both showing zip on the flows."

"We copy," Cap Com said. Panic had gripped the Command Center. Everyone was racking their brains trying to come up with an effective solution to the problem.

"Houston, are you still reading 13?" Swigert's voice said, thousands of miles away, somewhere between the Earth and the Moon.

"That's affirmative. We're still reading you. We're still trying to come up with some good ideas here for you."

"Let me give you some readings... Our oh-two cryo number two tank is reading zero... did you get that?"

"Oh-two quantity number two is zero," Houston confirmed.

"And it looks to me, looking out the hatch, that we are venting something. We are venting something out into space. It's a gas of some sort."

With this new piece of information, the scientists conferred. After a few moments, they had a consensus.

"We'd like you to power down until you get an amperage of ten less amps than what you've got now."

"It looks like oh-two tank one pressure is just a hair over two-hundred."

"We'll confirm that."

"Does it look like it's still going down?"

"It's going slowly to zero, and we're starting to think about the LM lifeboat."

"Yes, that's something we're thinking about too."

I was still lying in my bed listening to the radio and reading a novel by one of my favorite authors entitled *From the Earth to the Moon* by H.G. Wells. I was barely listening to the song that was playing on the radio, when it was interrupted by an urgent sounding voice.

"We interrupt this broadcast to bring you an emergency announcement. Approximately one hour ago at one-thirteen in the afternoon central time, Apollo 13 encountered a potentially life threatening accident. Details are still coming in. We switch you now to Mission Control in Houston..."

"Here in Mission Control we are now looking toward an alternative mission, swinging around the Moon and using the Lunar Module power systems because of the situation that has developed here this afternoon."

The local announcer came back a few seconds later. "Once again, ladies and gentlemen, Apollo 13 has encountered..."

CLICK!

I turned off the radio, my book and injury both temporarily forgotten, and sat in stunned silence.

Sister Mary Joseph sat behind her ornate maple desk, a gift from the Archbishop when she became principal of Saint Anthony's seven years ago, after Sister Mary Ambrose had retired from the post. Since the school's inception in 1937, a nun of the Dominican order had always held the position.

She had been born in a convent in 1924 under Dickensian circumstances. She never knew her parents; all she knew was that her mother was unwed and died because of complications at childbirth. The Dominicans took her in, named her Mary, after the Virgin Mother, and was raised in the convent. She was twenty-four years old when she took her vows, chose the name Joseph, and became a religious sister. Two years later, she completed her education and began teaching. Her first assignment had been at Saint Peter the Apostle school in Hackensack, New Jersey, where she taught fifth grade for sixteen years before being transferred to Saint Anthony's to take the job of principal.

The practice of teaching had certainly evolved since she started out as an educator, and sometimes she longed for the old ways. In her day, a cheater would receive a good rap on the knuckles with a ruler. Bullies would get twenty whacks on the behind with the paddle. If she tried that today, a disgruntled parent was likely to bring a lawsuit against the school for child abuse. In her opinion, modern children were too coddled.

But such was the world they lived in today. She had lived through the stock market crash and the Great Depression it had brought when she was a little girl, World War II, and the Korean War, but never before had she seen anything as tumultuous as the past decade.

The 1960's saw the world on the brink of nuclear war with Cuba; the political assassination of President John F. Kennedy; and then, five years later, those of civil rights leader Dr. Martin Luther King and the late president's own brother, Robert Kennedy, less than two months apart; another war, this time in a tiny southeast Asian country called Vietnam; hippies; and an entire youth culture completely transformed by four long-haired pop stars from England. Like many adults of her generation, she was delighted by the news of their disbanding this past weekend. Perhaps now things could get back to normal. But probably not, the damage was already done. In the words of another current pop icon, Bob Dylan, from that song some of the younger Sisters were fond of, *"the times they are a changin'."*

Today was certainly proof of that. One of her second grade students had stabbed another student with a pencil. Never before had she witnessed such violence on her watch. The attack was unprecedented, and she was unsure of the appropriate disciplinary action. She immediately dismissed the idea of calling law enforcement; the school had never taken such drastic measures against one of their students and would not start now—this would be handled internally. She was considering expulsion, but was leaning more toward suspension, especially this close to the end of the school year. As she weighed her options, the intercom on her desk sounded.

"Yes?" she said after depressing the "Talk" button.

"Mrs. Anderson is here," her secretary informed her.

"Send her in."

Butch sat nervously on the long wooden bench outside Sister Mary Joseph's office, trying to decipher what was being said behind the closed door. He couldn't make out the muffled conversation between his mother and the principal, but he could tell by their raised voices emanating from within that it couldn't be good.

He had sat in this chair many times before, but never for something so serious. He wasn't even sure why he did it. He hadn't really thought it through. The idea of putting a pencil on McBride's seat popped into his head and he did it. He hadn't expected him to actually sit on it. He thought he would have seen it first and caught himself before he sat down. But he didn't, and now Butch was in deep trouble. He might even get kicked out of school. He leaned in closer to the door in an attempt to listen more closely, but it proved futile.

Gloria Thompson, the school secretary, sat across the room stealing glances over the top of her horn-rimmed glasses at the boy on the bench. She was a small, round woman in her early fifties with graying black hair pulled back in a tight bun and had been secretary at Saint Anthony's for seventeen years. Orderly and efficient, she had her finger on the pulse of the school. Regardless of the circumstances, she was the first person to be notified or informed of any interaction within these walls; nothing happened at Saint Anthony's without her direct knowledge.

She shuffled and reshuffled the papers on her desk, surreptitiously watching Butch squirm in his seat. She'd seen his type come and go countless times over the years—she could spot a bully from a mile away. He may be able to fool most people with his blonde hair, sparkling blue eyes, and an almost angelic smile—he was able to feign innocence well—but she could see right through his façade.

She averted her eyes when Butch caught her staring. She didn't even want to make eye contact with the little cretin. Like him, she waited anxiously to learn the results of the meeting, but unlike him, she hoped for dire consequences. After what seemed like an eternity, the yelling stopped and the door flung open, banging the wall and causing both she and the boy to jump.

Rachael Anderson stormed out of the office looking furious, followed by Sister Joseph. Rachael grabbed Butch's ear, pulled him roughly off the bench, and frog-marched him out of the building to a refrain of, "Ow! Ow! Ow! Ow!"

"I almost feel sorry for him," Sister Joseph said before returning to her office.

"I don't," Mrs. Thompson said sotto voce.

Butch's mother pulled into her parking spot in front of the rundown duplex. She slammed the dented car door and stomped up the front porch steps, fiddling with her keys. Butch got out of the back seat just as Rachael pushed open the right half of the side-by-side doors and disappeared up the stairs into the second-floor apartment. Butch took his time, delaying the inevitable onslaught that was sure to come.

They lived in a small, two family house that was badly in need of repair. The front porch sagged on the right side and the wood was rotting. The screens on both the upstairs and downstairs front doors were ripped and hanging loose, on the windows there were no screens at all. The front yard, if you could even call it that, was a field of dirt and clumps of weeds, it had been years since anything resembling a lawn had grown there. The house itself was grey, the decades old paint peeling away. The overall look of the place was depressing.

Inside wasn't much better. The cramped, two-bedroom flat was barely big enough for one person, let alone two. The living room at the top of the stairs was the largest room in the house, with barely enough room for the used threadbare couch and chair and an old black & white television set in need of a new picture tube. One sad looking floor lamp in a corner provided the room's only source of light, save for the dirty window that let in almost no outside sunshine through the perpetually closed blinds. An ugly, loose, wobbly black wrought-iron railing surrounded the open stairwell. A generic still life print, probably purchased at a flea market for under a dollar by the landlord, hung on the wall over the TV. It was there when they moved in and had never been replaced. The wall-to-wall carpet in the entire apartment was old and dirty; a dull, ugly beige with well-worn paths and random stains throughout.

A long hallway led to a tiny bathroom with a sink, toilet, and shower; no bathtub. You had to close the door just to use the sink and your knees were mere inches from the wall when you sat down to use the toilet. The fixtures all appeared to be from the turn of the century, and probably were. The plumbing was a joke; there was hardly any water pressure and only one inadequate hot water heater for both apartments. The loud, clunky radiators hardly worked and there was no air conditioning. It was freezing in the winter and stifling hot in summer.

The "master" bedroom at the end of the hallway, next to the bathroom, was a twelve-foot by twelve-foot room with one window painted shut and a tiny closet. Butch's room was next door, directly across from the bathroom. The narrow kitchen was off the living room across from the stairs. A twenty-year-old noisy refrigerator that ran constantly and a two-burner gas stove took up one side, a sink, flanked by four cabinets—two above and two below—with very little counter space on the other. A compact two-seat table was propped against the far wall, a simple round clock hanging on the wall above it. A beige wall phone was bolted next to the open door frame, a free church calendar hung next to it. Butch could already hear his mother yelling inside.

He entered the apartment and quickly shut the door, hoping the downstairs neighbors, an elderly retired couple who never left the house, couldn't hear his mother's profanity filled tirade coming from the kitchen, though he was certain they probably could.

He knew she'd already been drinking that afternoon, he just didn't know how much. It all depended on what time she'd dragged herself out of bed. She usually slept until noon, sometimes earlier, but most times later. He suspected today was probably the latter;

she'd hit the bottle pretty hard last night. And she'd held it together pretty well at school and drove okay, so she wasn't that hammered yet. That would change though. Especially after being called in for a parent conference with Sister Joseph to learn that he'd earned a three-day suspension for stabbing another kid in the rear with a pencil. He was in for it now. He didn't mind the yelling so much, he could always tune that out; it was the beatings he dreaded.

He deserved it, of course. It was all his fault his father had left them, just like his mother reminded him daily. The level of abuse brought down on him depended on a number of factors; the weather outside, the time of the month, the ugliness of her mood, and of course, the amount of booze she consumed.

It would start with yelling, then progress to slapping. If she was really mad she would bring out his father's old belt. Sometimes, she would wake him up in the middle of the night just to beat him with the leather strap. Today would be a belt day, he already knew.

Sean met Tim in the park by the high school like they'd planned, and then walked the few blocks to the garden apartments where Joker lived.

"Timmy! Ringo!" Joker said, opening his door wider to allow entry. "Come on in."

They went inside and, just like the last time, the first thing Sean noticed was the smell. Like a mix of pot smoke, rotting garbage, and body odor. He didn't know how anyone could live like that. He could tell Joker wasn't real big on personal hygiene—he was still wearing the same dirty jeans from last week.

"Follow me," Joker said and flashed the widest grin and craziest eyes Sean had ever seen before disappearing into the back room.

Tim and Sean followed him through to the next room. It was just as messy as the rest of the apartment with dirty clothes thrown in piles all over. Against one wall was an unmade queen-size mattress and box spring sitting directly on the floor—no frame or headboard necessary. An old dresser stood next to it. On the wall over the bed was an American flag. Also mounted on the wall were two army rifles, several handguns and assorted combat knives. Sean stared at the weapons.

"Pretty cool, huh?" Joker said. "Souvenirs from 'Nam. Have a seat."

Sean looked around looking for a place to sit. Tim went over to the bed, moved aside a pair of crumpled jeans, and sat on the edge. Sean tentatively sat down next to him.

"Alright Ringo," Joker said. "Did Timmy tell you why I asked you here today?"

"I didn't get the chance," Tim said.

"How would you like to make some serious money?"

"Sure," Sean said, his eyes lighting up. "Like, how much?"

"Enough to buy your boat," Tim chimed in.

"What would I have to do?"

"Just give people what they want."

Sean stared blankly at him. "What do you mean?"

Joker went to a desk in the corner piled high with debris and a cardboard box. He opened the box and pulled out a large scale—the kind with three beams Sean had seen the pharmacist use at the drug store. He reached back inside and took out a large clear plastic bag filled with more marijuana than Sean had ever seen before. It must've weighed over ten pounds.

"I need someone to set up business in your school. I see a golden opportunity for both of us. All those Catholic school kids ripe for the picking. You pass out a few joints for free, and I guarantee they'll be lining up to buy from you."

"I don't know..."

"Listen, Ringo, I like you. It's easy money. Are you in or out?"

"Come on, man," Tim said. "Between you and me, we can make a fortune. What do you say... *partner*."

"I... I guess so," Sean reluctantly agreed.

"Excellent!" Joker said, grinning his unnaturally wide smile.

"You won't be sorry," Tim said through his own grin.

"Okay," Joker said, all business. "Come over here and I'll show you what I need you to do...."

It was almost suppertime when Sean found himself walking home alone with several ounces of marijuana in two-dozen little baggies inside his knapsack. He still wasn't exactly sure what had happened. The entire afternoon was a blur. He turned into his driveway and entered the house through the side door, relieved that at least he wasn't late for dinner again.

I awoke with a start from the sound of the kitchen door slamming shut. I never realized how loud it was from up here. I must've fallen asleep listening to the radio. I heard Sean and Mom talking downstairs and turned the volume down so I could hear what they were saying, but I guess the sound didn't travel as well as I thought because I still couldn't make anything out. A moment later Sean came in, out of breath, and threw the green canvas army-surplus knapsack he used to carry his books on his bed.

"How are you feeling? Mom said you got a pencil up your butt."

He laughed at that. I gave him a look that let him know I didn't think it was so funny. "Sorry," he said, still laughing a little. "Seriously though, are you okay?"

"Yeah, I guess. It's sore, but I'll live."

Sean started changing out of his school clothes, so I turned the radio back up. I tuned it to Ten-Ten-Wins, the all-news station, right after the story broke.

"Since when did you start listening to the news station?"

"Since there was an accident on board Apollo 13. Some kind of explosion. They don't know if they can even make it back to Earth. Didn't you hear about it?"

"No. When did this happen?"

"A little while ago. Here, listen," I said and turned the radio up.

"...reports are still coming in from NASA as to what emergency procedures are underway to bring these brave men home. To recap, this afternoon at one-thirteen central time, Apollo 13 reported a major malfunction aboard their space capsule with these fateful words...." The live broadcast switched to a recording, *"Houston, we've had a problem,"* then returned to the local announcer. "Every effort is being made to..."

I turned the volume back down.

"Man, what a drag," Sean commented.

"What a drag?" I repeated, incredulous. "Is that all you can say? Those are astronauts up there! Real live people! National heroes! They might die! Don't you even care?!"

"Jesus Christ, Billy, calm down. I'm sorry, okay? What the hell do you want me to say?"

I gasped. Not only did Sean just take the Lord's name in vain, he swore on top of it! In the same sentence!

"Oh grow up," he said. "Don't look at me like that."

"You said 'Hell'."

"You're damned right I did. I say a hell of a lot more than that, too. What are you gonna do, tell on me now?"

"I told you I didn't..."

"Save it. You tell on me again and I'll make you wish you were never born."

I picked up my stuffed Astronaut Snoopy and held him tight, cradling him in my arms as if he might protect me from the stranger in front of me that only looked like my brother. It was an eerie feeling, like a scene from that science-fiction movie *Invasion of the Body Snatchers* where aliens took over people's bodies. Where did my brother go that I loved so much? It's like I didn't even know him anymore. I was scared, not because he threatened me again, but for his heart and soul. I didn't want to, but I couldn't help it—I started crying again.

"Knock it off you big baby, or I'll really give you something to cry about," he said, and then turned his back on me. He turned on his stereo and flipped the switch on the turntable to automatically play the record already on the platter. He flopped on his bed as Mick Jagger's voice filled the room, respectfully asking permission to introduce himself.

I recognized the song, *Sympathy For the Devil* by The Rolling Stones. Sean had been playing The Stones a lot lately, ever since The Beatles broke up. I thought the song was appropriate, because this had to be Hell.

NINE

Captain Billy Apollo pulled free of the creature's grip and managed to land a fierce blow to its head. That gave him the time he needed to roll to the side, aim his gun and fire, finishing it off—the monster froze momentarily, its entire body glowing a brilliant white before disintegrating into nothingness.

"What was that thing?" Empress Lucinda said.

"I don't know, but let's not hang around to see if there are any more of them. Come on, my ship is this way."

Lucinda followed Captain Apollo through the maze of rocks. They rounded a corner and immediately came to a halt. Just ahead, The Butcher and Joemar were searching, guns drawn. Fortunately, their backs were turned and the captain and Lucinda were able to retreat behind a boulder before they were spotted.

"What now?" Lucinda said. "They're directly between us and your ship."

"Not for long. Wait here," Captain Apollo said and darted behind a ridge. Lucinda waited nervously, stealing glimpses at the two bandits only a few dozen yards away. She'd been waiting less than two minutes when the captain suddenly reappeared at her side.

"Miss me?"

"Yes. Where did you go?"

"Just over the ridge. Get ready."

"For what?"

BOOM!!!

A powerful explosion shook the ground as small rocks and dust rained down on them.

"That," Captain Apollo said. He looked around the boulder and watched the Butcher and Joemar run off in the direction of the blast. "Come on!"

He grabbed Lucinda's hand and pulled her with him as he made a beeline for his ship. They sprinted together across the canyon, up the gangplank, and into the ship. He closed the hatch and went straight to the cockpit.

"Strap in," he said. Lucinda buckled herself into the co-pilot chair while the captain fired up the engines. With the ease of a seasoned veteran, the ship was airborne and heading toward open space.

"They've started their ship," Lucinda said, reading the ships scanners. "They'll be within interception range any minute."

"Not if I can help it," he said. Then, into his microphone he said, "*Constellation One*, I have an enemy ship on my tail. I could use some help."

BOOM!!!

As if in reply, his ship was rocked by a laser blast. He was momentarily blinded by a shower of sparks that exploded from the forward control console.

I squinted my eyes from the sudden burst of light when Mom pulled open the dryer door without warning.

"Come on out, space man. I have laundry to do."

"But Mom, I was in the middle of a battle with an enemy ship."

"You can finish it another time. Out. I let you stay home today so you can rest, not so you could play in the dryer."

I climbed out slowly and carefully. I was still pretty sore. The doctor said that if I moved too quickly or extended myself too much I could re-open the wound.

"Why don't you go upstairs and watch TV?"

"There's nothing good on during the day. It's nothing but game shows and soap operas," I lamented.

"Then go read a book. Or play with your G.I. Joes. I'm sure you can find something to do besides play in my clothes dryer. I want you to find a new place to play. You're getting too big for that."

"But Mom..."

"No buts. No more playing in the dryer. I mean it. Go on now, go find something else to do upstairs."

"Yes ma'am."

I went up to my room and sat on the bed. What was I gonna do? The dryer was my spaceship, but now I wasn't even allowed to play in it. It's not fair! Somehow, I would find a way. I didn't like to disobey Mom, but this was my spaceship we were talking about! The safety of the galaxy hangs in the balance! Besides, what she didn't know wouldn't hurt her.

I put that aside in my mind for now—I would cross that bridge when I came to it. I started thinking instead about Apollo 13 and the accident yesterday, and all the questions I had, when I suddenly remembered something. I just had to find it, and I thought I knew where it was.

I stood on my tiptoes balancing precariously on Sean's wooden desk chair, searching the shelf in our shared clothes closet for my *How and Why Wonder Book on Space Exploration*. The *How and Why* series published science books for young readers on a multitude of subjects. They were really awesome books; I owned about a dozen on a variety of subjects: dinosaurs, reptiles, birds, fish, rocks, physics, the human body, etc. I had gotten the one about Space Exploration last year at the Hayden Planetarium gift shop—right before Apollo 11 became the first manned space craft to land on the Moon—when my class went on a field trip to the Museum of Natural History in New York City.

I wanted to see if the book could offer any insight into what was happening aboard Apollo 13 right now. The radio said they had some kind of short onboard and they were leaking some kind of gas and that NASA was trying to figure out how to get them home. They said they had it under control. It sounded pretty serious to me, but I was having trouble understanding everything they were saying about it. I thought that maybe my *How and Why* book could help me make sense out of it all. Maybe I could even help them figure out how to get them home. I was the captain of my own starship after all!

Finally, I spotted the books toward the back of the closet, but they were just beyond my reach. I was going to need a boost. I got off the chair and looked around the room for something to stand on. I put my foot on my space helmet sitting on the floor by my bed and put my weight on it to test it out. It seemed sturdy enough. I bent down to pick it up a little too fast—a wave of pain in my posterior reminded me to move a little slower. The pills Sammy's dad gave my mom for my pain worked pretty well, unless I moved too suddenly. Carefully this time, I picked up the helmet and placed it on the chair. I climbed on top and balanced myself on its rounded top. This was much better! I grabbed hold of an old shoebox on the shelf with my left hand to steady myself, and reached in the back for my book with my right.

Suddenly, my weight shifted and the plastic helmet under me slid across the seat of the chair. In one motion, the chair, the helmet, the shoebox, the books, and me all came crashing down together. The chair lay on its side; the helmet flew across the room; several of the books lay open across my chest with the rest scattered around me; the shoebox spilled its contents; and I lay on my back, one leg draped over the back of the overturned chair. Another jolt of pain shot through me.

"Ow!" I hollered, louder than I meant to.

"Billy?" Mom yelled from the bottom of the stairs.

"Yeah?" I yelled back.

"Are you okay? What was that noise?"

"Nothing, I'm fine. I just dropped something."

"You should be in bed resting. You know what the doctor said."

"I know," I said, and that seemed to be the end of it. At least she didn't come upstairs again. When we first got home yesterday, she was checking up on me every ten minutes. I mean, I'm glad she cares and all, but enough already!

I picked myself up and up-righted the chair. I started gathering up the spilled contents of the shoebox; a dozen baseball cards, a lucky rabbits-foot, some Boy Scout merit badges—when all of a sudden I froze in shock and horror. Lying among the miscellaneous forgotten items was half a pack of Marlboro cigarettes, several books of matches, a little cardboard package filled with white papers that said *Zig-Zag* on the front... and dozens of plastic sandwich baggies with some kind of dried green plant inside. I picked one up and opened it and brought it up to my nose. The odor was strong and it smelled to me almost like a skunk. Even though I'd never seen or smelled it before, I was pretty sure I knew what it was—marijuana! Oh no! My big brother was a pothead! This explains why he's been acting so strange lately.

I dropped the baggie on the ground like it was a hot potato burning my hand and pushed myself away with my legs, backpedaling until I was up against the far wall. I was in a panic now, breathing hard and sweating. I didn't know what to do. Should I tell Mom and Dad? This wasn't like smoking cigarettes, this was drugs! Should I call the police? I didn't want Sean to go to jail, but I didn't want him to die of an overdose either.

I promised Sean I wouldn't tell on him, but this was different. Wasn't it? I decided I would keep his secret—for now anyway. I didn't want Sean mad at me any more. I would wait until the time was right—when he was in a good mood—and I would talk to him about it. Until then, I would just pretend everything was okay. I put everything back in the shoebox and put it back on the shelf, put the chair and my helmet back where they belonged, picked up the scattered science books and sat on my bed with my *How and Why* space book. I opened it and tried to read, but it was no use. I closed my eyes and tried to rest, but sleep wouldn't come. I had to think of a way to save Sean, whether he liked it or not.

I awoke with a start. I was dreaming about getting ambushed at the underground fort again, only this time not as Captain Apollo but as myself, and this time, instead of a monster jumping out to grab me, it was Sean.

I looked over at the clock. It was only 2:17 in the afternoon. I swung my legs over the side of the bed; the sudden movement sent a jolt of pain through me, reminding me why I was not in school today. I remembered my discovery earlier in the closet, and a wave of fear and anxiety mingled with the pain and had a party inside my head. I got out of bed slowly this time, put on my robe and went downstairs.

In the kitchen, Mom was busy making something. She had out her electric stand mixer, cake pans, measuring cups and spoons, and a counter full of baking ingredients. Her apron and shoes, not to mention the floor, were coated with a light dusting of flour. She didn't hear me over the noise of the mixer when I sat down at the table.

"What'cha making?" I said, startling her and causing her to spill the teaspoon of vanilla extract she'd measured out. *Real* vanilla extract, not that imitation stuff—only the best ingredients went into my mom's cooking.

"Oops, sorry."

"That's okay, Sweetheart, I didn't see you come in," she said, wiping up the spill with a wet dishtowel. "I'm making a cinnamon raisin bundt cake for dessert. Would you like to help?"

Would I! "Sure!" I said, hopping up and rushing to her side to await instructions. I loved helping Mom in the kitchen. Ever since I was little, she would let me help around the kitchen, teaching me the finer points of cooking and baking, and I absorbed it all like a sponge. I could measure dry ingredients the right way (*scrape* flour and white sugar, but *pack* brown sugar), I knew how to cream butter and sugar together, and even to crack open eggs without getting any pieces of shell in them (most of the time). I was the official potato masher, and lately Mom had been teaching me how to make gravy from scratch. And the best part was I was good at it!

"Wash your hands first." I did.

For the next twenty minutes, we worked together like a well-oiled machine. I would measure out what she told me to and add them at the right times. I greased and floured the cake pan and held it steady while she poured in the batter. When it was in the oven, I helped put away the ingredients and wipe down the counter. Somehow, it got quite a bit messier when I helped. Mom washed the mixing bowl and measuring cups while I swept the floor. When we were done, she sat down with a cup of coffee.

I decided it was time to play with my turtle. I carefully picked up Oliver by the sides of his shell and put him in the palm of my hand. He was only about three inches long from head to tail, and maybe an inch and a half wide. I let him crawl around, his tiny toenails tickling my skin as he explored my hand and forearm.

"When was the last time you cleaned his bowl?" Mom said.

"I don't know. A couple weeks," I said absently. I was engrossed in watching the little reptile maneuver the contours of my hand.

"Why don't you do it now?" It was not a suggestion.

"Okay," I said. I put Oliver on my shoulder, got up, and went to the sink. I put the stopper in the drain, lifted the lever and started filling the sink with water, just as I had done dozens of times before. While the sink was filling, I brought over his bowl—it was kidney shaped with an island in the middle and a little plastic palm tree. I took Oliver from my shoulder and dropped him into the half-filled sink.

The moment I put him in the water, he started swimming around faster than I'd ever seen before. His little legs were kicking so hard it looked like he was trying to win a race.

"Wow! Look at him go!" I exclaimed. Suddenly, he was *Super-Turtle*! The water coming from the faucet flowed hard and fast creating a current where Oliver swam around and around. Mom got up to watch. "He must really love being in deep water again."

"I think that's enough water," Mom said. The sink was three-quarters full.

I turned off the water and Oliver stopped swimming—and sunk to the bottom. He not only stopped swimming, he stopped moving altogether. The grin that had been plastered on my face faltered. What happened? He was so happy a second ago. I reached my hand in the water and immediately pulled it out. It was hot! Scalding hot! I reached in again and grabbed him, pulling him out, but I was too late. Oliver was dead. I'd killed my pet turtle!

"NOOOOOOO!!!" I screamed.

Shock, horror, rage, guilt, and grief hit me all at once, overloading my emotional sensors. I ran around the house in circles, not knowing which way was up. Mom tried to calm me down with reassuring platitudes, that everything would be all right, but it was no use. I couldn't hear her over my own internal dialog telling me I was a murderer!

I ran screaming to my room, diving into bed and burying my head under my pillow, crying hysterically. Mom came up and sat by my side, rubbing my back, but I was beyond consoling. After a while, I have no idea how long, she left me alone to cry myself out.

It was nearly four o'clock by the time Sean reached the fence separating the fields from Old Man Hughes's property. He had just come from Jimmy's garage where they held an impromptu band meeting. Tim was not included as he was the subject of discussion. Apparently, Jimmy and Ben were having misgivings about their absent bass player.

"We just don't think he's right for us," Jimmy had said.

"Why not?" Sean had asked.

"We don't trust him," Ben told him.

"Tim's okay," Sean said. It was the second time this week he'd had to defend his friend.

"Tell him," Jimmy said.

Ben hesitated at first but then said, "I saw him in the park yesterday where all the hippies hang out. He was smoking marijuana." Sean feigned shock, but Ben continued, "I know he's your friend and all, but we talked it over and I think we need to find someone else."

"Who are you gonna find to replace him in time for the Battle of the Bands?"

"I know a guy in the neighborhood who plays bass," Jimmy said. "He's really good. And he already knows most of the songs."

"Since you're closest to Tim, we thought you should be the one to break it to him," Ben said.

"What if I say no?"

"Sorry man," Jimmy said. "It's him or us."

And just like that, Tim was out of Octopus's Garden. He felt guilty, since they were kicking Tim out because he smoked pot. Sean not only smoked it too, but he was dealing it now as well. He hoped they didn't find out. He didn't want to get kicked out too.

He had agreed to sell pot for Joker for a number of reasons: first, he didn't want to appear "un-cool" in front of Tim, especially when he was the one who had vouched for him; second, the lure of easy money was very tempting; but mostly because Joker didn't seem like he was going to take "no" for an answer. The weapons on the wall had frightened him. Before he'd left the house, Joker had taken out a big wad of money from his pocket, all one-hundred dollar bills, and peeled one off, handing it to Sean and saying, "Consider this a down payment. Do a good job and there's a lot more in it for you."

The thing that scared him the most though, and the thing that he was having the most trouble wrapping his head around, was that he was now a drug dealer. The one person he was most worried about finding out, even more that his band mates, was Billy.

Tim had been right about Billy. He turned out to be nothing but a little tattle-tale. Everything had been so much better before Billy came along. If not for him, Sean would already have his boat. His friend Mark at Hardwick Beach, where they had their summer bungalow, had gotten one last summer. It was a fourteen foot Boston Whaler with a Mercury 350 outboard motor, and it was about the grooviest thing Sean had ever seen. When Mark took him out in the bay for a ride, it was the most exhilarating feeling in the world. The wind in his face, and the freedom of the open water as they speeded through the waves enthralled him like nothing before. He was green with envy and he wanted one more than he ever wanted anything in his life. He had money in his savings account so it's not like they couldn't afford it. It was Billy. They were afraid something would happen to their precious little baby.

He knew Billy was his parent's favorite, but did they have to make it so obvious? It's like they just ignored him now and paid all their attention to *perfect* Billy. Like everything he did was *so* special. Oh look, *perfect* Billy drew a picture and won a prize! *Perfect* Billy sang at some stupid hotel in New York and they wrote about him in the paper! *Perfect* Billy got another A on his science test! He was sick of it.

Tim was right about grownups too; they just didn't care. The more he hung out with his new best friend, the more sense he made. Tim was older by a year, wiser, and next year he would be in high school—*public* high school. He, along with his friend Joker's help, had turned on his mind and opened his eyes. Everything that was happening today: youth culture, hippies, flower power, anti-war protests, rock & roll—it was all under siege by *The Man.*

The Man, they explained, was adults. Never trust anyone over thirty. Tune in, turn on, and drop out. Everybody look what's goin' down. All we are saying is give peace a chance. Everybody must get stoned! These were the anthems of the day, and he embraced them whole-heartedly. The more he thought about these things on his walk home from school, the angrier he became.

Sean didn't like the idea of having to be the one to tell Tim he was out of the band, especially since he was against it, but Jimmy and Ben didn't give him much of a choice. In the end, he decided the best thing to do was to call Tim and see if they could get together later. Ever since Tim found out about the underground fort, he'd been trying to talk Sean into sneaking out at night and meeting up with him there. Tonight would be the night. Man, he wished he had a cigarette now. Or better yet, a joint.

He hopped the fence behind Mr. Hughes's garage, sneaked

around the other side, and froze in his tracks. There he was! Old Man Hughes was in his yard, kneeling in the grass next to his flowers that ran along the side of the house, weeding. He had on a pair of old denim overalls with a red flannel checkered shirt frayed at the elbows. A white handkerchief stuck out of his back pocket, which he used to wipe his brow. His grey hair hung loosely over his face, three days worth of white stubble, giving him a scruffy appearance, his left eye was covered with a black patch; all he needed was a peg leg and a parrot on his shoulder and he would look just like Long John Silver from *Treasure Island*. On the ground beside him were various garden tools and something long, thin, and round that looked to Sean like a shotgun barrel!

He was trapped. There was no way he could make it past him without being seen. He could make a run for it, but he was terrified of getting a butt-load of rock salt. He could try to wait him out and hope Mr. Hughes went inside. After what seemed like an eternity, but was in reality only about ten minutes, Mr. Hughes slowly got off his knees, his joints popping loudly, and walked around to his back steps and into the house.

Sean hesitated for about half a minute before making a break for it, then took off running. He was mid-way between the garage and the neighbor's hedges when the back door opened and Mr. Hughes came out again. They locked eyes and Sean froze.

"Hey you!" Old Man Hughes shouted, clamoring down the porch steps. "Get over here!"

Sean tore out of there as fast as his legs would carry him, when he heard the *BANG!* of a shotgun and saw a small bush explode beside him.

"Get back here!"

Sean screamed and ran past the neighbor's hedges and down the street toward home without looking back.

I opened the top right hand drawer of my desk and rummaged around inside. It was my junk drawer and I kept all kinds of odds and ends in there. I was looking for the extra-large plastic container I got from the twenty-five cent gumball machine at the supermarket. It originally held a rubber toy lizard inside, and now I wanted to use it as a coffin for poor Oliver.

I was still rooting around in the drawer when Sean came into the room and tossed his knapsack on the bed and began changing out of his school uniform. I watched him out of the corner of my eye, trying to tell if he was high or not. If he was, I couldn't tell.

"What's wrong with you?" he said when he caught me watching him.

"Nothing," I said defensively, then corrected myself.

"Well, actually, that's not true. I accidentally killed Oliver."

"How'd you manage that?"

"I was cleaning his bowl and I turned on the hot water by mistake."

"Nice going."

"I didn't mean to, I'm still not used to the new faucet."

"Sorry, man," he said sympathetically. "That stinks. I know what he meant to you."

"Yeah," I agreed sadly. "I'm gonna bury him in the backyard. Wanna help me?"

He laughed at me and said, "No thanks. I'm not into reptile funerals." He started to change out of his school clothes, then remembered, "Oh, you'll never guess what happened."

"What?"

"When I cut through Old Man Hughes's property coming home today, he was outside in his garden and he saw me. He tried to pump me full of salt, but he missed."

"He shot at you?!" I said, shocked.

"Yeah, but I got away. It was a close call though."

"Man, I'll say! Maybe we shouldn't use that short cut anymore."

"Nah, him being outside was just a fluke. Besides, do you want to walk all the way around the long way?"

"No, not really."

"Just be extra careful from now on."

He finished putting on his play clothes and walked out of the room, laughing to himself and shaking his head.

I went back to foraging around in my drawer past my Duncan Butterfly yo-yo (I still needed to get a replacement string for that), a deck of playing cards, several empty PEZ containers, a box of crayons, a bag of marbles, and countless small toys, until I finally found it. I popped the top off and eyeballed the interior—I was almost positive he would fit inside.

Next, I opened my bottom drawer and took out my label maker. I carefully lined up each letter, O-L-I-V-E-R, and squeezed hard. I squeezed out three blank spaces, cut off the label, and stuck it in my pants pocket. Then I put the label maker away and went downstairs to the back porch where I'd put Oliver's bowl.

His limp little body was still on the plastic perch where I'd left it. He was beginning to smell. I carefully lifted him out and put him inside the plastic container. It was a perfect fit. I snapped the lid on, opened the back door to the backyard and set it down on the stairs. I sniffed my fingertips and decided I needed to go back inside and wash my hands before I went any further.

When my hands were clean, I ran downstairs to the workbench where my mom kept her gardening stuff. I found the hand-held shovel and brought it outside. I retrieved the plastic shell, now Oliver's coffin, and carried it to the far corner of the yard, where I'd already put the flat rock I'd found earlier to use as his gravestone.

Tears ran down my cheeks as I dug a hole about six inches deep and laid the "coffin" inside. I gently covered it over with dirt and set the stone at the head of the grave. I took the label from my pocket, pulled off the protective backing, and stuck it onto the rock.

I sat back on my calves, kneeling before the grave and closed my eyes. I made the Sign of the Cross and entwined my fingers together.

"Dear God," I began, "Please watch over Oliver in Heaven. He was a good turtle and didn't deserve to die. And please watch over Sean. I'm worried about him. I don't want him to be a drug addict. Help him to be like his old self again. I miss him. Amen."

I made the Sign of the Cross again, brushed off my hands and went back into the house.

Sean waited until he was sure both his parents and Billy were asleep. As quietly as he could he slipped out of bed and got dressed. He reached into his closet and took his shoebox from the shelf, fishing out his cigarettes and matches. He left the grass behind. If he was stopped by the cops, he didn't want to have it on him. Besides, Tim always had some.

He took his flashlight from his dresser drawer and tiptoed out of the room, silently closing the door behind him. Carefully, he sneaked past his parent's bedroom and down the stairs, avoiding the one that always creaked when you stepped on it. Two minutes later, he was out the kitchen door and headed for the short cut through the power company fence.

I couldn't sleep if I'd wanted to with everything that was racing through my head. Sean was in bed, but I knew he was awake and only pretending to be asleep, so I pretended I was too. Earlier, I'd seen him sneak into Dad's office. I was outside the door listening when he called someone and arranged to meet later tonight. I didn't know what Sean was up to, but after I found those bags of marijuana in his closet today, I decided I was going to watch him closely.

Right after Sean sneaked out of the room I hopped out of bed, threw on my clothes as fast as I could, and followed him. I stayed low and kept a safe distance away, but close enough so I didn't lose him. The Moon was almost full, so I could see fairly well. I couldn't look at the sky without thinking about the astronauts stranded up there somewhere in their damaged capsule. I said a little prayer that they would get home safe.

I followed Sean through the power company fence, out the other side, down the hill, along the tracks, and into the woods. When I entered the woods, I had to be more careful. I didn't want to get too close or Sean might hear my footsteps crunching leaves. It was easy to follow at a distance since Sean was using his flash-light now.

I also realized where we were headed—the underground fort. I still had nightmares about that place and was nervous and more than a little scared to go back there.

Up ahead, Sean extinguished his flashlight so I knew he had reached his destination. I was frightened now. I was alone, in the dark, walking ever closer to the source of my fear. As I made my way toward the spot where Sean's light went out, my heart started beating faster. I knew I was near because I could hear voices. Then I saw the glow of faint light coming from under the ground. I made it. I inched closer until I could hear.

Sean leaned his flashlight on the ground against the earthen wall, aiming the beam at the plywood ceiling, lighting up their underground lair. Tim was already down there, waiting for him. Sean got comfortable, stretching out his legs and leaning against the wall next to his friend.

"Thanks for meeting me out here so late," Sean said.

"Hey, no sweat man. So what's up? Why all the cloak and dagger stuff?"

"I got some bad news."

"Uh-oh, I don't like the sound of that."

"Jimmy and Ben voted you out of the band."

"What? What for? What did I do?"

"Ben saw you smoking grass in the park. He says he doesn't trust you."

"You know what?" he said, reaching into his shirt pocket and pulling out a joint, which he put between his lips, smiling mischievously. "Who needs 'em."

"You mean you're not mad?"

"Nah. I was gonna quit anyway," he lied, using his Zippo to light the joint.

"Man, you're taking this a lot better than I would."

"What am I gonna do, cry about it like a little kid? We're still friends, right? That's all that matters."

"Right on!" Sean said, relieved. He'd been afraid Tim was going to dump him when he heard the news. They passed the joint back and forth until it was too small to hold without burning their fingers.

"Speaking of little kids," Tim began, "how's your brother doing? I hope he recovered okay from me jumping out at him like that. I didn't mean to scare him that bad. But man, you should have seen his face!"

"Yeah, you got him good. The little turd woke everyone up yesterday screaming in his sleep. He said a monster reached out and grabbed him."

"Oh man. Now I feel bad."

"Don't. He's a little wuss anyway. Maybe now he'll grow a pair."

"Lighten up on him, man. He's just a kid."

"Easy for you to say. You're not related to him. I swear to God, my life would be a lot easier if he wasn't around."

"Oh come on. I know you don't mean that."

"Yes I do! The kid's a pain in my butt. He's the reason I can't have a boat. My parents are afraid he's gonna fall out and drown or something, as if I would ever get that lucky. They think he's such a perfect little angel. It's like I'm not even there sometimes. Everything was fine until *he* was born. I swear, sometimes I wish he would just drop dead!"

I recoiled at my brother's words. I backed away in shock until I couldn't hear them anymore, then I turned and ran. I still couldn't believe what I'd overheard. Not only had Sean been in the fort when that other guy he was talking to jumped out and scared Lucy and me, but he was laughing about it and calling me a wuss. And then he said he wished I were dead! Why? What did I do that was so bad? Why did he hate me so much? I could barely see through my tears I was crying so hard, but I just wiped them away and ran home as fast as I could.

Tim lit a cigarette and leaned back against the wall. "You know what? I'm glad they kicked me out."

"I stuck up for you. They said if I didn't go along with it then I was out too."

"Don't sweat it," he said, taking a puff from his cigarette. "So who they gonna get to replace me?"

"I don't know. Some kid Jimmy knows in his neighborhood."

"Well, I hope he can play."

"Me too."

They let a moment of silence pass between them.

"I better get going, it's late," Sean said, picking up his flashlight.

I had already stopped crying by the time Sean sneaked back into the house. I waited until he got undressed and back into bed before I spoke.

"I followed you tonight," I whispered in the dark.

"What?" Sean whispered back, fear and worry in his voice.

"Out in the woods. I followed you. I know you smoke pot. I accidentally found it in our closet this afternoon, and I smelled it out in the woods tonight. Don't bother trying to lie about it."

The next thing I knew, Sean was out of bed and moving across the room. My eyes blinked when he switched on the light. He hovered over me, his face red with anger.

"You followed me?" he said, incredulously. "And you were snooping around in my stuff?"

"I wasn't snooping! It fell on the floor."

"Shut up," he hissed. "What did you tell Mom?"

"Nothing. I didn't say anything. Yet. But this is serious."

"You better keep your mouth shut."

"And what if I don't? Are you gonna kill me? I know you wish I were dead. I heard you!"

Before I knew what was happening, Sean reached down and snatched my Astronaut Snoopy doll off my bed and held it out, one hand gripping his head.

"No!" I whisper-yelled. "Please, Sean, don't!"

Without warning, Sean viciously pulled his hands in opposite directions, decapitating my beloved beagle. I stared at him uncomprehendingly. He threw the two pieces at me, stuffing protruding from both ends. I picked them up, tears flowing down my cheeks again, but no sound came out. First Oliver, now Snoopy.

"That's what you get for spying on me! Next time that's you!"

I stared at the alien invader that had taken over my brother's body. I forced myself to stop crying. I had come to a decision. In a very calm, steady voice I said, "Don't worry Sean. I'm not gonna tell Mom and Dad. And I'm never gonna bother you again. Have a nice life."

And with that, I lay down, pulled the covers over me and closed my eyes. I rolled over and turned my back on him—forever.

TEN

"Mayday. Mayday. *Constellation One*, come in."

"This is *Constellation One*," Matt Sherman's voice said. "Good to hear your voice, sir."

"Matt? Where's Shondo?" Captain Apollo said with surprise. "I left him in charge."

"Aye sir, you did. I'm afraid Mr. Shondo's missing, Captain."

"What do you mean he's missing?"

"Just what I said, sir. He's no longer on board the ship."

BOOM!!!

The small fighter was rocked by a laser blast.

"Never mind that now," the captain said, "I'm under attack and I'm venting plasma. Rendezvous at coordinates two-two-mark..."

"I'm afraid that's impossible, Captain. We've had problems of our own. We were attacked by the *Black Widow*. Main drive has been disabled."

BOOM!!!

"Communications out, Captain!" Lucinda barked. "Propulsion

systems out. Shields down to twenty percent. One more blast and we're finished."

"Where are they?"

On the viewscreen, he got his answer. A giant, terrifying monstrosity of a ship filled their field of vision. It was the *Black Widow*, known throughout the quadrant as the most notorious ship in the galaxy, commanded by none other than Mack the Black, ruler of the Dark Realm. The weapons on board that ship could blow them into space dust with one blast. She was toying with them.

"*Constellation* fighter. Surrender and prepare to be boarded," a familiar voice said.

No. It couldn't be. But it was!

"Shondo!"

The only reply to Captain Apollo's disbelieving exclamation was Mack the Black's maniacal laughter.

The fighter was captured by a tractor beam and pulled into the *Black Widow's* cargo bay. It would have been futile to attempt to fight. Captain Apollo concluded that at this point, their best, if not only option, was to allow themselves to be taken captive and find out what they wanted, and even more important, what could have caused Shondo to betray him, their friendship, and the fleet.

Shondo... a traitor? He still couldn't believe it.

The fighter hatch opened. Standing before them was Mack the Black, an appropriate moniker considering her flowing black robes, a matching veil surrounding her grotesque reptilian face. The effect was both ominous and repugnant. Flanking her right was Shondo, stone faced and staring straight ahead. On her left were the Butcher and Joemar, both looking considerably battered since their last encounter, no doubt punishment inflicted by their host for allowing their captives to escape. Surrounding them, with every weapon trained on the fighter hatch, were two full battalions of her troops, all dressed alike in head to toe black armor with red pinstripes.

"Greetings Captain. Your Highness," Mack the Black said with mock respect. "I trust my invitation was not too... subtle."

"What is it you want? What have you done to my First Officer?"

"Why, I haven't done anything to him, Captain. Have I Mr. Shondo?"

"No," Shondo said. "On the contrary Captain. It is *you* who are responsible for my defection."

"I don't understand," Captain Apollo said, bewildered.

"In due time, Captain," Mack the Black said. "As for what I want... I want what's embedded in the Empress's pretty little head. And you, my dear Captain, are going to help me."

"I'll never help you," Apollo shouted defiantly.

"We'll see about that," Mack the Black intimated.

"If you think..."

"Guards!" she shouted, cutting off Apollo in mid-sentence. "Take them to their cells!"

Instantly, they were surrounded, led by Shondo pointing a laser gun at his former friend and captain.

"I suggest you cooperate, Captain," Shondo said. "I would hate for anything to happen to you."

Captain Apollo and Lucinda were silent as Shondo led them away.

Phil McLean sat behind his desk in front of the classroom as his second grade class worked on the assignment. They were supposed to be writing a brief paragraph on how the Apollo 13 accident affected them. Judging by the pre-bell chatter when they filed in and took their seats this morning, their minds were more on the return to school of Billy McBride and the three-day vacation of Butch Anderson.

It had only been two days since the infamous pencil piercing had occurred—in his class—and he was trying to divert the class's attention onto more academic topics. Fortunately, with second graders, that was fairly easy to do.

He'd been teaching second grade school children for eight years, ever since he got his Masters in physics from MIT. He really loved teaching, though the pay wasn't the greatest. He considered it his calling and he had a real knack for it. He tried to make learning fun and he'd found no greater satisfaction in life than being able to help mold young minds. The look in a child's eyes when a complex concept took hold—the spark of understanding—when they "got it" was all the reward he needed.

He usually tried to begin the day's lessons with a game, something silly to start the creative juices flowing. Sometimes he would scramble a word or phrase on the blackboard and have the class try to figure it out. Yesterday, he jumbled the song title *Maxwell's Silver Hammer* from The Beatles album *Abbey Road.* It took the class ten minutes to unscramble it. Other times, if a class seemed especially distracted or fatigued, usually right after lunch recess when the afternoon doldrums have taken hold, he would liven things up with "finger exercises," a game he invented that never failed to entice laughter among his pupils. Not today though. Before the students arrived he had written the quote "Houston, we have a problem" on the blackboard.

Mr. McLean stood and walked around to the front of his desk and leaned on the edge, looking solemnly at his class.

"Okay, pencils down."

The sound of two dozen pencils simultaneously dropping to the desk was followed by the rapt attention of all eyes in the room. Well, almost all.

"Mr. McBride?" Mr. McLean said. The boy apparently didn't hear him and continued staring out the window, lost in a day-dream. He tried a little louder...

"Billy!"

I jumped at the sound of my name, followed by the sound of laughter. "Yes sir?"

Mr. McLean was sitting on the edge of his desk smiling at me. At least he wasn't mad at me. Then again, Mr. McLean almost never got mad. Not at me anyway. He was cool. Now, if it had been Mack Truck's class...

"I know you were absent yesterday, but can you tell us anything about the accident on board Apollo 13?"

"Yes sir," I said, standing up slowly beside my desk and trying not to wince in pain.

"You don't have to stand if it's too uncomfortable."

"No sir, I'd prefer to stand." Some kids giggled at that.

"Whatever you like. Go ahead"

"Well, there was an explosion and they started leaking oxygen into space."

"That's right. Anything else?"

"They also lost fuel. They don't know if they can make it home."

"And therein lies the tragedy. Thank you, Billy." I sat down.

"Three brave Americans, men who have trained all their lives, will probably never set foot on their home planet again. Their sacrifice, the ultimate sacrifice, will never be forgotten."

I raised my hand.

"Yes Billy? You have something to add?"

I stood up again.

"There's still a chance they could make it back. NASA thinks they can orbit the Moon and use the Moon's gravity to whip around and push them back in the direction of the Earth. The same way the *Enterprise* can slingshot around the sun to travel through time on *Star Trek*."

This caused spontaneously laughter among my classmates. Someone said, "What a geek."

"Thank you Billy," Mr. McLean said, smiling. "Unfortunately, this isn't *Star Trek*. But you're right. NASA is working on a way to try to bring them home. The problem is they only have one shot at it, and time is working against them. The odds of success aren't in their favor. All we can do is hope nothing else goes wrong and pray they get home in one piece."

A low murmur filled the room as the gravity of the situation sunk in around me.

"Now, pass your paragraphs forward. I'm not going to grade them, but I'll take them home and read them and then tomorrow we'll read a few of the best ones aloud."

As the class passed their papers forward, I raised my hand. "Mr. McLean?"

"Yes Billy?"

"Do you think they'll make it?"

"I don't know, Billy. I just don't know."

I was hiding behind the dumpster next to the cafeteria door when Matt and Lucy found me. Immediately after lunch, I'd bolted from the cafeteria as soon as the recess bell rang and hid from Joey Martino. Butch may have been suspended, but I was by no means safe. Joey had made that abundantly clear this morning when he approached me before school began.

"Don't think just because Butch isn't here we're not gonna get you," he'd threatened. "What he did to you on Monday is nothing. He'll be back on Friday, but in the meantime, I'm still here. You won't know where and you won't know when, but we're coming for you, McBride."

I had managed to remain hidden a whole ten minutes when Matt and Lucy found me.

"What are you doing back here?" Lucy asked.

"Hiding, what does it look like?" I said, sounding a little more irritated than I'd intended.

"I thought we were gonna play Spaceship today," Matt said, obviously disappointed.

"What's 'Spaceship?'" Lucy said.

"It's a game we play. Billy's the captain of a starship and I'm the engineer, like Scotty. Sometimes his brother Sean plays too. He's the First Officer."

"Sounds like fun. Can I play?"

"Not today. I'm not up to it," I said, which was the truth. "And Sean's not playing anymore. Ever."

"Why not? I liked it when he played too."

"I don't want to talk about it," I said with finality.

Across the playground, we could hear the sound of jingling bells approaching. That could only mean one thing.

"Ice cream!" Matt yelled and took off in excitement.

The bells grew louder and stopped just outside the open gate outside the playground. A crowd quickly formed beside the truck.

"Wanna get some ice cream?" Lucy said. She obviously did.

"Nah. I think I'll just stay here."

"I don't know why you're hiding. Butch isn't even here."

"Joey Martino is. He already threatened me this morning."

"He's not going to do anything without Butch calling the shots. That hound dog is all bark and no bite."

"What is that, Texas wisdom?"

"Yes, and if you were smart you would listen. Why is he even after you in the first place?"

"I can't tell you."

"You mean you're afraid."

She hit the nail on the head. I lowered my eyes and nodded. "If I tell you, do you swear you won't tell anyone?"

"What is it?"

"Swear first."

"Okay, I swear," she said, rolling her eyes.

"Okay. Remember the other day at gym when we were changing? Well, I saw bruises all over Butch's back where his shirt lifted up. And he had all these red swollen marks, like someone hit him with a belt. His legs too. I think someone's beating him up at home. I know he's a bully and all, but I feel kinda bad for him. I'm scared Luce."

"Oh my God! Billy, you have to tell someone!"

"No! He said if I tell he'll do something bad. And not just to me!"

"Then I'll tell."

"You just swore you wouldn't! You promised!"

"Yeah, but that was before I knew what it was."

"Please Lucy! He knows I know. He'll know it was me who told. Promise you won't say anything. I'll think of something."

"Okay Billy, but this is really serious."

"I know. I just need time to think."

"Okay, but no more hiding. Deal?"

"Deal."

"Good. Now let's go get some ice cream."

Sean, Ben, and Jimmy sat along the fence eating ice cream. Sean spotted Billy and Lucy walking across the playground headed for the Good Humor truck. Billy saw Sean watching him and their eyes locked, each shooting daggers at the other. Sean was the first to break eye contact, suddenly finding something infinitely more interesting to look at by his feet. Ben noticed the staring contest between them.

"So what's up with you and your brother?"

"Nothing. Forget about it."

"I heard that Butch kid made him sit on a pencil," Jimmy said. "Ouch."

"He got what he deserves."

"Did you guys have a fight or something?" Ben asked.

"You could say that. I don't want to talk about it."

"Okay man, it's cool."

"Did you talk to Tim yet?" Jimmy said.

"Yeah," Sean said. "I talked to him last night."

"How'd he take it?" Ben said.

"Fine."

"That's good. I was afraid he'd make a big stink about it," Jimmy said.

"To tell the truth, I don't think he really cared."

"We should start rehearsals as soon as possible with the new kid," Ben said. "What's his name again?"

"John Grady," Jimmy said.

"Right, John. Can you come over today after school Sean?"

"Not today," Sean said. He just didn't feel like it.

"Are you sure? We need to start right away if we're gonna be ready for the Battle of the Bands."

"I said no!" Sean yelled, catching his band mates off guard.

"Okay, take it easy man," Ben said. "It's cool."

"Sorry," Sean said. "I guess I'm just a little on edge."

"It's okay," Jimmy said.

But it wasn't.

Lucy and I were almost to the front of the ice cream line. Matt had already gotten his and was almost done eating it. I kept looking over to where Sean was hanging out with his friends to see if he was still watching me, but he was too busy talking, which was fine with me.

I turned to look the other way and saw Joey about ten yards away, leaning against the brick wall of the school and staring threateningly at me. I tried to avoid his gaze, but I couldn't help glancing his way every few minutes. Joey never looked away; every time I looked over, he was staring right at me. The longer he stared, the more anxious I became.

"Oh, just ignore him," Lucy said.

"I can't."

"He's just trying to scare you."

"It's working."

"When are you just going to stand up for yourself? Then they'll leave you alone."

"Not today."

Lucy sighed heavily. We finally made it to the front of the line, the only two customers left, when the bell rang.

"Figures," Lucy said.

"You go back. I'll get the ice cream. We can eat it real quick before class starts."

"Are you sure?"

"Yeah, go ahead. I'll catch up."

"Okay," she said and ran for the door, just as the second bell rang.

I gave the Good Humor man my order. It took slightly longer than I anticipated getting our ice cream and paying the man. Just as I turned to head back to school, I could see the last of the kids walk through the doors. I was late! I broke into a full sprint, reaching the doors just as they were closing.

Sister Janet, the young nun who taught us Art on Friday, was the door monitor today. She was so nice; she actually held the door open for me!

"I'm sorry I'm late. I was in line for a really long time and finally got to the front and then the bell rang and the ice cream guy was really slow and then..." I was talking very fast and stringing my words together.

"Whoa, slow down," Sister Janet said. "Take a breath."

I did as I was told and relaxed, smiling up at this very understanding nun. She really was as nice as everybody said.

"I'm sorry Billy, but you can't bring those to class," she said, looking at the ice cream bars in my hands. I was surprised she knew my name, but I was disappointed I couldn't have the prize I'd waited so patiently for and cost a good chunk of my birthday money. I was about to toss them in the trash when she stopped me.

"Wait."

I looked into her eyes hopefully.

"I said you couldn't take them to class. I didn't say you couldn't have them later. There's a little refrigerator in the Teacher's lounge. You can put them in the freezer and pick them up after school."

My frown turned into a smile and I beamed up at her. "Well go on," she said. "Hurry up, before class starts."

"Thank you, Sister," I said and ran toward the lounge. I almost made it to the door when I heard:

"McBride! Freeze!"

I stopped dead in my tracks and froze. Barreling down the hall at me was Sister Mary Andrews, the assistant principal, the oldest—and maybe meanest—nun in the school.

"Just where do you think you're going?" She was not in a good mood, but then, she was never in a good mood.

"Sister Janet told me to put this in the freezer," I said, holding out the melting ice cream bars.

"Where did you get ice cream?"

"The Good Humor man. There was a truck..."

"Disobedient McBride! You know you're not allowed off school property."

"But everyone else..."

"I don't care. Go on, put it in the freezer and get back to class.

But you are never to go off school property again while classes are in session. Do I make myself clear?"

"Yes Sister," I said.

"Hurry up then."

I ran through the lounge door, deposited the ice cream bars in the freezer, and ran to class. That was the last time I ever saw them. I was so terrified that I never even tried to get them after school.

Matt practically skipped down the steps when school let out. Billy was back, Butch was suspended for three days, and any day without Butch was a good day. And with Butch gone, Joey was like a cat with his claws removed. He turned and headed through the playground to the hole in the back fence. It was such a beautiful spring day, he'd decided to walk through the fields instead of taking the bus. He used the fields to walk home the same as Billy did, just in the opposite direction.

As he thought of Billy, it made him realize just how much he loved it here. Of all the places he had ever lived, he loved New Jersey the best. He even loved his school. For the first time, he had real friends. But Billy was special. In his whole life, he'd never had a best friend like Billy before, and he probably never would again. They were like brothers. He still couldn't believe Butch had stabbed him with a pencil.

He felt the sun on his face and loosened his tie as he walked across the playground. It was getting warm; soon it would be hot with stifling humidity, but right now, it was perfect weather. Days like this always reminded him of picnics with his mom.

He tried to remember his mother's face, but he found it harder and harder as time passed. His father didn't have any pictures of her, at least none that he displayed. He probably had some somewhere. He remembered his mother was beautiful though. She had dark hair, and she always smelled so pretty. And he remembered her laugh—loud and joyful, and it always came easily. They laughed together a lot.

And then the laughter went away, and she was gone. "Mommy's gone to Heaven," his father had told him. Back then, he thought Heaven was a place you could visit, like going to Grandma's, and that she was coming home again. But she never did. He missed her a lot.

"Hey, fatboy!"

Matt was pulled out of his reverie by the sound of Joey's voice. He looked up to see not only Joey, but Butch too, and they were closing the distance between them across the asphalt. Oh no, what was Butch doing here? He's supposed to be suspended! Butch had a baseball in his hand and Joey had a baseball bat slung over his shoulder, with a pitcher's mitt hanging from the end.

"What are you doing in our playground?" Joey demanded.

"It belongs to everyone," Matt said.

"Maybe during the day," Butch said, "But after school it's *ours*, and you're not allowed."

"Or what? You gonna stab me with a pencil too?"

"Shut your mouth. That was an accident," Butch insisted.

"Yeah, you 'accidentally' held a pencil point up on Billy's chair."

"How about I 'accidentally' kick your butt?" Butch said. Joey put his hand to his mouth and giggled.

"I'm not afraid of you," Matt said, terrified but holding his ground.

"Oh no? You should be."

"Why can't you just leave us alone? We never did anything to you."

"Go on," Butch said. "Get out of here before I do something to *you.*"

Matt turned and started back toward the fence. He got about twenty feet away before Butch wound up and pitched the baseball as hard as he could at the back of Matt's head. The sound it made when it impacted with his skull was a sickeningly spongy *thwack!* Matt fell sprawling to the ground like a marionette with its strings cut, a puddle of blood forming around his head.

Butch and Joey stared at the limp body on the ground, their eyes bulging and their mouths hanging open in shock. They turned to look at each other, screamed, *"AHHHHHHHHHH!!!,"* and took off running, leaving Matt bleeding on the ground.

Lucy sat on a branch of the old apple tree by the side of the house. From up there, she could see both the front and back of the house. She watched her father in the backyard as he arranged charcoal briquettes into a neat pile inside the Weber barbeque grill. Daddy was born and raised in Texas, and if there was one thing he knew about, it was barbeque.

This was Lucy's favorite spot in the world. She could sit up there for hours, just thinking. From her perch high up in the tree, she could see for miles beyond her own property, but no one could see her. Not unless they were really looking, but no one ever did.

On a clear day, she could see the New York City skyline from here, about ten miles to the east, the Empire State Building standing tall and majestic in the distance. She imagined the millions of people living and working there, all running around in their busy lives, never slowing down in the city that never sleeps. No wonder they called it the Rat Race.

Today, she mostly thought about Billy and Butch, and found herself in a conundrum. On the one hand, there was Billy—probably the kindest person she'd ever met. He was smart. And caring, and creative, and wouldn't hurt a living soul. The kind of person who would literally give you the shirt off his back. Sure, he was different, maybe even a little weird—okay, more than a little—but that just added to the charm of who he was as a person. He was her best friend, and she hated to admit it, but maybe she even loved him. A little. For a boy.

And then there was Butch, probably the meanest kid she'd ever met. He was the complete polar opposite of Billy. A bully who preyed on anyone weaker than him. Anyone who let him, and unfortunately, Billy let him. Yet somehow, he almost always got away with it too. Or, he let someone else take the blame—she'd seen it with her own eyes. The only reason he got in trouble for stabbing Billy is because he did it in the middle of class in front of everyone.

She still couldn't believe all he got was a three-day suspension. If this were Texas, he would be kicked out, at the very least. She wished with all her heart Billy would stand up to him and fight back. Give that no good punk Butch a taste of his own medicine and stop the bullying once and for all.

Yet today shook her, and she didn't know what to do. If what Billy suspected was true, if Butch was being abused at home, then they should tell someone. No one deserved that, not even a bully. In fact, that's probably what made him a bully in the first place.

But Billy made her promise not to tell anybody. She knew he did it out of fear. Butch terrorized him and he was afraid of some kind of retribution. But that didn't make it right. By keeping quiet about it, didn't that make Billy just as guilty as whoever was hurting Butch? And by her promising to remain silent too, wasn't she guilty as well? She didn't want to break her promise, but she couldn't, in good conscience, stand around and let Butch get beaten, even if he was a total butthead. She just didn't know what to do.

Her father was tending to the grill. The flames had died down and the briquettes had turned an ashy white with red-hot centers. He spread them evenly with long-handled tongs and put the metal surface grate in place. Lucy climbed down and approached him just as he was laying the first steak over the fire.

"Hi Daddy."

"Hey, Pumpkin," he said, "where'd you come from?"

"Oh, around," she said, not wanting to divulge her secret spot. "You're home early."

Her father worked in New York, one of the rats in the race. He worked at a big national bank and was transferred from Houston last month. It was supposed to be a big promotion, only now he was hardly ever home anymore because of the long commute to and from work.

"Yep. I finished my meetings early, so I decided to take the rest of the day off, get home to have supper with my darlin' girls for a change."

Lucy had two sisters, one older and one younger. Emma was eleven, and Clara was six, making Lucy the middle child, which she hated. Both of her sisters were the sweet, frilly type, all pink dresses and ribbons, probably inside playing "house" or some other such nonsense. Blech!

"Daddy, can I ask you something?"

"Anything Pumpkin."

"If you had a secret, and you promised not to tell anyone, but you knew you probably should, would you break that promise?"

"Well, now, that's a tough one. I guess it all depends."

"On what?"

"For one thing, who you made the promise to, and why. Is it someone who's gonna get hurt if you tell? Did they threaten you into making the promise? How close are you to the person, and do you want to risk losing them as a friend if you break it?"

"What if it might hurt someone else besides the person you promised? And what if the person who might be getting hurt threatened the person you made the promise to?"

"Well..."

"And what if you can stop someone from getting hurt if you tell? Even if that person kind of deserves it?"

"I guess I would say do what your heart tells you is the right thing to do. I think you already know the answer."

Lucy nodded her head and looked at her father and made her decision. And then she told him everything.

Max sat in the waiting room of Passaic General Hospital waiting for any word on Matt. He had been in surgery for over two hours now, and no one could tell him anything. He hated hospitals. They always reminded him of when his wife, Amy, had gotten sick four years ago. He didn't know what he would do if he lost Matt too.

Max and Amy had met fourteen years ago at B.C.—Boston College. He'd been in his third year as a music major and she was a freshman majoring in psychology. He remembered the night they met, at a party in one of the dorms. She was fresh off the farm from Kansas and a little awkward in the social department, but to Max, she was utterly charming. He wooed her that night from the piano, playing only for her in a room full of people. He immediately won her heart and they dated for the next three years, marrying one another immediately after she graduated. Matt arrived thirteen months later. Her career took a back burner so she could raise their child, but she didn't mind. She loved being a mother. The boy was only five when she died of an inoperable malignant brain tumor.

It had been hardest on Matt. Max was broken hearted, of course, but she had been diagnosed six months before the inevitable and he had time to prepare himself. Poor little Matt couldn't understand where Mommy went and why she wasn't coming back. Max thought it would be best for both of them if they moved to a new city, away from the home they'd all shared together and the ghosts of the past.

He'd applied for, and received, a position at Kendall College in Chicago. At first, it seemed like an exciting career move, but he soon grew to dislike intensely the internal politics of the school in general and the music department specifically. He could also see that Matt was not adjusting well to city life, and had difficulty making new friends at school. Since his mother's death, he had become withdrawn. The other children thought he was weird and teased him mercilessly. So, he put in applications at other colleges and two years ago, he was offered a job at Rutgers University in Newark, New Jersey.

The suburbs proved to be exactly what they both needed, though at first, Matt had trouble adjusting to this new school as well. Max enrolled him in a Catholic school—Amy had been Catholic and he promised her he would raise Matt in the Catholic faith. Although he personally considered himself an agnostic, he dutifully took Matt to Sunday Mass every week.

Then, Matt befriended Billy McBride, and everything changed. The boys became inseparable and he watched with delight as his son slowly came out of his shell. It was a beautiful thing to see. They had each found a kindred spirit. They loved the same music, the same television shows, even the same foods. They were wild about monster movies, science fiction, and even the Marx Brothers. And they both shared an affinity for anything to do with NASA and the space program. It was as if they were cast from the same mold.

And then, in the blink of an eye, everything came crashing down. He'd been teaching class at Rutgers when the call came through that his son had been found in the schoolyard by one of the priests, apparently the victim of a stray baseball. The bloodied ball was found near where his son lay bleeding. Whoever threw it didn't have the guts to stick around or even alert anyone.

Max put his face in his hands and softly wept.

Sean was anxious riding his bike to Joker's apartment. He had two-dozen baggies of grass in his knapsack and if the cops stopped him, he'd be busted. It was the first time he was going over unannounced and without Tim accompanying him. He decided he wasn't going to be Joker's pawn and had to return the pot he was given to sell, but he was afraid of how Joker would react. He didn't seem like the most stable person he'd ever met. He'd heard about how some guys came back from Vietnam a little crazy, and he figured Joker was probably the poster child.

He got to Joker's building and parked his bike around back and walked down the stairs to the basement apartment. He hesitated a few seconds, gathering courage before ringing the bell. Joker came to the door wearing washed-out jeans and nothing else. His hair was all over the place and he had dark circles under his wild eyes. Even though it was well into the afternoon, he looked like he just woke up. It took him a few moments to focus and recognize Sean.

"Oh, hey, Ringo. Come in," he said, opening the door so Sean could enter. "What's up man? Where's Timmy?"

"I don't know, I came by myself. I hope that's okay."

"Yeah, yeah, sure." Joker walked into the living room and sat on the couch. Sean followed him but remained standing. This wasn't a social call.

"You want a bong hit?" Joker asked, filling the bowl of his water pipe with a large, green bud.

"No thanks."

"Suit yourself," he said, and proceeded to indulge in a massive bowl-full. He exhaled a huge cloud of smoke, coughing out half of it.

"So," he said when he recovered from his coughing fit, "What brings you to my humble abode?"

Tim opened his knapsack and threw the baggies of pot on the coffee table along with the hundred-dollar bill Joker had already given him. Joker's trademark smile immediately disappeared.

"What's this?"

"I'm not gonna sell pot for you."

"Yes you are. This isn't like a job at the grocery store that you can just quit if you don't like it. You're mine now."

"Just take your drugs and leave me alone. I'm not gonna do it."

"Let me explain how this works. You sell my grass or you get hurt."

"You can threaten me all you want, I'm still not gonna do it." Sean was scared and his voice was shaky, but he held his ground.

"No? Timmy told me you have a little brother. It would be a shame if he had an accident."

"Leave Billy out of this."

"That's up to you. You can pick up that grass and walk away, or little Billy never walks again. Your choice."

"I hate you."

Joker laughed. "Just have that batch sold by next weekend or else. And don't think I'm kidding. I have no qualms about hurting a kid. Back in 'Nam I killed plenty."

"You're a psycho," Sean said, picking up the baggies from the table and roughly shoving them back in his knapsack.

"Sticks and stones, kid. Sticks and stones. Now get out of here, and don't come back 'til it's sold."

ELEVEN

Mr. McLean was at the head of the classroom teaching, but don't ask me what he was saying. All I heard was, "Wah-wah-wah," like the teachers in a *Peanuts* cartoon. I knew we were in English class, and he was talking about adjectives or adverbs, or one of those ad-things, but that's about as far as my comprehension went today. I couldn't focus on schoolwork if my life depended on it. The thoughts in my head were spinning round and round going over everything that had happened recently, beginning with The Beatles breaking up.

I'd been stabbed—the pain in my seat had gone from sharp spasms to a dull ache, but even a small shift in my posture reminded me it was there—Apollo 13 had a major accident, I discovered my brother was on drugs, I killed my pet turtle (*murderer!*), and I witnessed the beheading of my constant companion. In my head, I knew it was just a stuffed toy, but in my heart, Snoopy was like my best friend.

Speaking of which, I had really been looking forward to seeing

Matt today, my real-life best friend and confidant. We hadn't really had much chance to talk this week, and I really wanted to fill him in on everything that was going on. I could always count on Matt to be there for me, even if it just meant listening. Matt was a good listener. Sometimes he even offered some good advice. Unfortunately, Matt was out sick today.

I supposed I could talk to Lucy, but I still barely knew her. It's true we had grown close in a short amount of time, but it was still only last week since she had come into my life. I didn't think I was ready to bare my soul to her just yet. Plus, she was a girl. I couldn't talk to her about my stab wound, for instance—that was guy talk.

"Billy McBride, please come to the office," the overhead speaker announced. Mr. McLean turned from the blackboard to look at me, and every eye in the classroom was trained on me. What now?

I got up from my desk and left the room. My footsteps echoed in the hall as I walked to the office. This must be about the ice cream I left in the Teachers' freezer. I walked into the front office and Mrs. Thompson looked at me with sad eyes before looking away. Okay, what was going on here? She picked up her phone, pressed a button, then covered her mouth with her hand and whispered something into the receiver. She nodded her head and cradled the phone.

"Go ahead in, Billy. They're waiting for you."

I opened the door to the principal's office and walked inside. Behind the desk, Sister Joseph was sitting down looking worried. But what really took me by surprise was the presence of Matt's dad. What was he doing here?

"Billy, please sit down," Sister Joseph said. I sat down, nervously looking back and forth between the two adults. Mr. Sherman's eyes were red and puffy, like he'd been crying. That made me scared. Adults, especially men, weren't supposed to cry. He knelt down beside me and took my hand, looking directly into my eyes. Uh-oh. This can't be good. I swallowed hard, but the lump that had formed in my throat didn't budge.

"Billy..." His voice choked fighting back tears. He cleared his throat and tried again. "Billy, there's been an accident." I suddenly sat bolt upright. "Matt's in the hospital. He's in a coma."

My tears were immediate. "What happened?" I demanded.

"Somebody hit him in the head with a baseball."

"Who?"

"I don't know."

"He's gonna be okay, isn't he?"

"Right now, he's stable. The doctors are doing everything they can. I know how close the two of you are. I wanted to be the one to tell you before you heard it from someone else." Matt's dad was crying now too.

"Can I see him?"

"Not now, I'm sorry."

"Please?" I begged. "I have to see him!"

"Maybe after school," he said. "I'll call your Mom and see what she says."

I was blubbering now. Sister Joseph came around to the front of her desk and pulled me to her, engulfing me in her arms, patting me on the back, and whispering condolences into my ear. Her shoulder was soft and warm and comforting, and I let out all the pain and hurt I was keeping bottled up inside. All of it.

I laid on the green leather lounge/bed in the nurse's office staring at the ceiling and counting the tiles, trying to keep my mind off everything. What started out as what I thought would be the best week ever turned out to be the worst. What else could go wrong? How much could one kid take? At least I stopped crying. I was all cried out.

After I'd used Sister Joseph's shoulder like a human box of tissues, she let me lie down instead of going right back to class. Who knew she could be so kind? I had always been afraid of her because she was the principal; now I loved her. I'd felt safe in her arms.

I was down to one row of ceiling tiles left to count, when the nurse came in to check on me.

"How are you feeling?" she asked.

"Okay I guess," I was feeling a lot of things, none of which I felt like sharing.

"It's lunch time. Ready to go back yet?"

"I guess so. I am kinda hungry." Actually, I was famished.

She helped me to my feet and said, "You're a brave little boy."

I smiled and blushed and left for the cafeteria. It wasn't really a cafeteria since they didn't serve food. We had to bring our own lunches. It was, in reality, just a really big room with four long, long, long tables with chairs on both sides.

After a quick pit stop in the classroom coat closet to retrieve my *Superman* lunch box, I joined Lucy at our usual spot in the lunchroom. The empty chair next to me only reminded me of Matt's absence.

"Where have you been?" Lucy said. "I thought you went home sick again, you were gone so long."

"No, I was just in the nurse's office."

"Is something wrong? You seem kind of out of it."

I nodded. "Matt's in the hospital."

"Oh my God! What happened? Is he okay?"

"He's in a coma. They don't know if he's gonna wake up. I really don't want to talk about it."

I robotically opened my lunch box and pulled out a Thermos of chocolate milk, a peanut butter and jelly sandwich, and a Twinkie. My favorite lunch. My mom made me the same thing every day. She wasn't being unimaginative, it's just that I complained whenever she tried to switch things up.

"Don't you ever get sick of peanut butter?" Lucy said.

"Nope," I said, taking a big bite to demonstrate. I was just finishing the first half of my diagonally cut sandwich when a hand reached in and snatched up my Twinkie. I turned around to see Joey grinning down at me.

"Hey! Give me that back!" I said, reaching for it, but Joey pulled his arm back, holding it just out of reach.

"What'll you give me for it?"

"I'll give you a fat lip," Lucy said.

"You gonna let a girl fight for you, faggot?"

"Just give it back," I pleaded, standing up to reach for it. Joey held it further out of reach.

"Butch will be back tomorrow," he said between giggles. "He told me to tell you we're gonna get you good for making him get suspended. Just like your fat friend."

I looked at him in astonished comprehension. "It was you."

"What?" he said, shrinking back.

"You hurt Matt, didn't you? You and Butch."

"I don't know what you're talking about." He sounded nervous.

Scared.

Lucy pushed her chair away from the table and kicked him in the shin.

"Ow!" he screamed, dropping the Twinkie into Lucy's hands.

"McBride!" bellowed Mack Truck from the front of the cavernous room. I was standing toe-to-toe with Joey. To the casual observer, or militant nun, it looked like I had just assaulted him. "Detention for fighting!"

"But I wasn't..."

"Don't talk back!"

"But he..."

"Sit down and shut up, unless you want to try for two detentions!"

Joey laughed in my face as I took my seat and then he punched the table, squishing my Twinkie before walking away.

"Thanks a lot," I said angrily to Lucy. "Now I got a detention because of you."

"I was only trying to help," she said defensively. She must've been shocked by the way I lashed out at her. I know I was, but I couldn't help it. I was an emotional wreck, and unfortunately, she was the one I decided to take it out on.

"I don't need your help!"

"I'm sick of watching them pick on you."

"So don't watch."

"Fine. Next time I'll let them do whatever they want to you and just walk away."

"Good," I said as the recess bell rang. Lucy picked up the destroyed dessert cake and threw it at me.

"Enjoy your Twinkie," she said, shoving her chair back violently as she stood and stormed away in anger.

I couldn't believe it. Now Lucy was mad at me too. This day just keeps getting better and better. Just when I thought things couldn't possibly get any worse, they did.

I sat by myself on the steps leading from the far side of the playground up to the church. It's not that I wanted to be by myself as much as I didn't have anyone to play with. Matt was in the hospital, Lucy was mad at me—not that I blame her—and Sean and I weren't speaking. I just finished saying a little prayer for Matt to be okay, when I heard someone come up behind me.

"Mind if I join you?"

I turned my head and saw Father Scott's kind face looking at me. I shook my head and scooted over a little to give him more room. He sat down next to me.

"Is everything alright, Sport?"

"My dad calls me Sport," I said absently.

"Is it alright if I call you that too?"

"If you want."

"Why aren't you out there playing with your friends?"

I shrugged my shoulders. "I don't feel like it." Neither one of us spoke for a couple minutes, and then I said, "Why does God punish you when you're being good?"

"Sometimes it isn't always clear why God chooses us to bear our burdens in life. We have to have faith He has a higher purpose. Do you feel like you're being punished?"

"Lately I do. I killed my pet turtle. I didn't mean to, but that doesn't change what happened. I feel like I'm losing everything that matters to me. First The Beatles, then Oliver, now Matt.... It's like, no matter how good I try to be, everything is going wrong and there's nothing I can do to stop it. It's like the whole world is out to get me."

"I know it can feel like that sometimes. I've felt that way myself a time or two." He paused, then said, "How's Matt? He got hit pretty hard."

"You know about that?"

"I'm the one who found him."

"His dad said he's in a coma. That's all I know. And it's all my fault."

"You mustn't blame yourself. You didn't do it. I wish I knew who did."

"It was Butch and Joey. I can't prove it, but I know it was them. Butch is after me and he took it out on Matt."

"Dear God."

"Maybe you could say a prayer for him. And me."

"You're always in my prayers."

I smiled at him.

"All I can tell you is it does get better. Have you ever heard the saying 'it's always darkest before the dawn'?"

I shook my head no, staring up into his eyes now.

"It means that just when things seem as bad as they can be, it gets better."

"I sure hope you're right, because I don't think I can take any more bad."

"Have faith in God. He hasn't abandoned you. I promise."

"Thanks Father," I said and leaned against him. He always made me feel better. He smiled at me and put his arm around my shoulder.

"Call me Scotty."

It was almost four o'clock by the time we arrived at the hospital. Usually we walk home from school, but today Mom was there to pick us up right as school let out. Sean didn't want to come with us, but Mom made him. He argued with her of course, trying to get her to drop him off at home first, but finally realized he wasn't going to get his way. He spent the rest of the trip with his arms crossed defiantly and staring out the back-seat window, as far away from me as he could get. That was fine with me; I didn't want to talk to him either.

Mom and I walked together through the visitor's parking lot to the main building. Sean didn't want to come in, so, to avoid another argument, she allowed him to stay in the car. Closer to the building were parked the expensive cars like Porches and Mercedes Benz and Corvette Stingrays and I knew we had passed into the doctors' parking lot. I loved Stingrays. I thought they were the coolest cars ever made and I wanted one when I grew up. For now though, I'd have to be happy with my Hot Wheels version.

The hospital was brand new and modern. At the entrance, you stepped on pressure sensitive pads and the doors opened automatically as you approached—just like *Star Trek!*

I wondered what other space-age gizmos they had here. We walked up to the admissions desk where a middle age nurse who reminded me of Ethel Mertz on *I Love Lucy* sat behind the desk dressed all in white with a nurses cap on her head.

"May I help you?" she said with a tone that sounded anything but helpful.

"Yes. We're here to see Matt Sherman."

The nurse looked through a rack of hanging folders on wheels beside her desk. Too bad they didn't have *Star Trek* computers too, I thought. That would sure make it easier to look stuff up. Maybe some day. Finally, she found his file.

"Here it is. He's in pediatrics. Fourth floor, room four-eleven. But he can't go up. No visitors under twelve."

"I called ahead and got special permission from Dr. Washington to allow my son to see his friend," Mom insisted.

"Hold on," the nurse said and picked up the phone and dialed a local extension. I could tell because she only dialed four numbers. A few seconds later, she confirmed what my mom had told her with the person on the other end.

"Take the elevator up to the fourth floor," Nurse Ethel said, "then follow the purple stripe to the pediatrics wing. Dr. Washington will be waiting for you at the nurse's station."

"Thank you," Mom said and took my hand. We followed the nurse's directions upstairs. As we made our way closer to the kid's section, I recognized all the pictures on the wall from the time I was here after my bike accident—*Mother Goose* and *Dr. Seuss* and *Peanuts*—the picture of Snoopy only reminded me of my doll and a fresh wave of resentment toward Sean ran through me.

"How you doing, champ?" Dr. Washington said, mussing my hair when we reached our destination. "Any problems in the region you were ass-aulted?"

I blushed and giggled at his naughty pun, but I could tell by Mom's expression that she did not approve of his salty humor. I guess it must be a "guy thing."

"No sir," I said. "It hurt the first couple of days, but now it's just a little achy when I'm sitting too long."

"Good. Sounds like you're healing nicely. You're very lucky. Another two inches to the left and it would have been a whole different story."

Everyone keeps telling me how lucky I was. So why didn't I feel lucky? "Can I see Matt now?" I said. I didn't want to talk about me anymore.

"Okay, come with me." We followed him to room four-eleven and stopped outside. "He's out of danger now, but he's still in a coma. Do you know what that means?"

"It means he's asleep and he can't wake up."

"That's right."

"Will he wake up?"

"We hope so. That's up to him. It could be a day, or a week, or even a year."

A whole year. I let that sink in. "Can I see him by myself?"

"I think that would be alright," Dr. Washington said.

I pushed the door open and stepped into the dimly lit room. At first, all I saw was an empty bed and a drawn curtain, but then I realized there was another bed on the other side. I moved further into the room, and for some odd reason found myself tiptoeing around to the other bed, though I knew its occupant wouldn't be disturbed.

There was Matt, looking too small lying in the middle of the big bed, covered up to his chest with a white blanket, his arms at his sides on top. The head of the bed was tilting up so he was half lying down and half sitting up. He had a tube going into his arm attached to a bag of clear liquid and a bunch of wires stuck to his head and chest going to a machine that went *beep-beep-beep* with his heartbeat.

I walked over to his side and took his hand. I could feel his warmth. I hadn't really expected him to grip me back, but I was still disappointed when his hand remained limp in mine.

"Hey Matt," I whispered. "It's me, Billy. I don't know if you can hear me or not. If you can, please come back. You're the best friend I ever had and I don't know what I'd do without you. You're gonna be okay once you wake up and then we'll do whatever you want. Just you and me. I need you. Sean and Lucy are both mad at me so you're the only friend I got left. Who else am I gonna play Spaceship with? You're the best engineer in the whole galaxy. I can't run the ship without you. When you wake up, I'll make you my First Officer. Please Matt. I lost so much in the past few days. I can't lose you too. I love you like you were my brother. I'll do anything if you just wake up. Please."

I was crying with my head on the side rail of the bed when my mom and Sammy's dad came in. I was still holding Matt's hand. She came around and stood behind me, putting both hands on my shoulders.

"Come on Honey, let's go," she whispered.

I wiped my eyes and stood, gripping Matt's hand. I didn't want to let go. Finally, I laid it down gently across his stomach.

"See you soon, buddy," I said and let my mother lead me out of the room.

As soon as they got home from the hospital, Sean stuffed half a dozen bags of dope in his knapsack and went to the park where all the burnouts hang out. If he was lucky, he could get rid of some of it today. At least he hoped so. He had no idea how to sell drugs.

He put his bike in the rack and chained the front tire. A few years ago, he never would have even thought about locking up his bike, but last year there had been a series of bicycle thefts in the neighborhood and his dad bought him a chain and padlock. Just one more sign that the innocence of the 60's was really over.

He'd been going to this park since he was a kid. It had the usual playground things like swings, monkey bars, a merry-go-round, a sandbox, basketball hoops, a tennis court, and even a baseball field. Billy and he had spent many Saturday afternoons here, but in the last year or so, it had been taken over by hippies. They were a motley crew with about a dozen of them ranging in age from around sixteen to mid-twenties, mostly high school and college dropouts. They all had long hair and looked as though they hadn't seen a bar of soap in a while. Not many kids played here anymore because of them. They were afraid of the drugs. Yet here he was.

He knew they mostly hung out around the baseball dugout. He didn't know how to approach them though. They weren't exactly his crowd. They were more Tim's friends.

He'd actually thought about calling Tim and asking him for help, he knew he hung out in the park and smoked dope with these guys—maybe he could get an introduction. Before he left home, he'd started to dial his number, then immediately put the phone down. He never wanted to see Tim again. He's the one that got him into this mess in the first place. He still can't believe he'd trusted him.

He slung his knapsack off his back and carried it in his hand. He did his best to look casual, but he didn't think it was working by the way they all stared at him. He was scared and nervous, and it showed. He didn't want to do this. Every fiber of his being was screaming at him to run away and get out of there. He had to remind himself he was doing this for Billy's safety. He didn't think Joker made idle threats and he wasn't going to take a chance. He steeled his courage and walked straight into the lion's den.

"What's the buzz, little man?" a guy that looked around nineteen or twenty years old said. He had shoulder length stringy blonde hair and wore a tie-dye t-shirt. The pungent aroma of body odor wafted into Sean's nostrils and almost made him gag.

"Uh...." Now that he was here, he had no idea what to say.

"It's cool, man, we're not gonna bite," another said, this one looked about sixteen.

"Haven't I seen you before?" said a third.

"I don't think so," Sean said nervously.

"Yeah, you pal around with that little pothead, what's his name."

"Tim," Mr. Tie-Dye said.

"Yeah, that's it, Tim. What's your name, kid?"

"Uh, Sean."

"Peace, Sean."

"Uh, peace," he replied awkwardly, causing mild chuckles from a few of them.

"What can we do for you? You wanna get high?"

He really didn't, but he wanted them to trust him, so he said, "Sure."

"Right on. Who's got a joint?" One appeared as if by magic, already lit. Sean took it and spent the rest of the afternoon getting high in the dugout, talking and laughing with the hippies.

He finally got around to his real motive for being there and broke out his knapsack. He ended up selling four of the baggies for ten dollars each. Mr. Tie-Dye, Dennis was his real name, sidled up to Sean and offered to buy Sean's entire remaining stock.

"I have two more ten dollar bags on me, but I have a lot more at home," Sean told him.

"How much is a lot?"

"Like eighteen more."

"Okay, I'll take all of it."

"All of it?"

"As much as you got."

"Wow," Sean said smiling. This was easier than he thought.

"I don't have the cash now. Can you meet me here at eleven o'clock tonight?" Dennis said.

"I guess so." Looks like he'd be sneaking out again. This was becoming a habit.

"Perfect. I'll meet you here later with the cash."

Sean got back on his bike and peddled home, relieved that he was getting rid of his entire consignment of marijuana in one transaction. Yet he just couldn't shake the feeling that he had sunk to a new low. Maybe now Joker would leave him alone. He would give Joker his money and that would be the end of it. Yeah, and pigs could fly.

After everyone was in bed, he sneaked down to the basement and got the rest of the pot from his new hiding spot behind the freezer (where Billy wouldn't find it), and rode his bike back to the park. It was pitch black out when he got there a little after eleven. Dennis was waiting for him under a streetlight by the fence near home plate. Sean waved and cruised over to the baseball field where they went into the dugout together. Sean gave Dennis the pot in exchange for one hundred eighty dollars cash. He hadn't even put the money in his pocket before six police cars surrounded the park, lights flashing.

That's when Dennis flashed his detective badge and said, "You're under arrest."

"Billy, wake up," Mom said, urgently shaking me.

"Huh..? Wha..?" I said groggily, half asleep.

"Get up," she said, pulling clothes from my dresser. "You have to get dressed."

"What time is it?" I said through a yawn. "It's still dark out."

"It's five-thirty. Hurry now and get dressed. We have to go pick up your brother."

It took me a minute to realize my mother was crying. The only other time I'd ever seen her cry was when I was in the hospital following my bike accident when they thought I might die. Something bad must have happened.

"What's wrong? Why are you crying?"

"Sean's been arrested."

I looked across the room at the empty bed. Sean must have sneaked out again last night. And now he was in jail. I got dressed and went downstairs where Mom gave me a package of Pop-Tarts and a glass of milk saying, "Eat those in the car." Twenty-five minutes later, we were walking in the front doors of the Passaic County Sheriff's Office.

I had never been inside a police station before. A uniformed Sheriff's Deputy was sitting behind an open window in the middle of a long wooden wall with a ledge about four feet off the ground. There were two other windows, both closed. It was just after six in the morning and there wasn't much activity yet. It reminded me of a bank.

"Can I help you?" the deputy said as Dad approached the window.

"I'm here to pick up my son, Sean McBride."

"Just a minute," he said, and then disappeared. He returned a moment later and handed Dad a stack of papers and said, "Fill these out."

Mom took a seat on a wooden bench along the sidewall while Dad stood to the side of the window filling out the paperwork.

I looked around the open room. There were two flags on either end of the wall; an American flag on one side, and the New Jersey state flag on the other. On the wall above the bench were two large framed photographs; one was of President Nixon, who I recognized, and the other was the Governor of New Jersey, who I did not.

Between the bench where my mom was sitting, and the wall of windows, was a closed wooden door marked Authorized Personnel Only. Covering the entire floor was a big circle with an eagle inside and the words Seal of the Great State of New Jersey encircling it.

Dad finished the paperwork and handed them back to the deputy.

"Wait here," the deputy said and disappeared again.

Dad took a seat on the bench next to Mom.

Sean sat on the narrow metal bed holding his legs, his knees touching his chin. He was shaking uncontrollably and crying; he had been since they locked him in the eight by twelve-foot holding cell. He still couldn't believe this was happening to him, but it was.

Nothing had prepared him for this.

As soon as Dennis, who turned out to be detective Murphy, told him he was under arrest, he shut down and went into a state of shock. Everything that happened after that seemed surreal, an almost out of body experience. He was handcuffed and placed in the back of the patrol car and taken to the Passaic County Sheriff's Department where he was booked and fingerprinted. After that, they took his handcuffs off and put him in a little white tiled room with a table and two chairs on opposite sides. On one wall was a large mirror that he assumed was two-way, like he'd seen on *Dragnet*. He sat in the room alone for what seemed like hours before Detective Murphy came in and sat across from him. He had thankfully bathed since that afternoon.

"Hello Sean. Can I get you anything? Coke? Water?"

"No thanks. When can I call my parents?"

"Soon. First, I need to explain some things. I already read you your rights. Do you understand you don't have to talk to me?" Sean nodded. "And you can have a lawyer with you."

"Yes."

"I can't promise anything, but if you cooperate, things could go a lot easier on you."

"I don't want to go to jail."

"I'll do my best to keep you out, but you have to help me. So, do you want to talk?"

"I guess."

"Okay, good. So, where did you get the pot?"

"I was forced into it. He said he would hurt my brother if I didn't."

"Whoa, back up. Who forced you?"

"He calls himself Joker. I don't know his real name."

"Tim Bennet mentioned someone named Joker."

"Yeah, Tim was in my band. I thought he was my friend. He's the one who got me into this."

"Okay, let's start at the beginning."

Sean told him everything he knew, starting with Tim taking him to Joker's apartment to get high and ending with Joker's threats against Billy. He agreed to help them get Joker in exchange for leniency.

In a way, he was almost glad he'd been caught. He never wanted to get involved in any of this in the first place. He still couldn't believe Tim had done this to him. He trusted him! He didn't care if Joker or Tim got in trouble; as far as he was concerned, they deserved whatever they got.

After his interview, they put him in a holding cell by himself. The first thing that surprised him was the amount of activity for the middle of the night. And it was so loud there. Even though he was in his own cell, he could still hear the other prisoners in the jail. There were criminals yelling and screaming on top of each other. He heard obscenities he'd never heard before. He was terrified.

He had no idea what time it was or how long he'd been here, he'd lost all sense of time and there were no clocks. He must've been here for several hours, at least. And there were no windows either, so he couldn't see if it was still night or if the sun had come up yet. It was very disorienting. But he had plenty of time to think.

He had no idea what he was going to tell his parents. This was the worst thing he'd ever done. He'd brought shame and embarrassment down on the family. The one thing he did know was that he was not going to lie to them. He would tell them everything. He just hoped they didn't kick him out of school. Right now, all he wanted to do was crawl into a hole and die.

He prayed to God to help him get out of this mess, and promised he would never do drugs again. He was sorry for behaving so badly lately, and swore he would go back to the way he was before he met Tim. Just please, God, help him get through this. And please don't let his father kill him.

He heard a key in the lock of his cell and the door swung open. A large Sheriff's Deputy stood outside.

"Let's go, McBride," he said briskly.

Sean got off the bunk, wiped his eyes, and followed the deputy through the jail.

The door marked Authorized Personnel Only opened and Sean walked through, head hung low in shame. Mom jumped up and ran to him, hugging him tight. Dad glared at him, barely containing his anger. I could scarcely even bring myself to look at him.

Sean looked a mess. I could tell by the tearstains down both cheeks that he'd been crying and his hair was sticking up in the back as though he'd just gotten out of bed and his clothes were all rumpled, like they'd been slept in. His cheek was red and it looked a little swollen, like he'd been punched in the face. On his fingers were grey smudges of ink stains that hadn't been completely wiped off after they fingerprinted him.

"Let's go," Dad said, putting an end to our awkward family reunion.

No one spoke on the ride home. Dad watched the road ahead; Mom stared out the window, every now and then she dabbed her eyes with a white lace hankie; Sean and I sat in the back, stealing angry sideways glances at each other.

We arrived home a few minutes before seven a.m. Sean leaped from the car and raced to the side door, entering the house and running upstairs to our room. In the confusion, Mom had forgotten to lock the door. Dad followed Sean into the house and angrily went up the stairs and into the room, slamming the door behind him.

Mom told me to stay downstairs so she could fix me breakfast. Neither of us spoke. We could hear Dad yelling at Sean upstairs. Though we couldn't make out what was being said through the closed door, we got the gist of it. I was glad it wasn't me up there. I'd never heard Dad so furious in all my life.

I still hadn't told my parents I had detention this afternoon, and with Dad in such a foul mood, I was afraid to. But I had to, so I gathered my courage before Dad came back downstairs.

"Hey Mom?" I said cautiously. "I got something to tell you."

"What is it?"

"I got a detention after school today. But it wasn't my fault, I swear."

I guess she was too weary to get mad. She said, "Okay. Come straight home after. And don't tell your father."

And that was the end of it.

Just as I was finishing my scrambled eggs, the upstairs door slammed shut and Dad walked into the kitchen all red in the face.

"Go get ready for school, Sweetheart," Mom said. I got up from the table and ran to my room. I entered cautiously, eased inside and gently closed the door behind me. Sean was on his bed crying. He looked so pathetic sitting there I forgot I was supposed to be mad at him.

"Are you okay?" I asked sympathetically.

"Leave me alone."

"I'm just trying to be nice. You don't have to bite my head off."

"Just mind your own business."

"You know, you're a real jerk. I was willing to forget all the mean things you said and did to me lately because we're brothers, but now you can forget it."

"Good. I don't need you anyway. I hate you."

"You don't mean that," I said, barely above a whisper.

He brushed past me, pushing me out of his way to go down to breakfast. Fine with me. No skin off my nose. Yeah right. I hated when we fought.

I slowly put on my school uniform. Normally on Fridays, I would put on my gym clothes under my uniform, but I was excused today because I was stabbed. Which reminded me, Butch's suspension was over and he would be back in school today. I would have to do my best to try and avoid him, but that was easier said than done. We're in the same class.

I went through most of the day on autopilot, going through the motions like some kind of zombie-student, but not really there. It hardly registered with me that Butch was back in school today. Even when Mr. McLean was talking about today being the day Apollo 13 would have one last chance to get home, I was barely paying attention.

"I'm sorry about yesterday," Lucy said later, on our walk from the school to the church basement for gym class. "I didn't mean to get you in trouble. Please don't be mad at me."

"Huh? Oh. Don't worry about it."

"What's the matter?"

"Don't ask," I said with a heavy sigh. "You don't want to know."

"Yes I do. I know you saw Matt yesterday. My mom talked to his father. And I know he's your best friend. Please talk to me Billy. I only want to help."

"I know you do, Luce. But you can't. That's the thing. No one can. And it's not just Matt either. It's a lot of things. It's Sean, and Butch, and the astronauts, and my turtle, and The Beatles. Sometimes I feel like I just can't take it anymore. Sometimes I think everyone would be better off if I just killed myself."

Without any warning, Lucy slapped my face. Hard. "Don't you *ever* say that again! I know I haven't known you very long, but I know you're a good, kind person. In fact, you're the best person I know. So you better not even *think* that for another second. Because I love you, Billy McBride, and I would never forgive you if you ever hurt yourself."

"You... you love me?" I couldn't believe my ears!

"Yes, I do. And don't make a big deal about it," she blushed.

Suddenly, it felt like a weight was lifting from my shoulders. Maybe Father Scott was right. She slipped her hand into mine and we walked hand in hand the rest of the way to the auditorium.

When we got to gym class, we split up—she went to the girl's side and I went to the boy's. Because I wasn't fully healed yet, I was excused and didn't have to participate, but I still had to be there. While everyone was changing into their gym clothes, I went to the Boys Room. When I was finished, I went to the sink to wash my hands. I heard the door open and looked in the mirror and froze.

"Hi McBride. Miss me?" Butch said, coming up behind me. Joey stood at his side. "I sure missed you."

"Hey Butch," I said, fear creeping into my voice.

"You and me got some unfinished business," he said, speaking directly into my ear. Joey was cackling like a mental patient.

"Can't you just leave me alone?" I pleaded, "I didn't do anything to you."

"You got me in trouble! And I'm gonna do to you double what I got!" Then he reached in the back of my pants, grabbed hold of the waistband of my underwear, and yanked up hard and fast. I heard and felt them rip as my feet were lifted from the floor. It was the worst wedgie I ever got. The pain between my legs made me yelp and I saw stars, but even worse was the realization that he reopened my stab wound. Tears came to my eyes and I collapsed to my knees when he let go.

"See you later, McBride," he sneered, and they both left me in a heap on the ground.

I picked myself up and went into a stall to assess the damage. My underwear was ruined beyond adjustment and I was bleeding again, though not badly. I held toilet paper on it until it stopped. Then I buttoned my pants, tucked in my shirt, and adjusted my tie. I pitched what was left of my underwear in the trash can and rejoined my class.

TWELVE

I sat quietly in detention waiting patiently for four o'clock. Freddie Weaver, the sixth grader who specialized in erotic art, was the only other kid in detention today besides me. I got the feeling he was in here a lot. He showed me one of his drawings once. I'm not exactly sure what I was supposed to be looking at, but I was pretty sure I didn't want to know.

Mr. Flowers, one of the seventh grade teachers, was the detention monitor today, so we didn't have any clandestine candy entertainment. But he did let us do our homework, so we didn't have to just sit there and stare at the wall.

When the hour was up, he wished us a pleasant weekend and let us go. I exited the building via a side door that let me out into the playground. I pretended I was James Bond and stealthily looked around corners for any sign of Butch or Joey. I didn't see them anywhere. It looked like the coast was clear. They probably didn't feel like waiting around for an hour after school.

I walked to the far corner of the yard where the hole in the fence led to the fields. Looking around one last time for Butch and seeing no one, I passed through to the other side. I barely made it a few yards when I heard behind me, “Going somewhere, faggot?”

I stopped in my tracks and turned around to face Butch and Joey stepping out from behind a bush. Joey moved to the other side, preventing me from running. I was trapped.

“Leave me alone!” I said.

“Or what?” Butch said, taking a few steps closer. “Your girlfriend’s not here to fight for you this time.”

“Why do you hate me so much?”

“I don’t like your face,” he said. He was only a foot away now.

“What did I ever do to you?” I said, backing up.

“Nothing. I just don’t like faggots,” he said, suddenly lunging forward, shoving me in the chest and knocking me to the ground. Joey laughed from the sidelines. Butch advanced on me.

“Get up,” he commanded, kicking me in the side. I winced in pain. “I said get up!” He emphasized the last word with another kick—this time in the ribs.

I held my side, pain registering on my face. I struggled to stand; Joey grabbed me under my arms and pulled me to my feet.

The next blow was to the solar plexus, knocking the wind out of me. I struggled to catch my breath, my lungs suddenly emptied of air.

“What’s the matter, faggot? Can’t breathe?”

I took a wild, awkward swing at Butch, but he easily dodged it. He kicked me in the butt as I flew past, opening my wound yet again and knocking me into the dirt face first. My left cheek and brow scraped against the gravel.

“Who said you were allowed to fight back?”

Joey laughed like crazy, something he was good at. I rolled onto my back and looked into Butch's face, a sadistic, murderous look in his eyes. I could only cry in pain. I hated Butch and Joey, but I hated myself more for letting them see me cry again.

"Please... no more," I begged.

"Pick him up," Butch ordered.

"Maybe he's had enough," Joey suggested.

"I said, pick him up!" he shouted, blind rage in his voice. Joey did as he was told. He lifted me to my feet again and held me in place. I was panting, whimpering, barely able to stand, even with Joey holding me up.

"This is for getting me suspended!" Butch shouted, and punched me full force in the face, over and over, with both fists, until I was battered, bruised, and bleeding. Finally, he stopped his merciless barrage, having spent all the pent-up fury inside of him from countless beatings.

Joey released my limp body and I fell to the ground, groaning and crying, barely conscious.

"Come on," Butch said, kicking me viciously one last time and leaving me, a broken heap on the ground.

Lucy was sitting in her tree thinking about Billy having to serve detention for something she did. She knew he didn't like it when she interfered, but she couldn't stand the way Joey was teasing him. She'd finally had enough when she kicked him in the leg.

She tried explaining to Mack Truck that it was her fault, not Billy's, but she thought Lucy was just trying to cover for her friend and didn't believe her.

She was looking out over the lawn in front when she heard kids approaching. She recognized the voices before she saw their faces. It was Butch and Joey, but she couldn't make out what they were saying. She got lower in the tree. She could hear them now as they walked past on the sidewalk.

"Do you think we should have just left him there?" Joey was saying.

"Don't worry about it," Butch said. He was flexing his fingers and shaking out his hands. Lucy thought she could see blood on his knuckles.

"I don't know, man. I think you might have gone a little too overboard this time. Maybe we should go back and make sure he's alright."

"I said don't worry about it," Butch insisted, and they passed out of range.

Lucy jumped out of the tree in near panic. They were talking about Billy, she was sure of it! They did something to him. Where would he be? They'd waited until detention was over, so he must be somewhere near school.

She ran from her yard as fast as she could and down the block toward the school. *It was a good thing she lived so close*, she thought.

She ran into the playground and began looking all over for him. She checked every place where she thought he might be, but still no Billy. Then she remembered he sometimes walked through the power fields as a short cut to his street.

She ran to the corner where the fence had a hole in it and stopped short. Then she saw him; he was lying motionless on the ground about twenty feet from her. And then she saw all the blood.

"Oh my God! Billy!!!" she screamed.

Someone was speaking. "Billy, can you hear me? Can you talk?"

"Luce?" I heard my voice say, barely audible. I blinked my eyes. "We have to get to my ship..."

"Ship? What ship? Billy, I don't know what you're saying."

"Shondo... traitor... Luce..."

"Who's Shondo? What are you talking about?'

I blinked a few more times, trying to focus, but everything was blurred. I groped around on the ground looking for my glasses. I found them a few feet away, the frame cracked and one of the arms bent at an odd angle. I bent it back as best I could and put them on. They were crooked, but at least I could see. I looked up into Lucy's eyes.

"Lucy?" I said, trying to sit up. "What happened?"

"Billy, are you okay?"

"What..."

She helped me to sit up. My hand went to my side. It hurt so much. "Butch and Joey beat you up. Do you remember that?"

I nodded my head—it was all coming back to me now. I touched my face and winced in pain. "My face hurts. And my side."

"Can you stand up?"

"I think so." Slowly, with Lucy's help, I got to my feet.

"How do you feel?"

"Like I got hit by a bus," I said and attempted to smile, but it hurt too much. I slowly started limping toward my house.

"Where are you going?"

"Home."

"Come back to my house. My mom can drive you."

I shook my head. "No, I'm okay," I said and kept limping along. "You go home."

She stood there watching me walk away. "You are so stubborn sometimes!" she yelled after me. "Just like a boy!" Then she added, "Call me when you get home!"

I lifted my hand and waved and kept walking.

Katherine opened the bedroom door and saw Sean was out of bed and dressed. After the morning drama was said and done, it was decided they would keep him home from school. He slept most of the day. He looked up at her, a sad expression on his face.

"Is Dad still mad at me?" he said as she walked in.

"I'm sure he is."

"I'm really sorry. I screwed everything up."

"You made a mistake, but we'll get through it together, as a family. The police said if you cooperate, they might not press charges. Apparently, they've been after this Joker character for some time. We know you'll do the right thing."

He nodded and hung his head.

"I'll do whatever they want. They tricked me, Mom. I swear I was forced into it. He said he would hurt Billy if I didn't sell drugs for him."

"I believe you."

"I tried to tell Dad, but he won't listen to me."

"He won't be home until later, but I'll talk to him. In the meantime, if you want to get back in your father's good graces, you could start by doing some chores around the house. Why don't you start by mowing the lawn in the backyard? It really needs it."

"Okay," he agreed.

"I have to go to the grocery store, there's nothing in the house for dinner. Keep an eye out for Billy. He had detention today, but he should be home soon."

"Do I have to?"

"Yes, you have to. He's your brother. What has been going on with you two lately? You've always gotten along so well."

"He's a little tattle-tale."

"What are you talking about?"

"He told you and Dad about me smoking."

"You've been smoking? This is the first I've heard about it."

"You mean he didn't..."

"No. Is that why you pulled the head off his Snoopy doll?"

"Oh, you know about that, huh?"

"I think you owe Billy an apology."

Sean sighed. "Yes ma'am. Please don't tell Dad about me smoking? I won't do it anymore, I promise."

"I won't. Now get started on the lawn. I want it finished by the time I get home. I'll be back in an hour."

I made it to the fence behind Mr. Hughes's garage. With great difficulty, I managed to climb over, almost falling on the other side. I limped around the garage without even looking.

"Hey! Hey you!" Mr. Hughes yelled. He was standing with a hose in his hand and a shotgun on the ground by his feet, watering his flowers. I stopped and looked at him. I couldn't run away if I wanted to—and I did. He dropped the hose and came running over.

"Are you alright, boy? What happened to you?"

"I fell down."

Mr. Hughes looked at me suspiciously with his good eye. "Fell down, huh? Looks like the ground had a mean right hook." I just continued to stare at him. "C'mon over here and sit down a minute.

Let me get you some ice," he said and disappeared into the house. A few minutes later, he came back outside with an ice pack, a first-aid kit, and a glass of water. He handed me the glass and two aspirin.

"Take these," he said. I took the pills with a sip of water. It was cool and felt good going down so I drank the whole glass.

"Here, put this on that cheek," he said, and put the ice pack to my face. I held it there. Then Mr. Hughes opened the first-aid kit and took out some cotton and peroxide. "This might sting a little." I shrank back and inhaled sharply, making an "Sssss" sound when he touched the cotton to my face. I relaxed after the initial shock was over and I let the man clean my wounds.

"Where'd you learn to do that?" I asked.

"First World War," he said. "The Big One. I was a medic. Now hold still." When he was done, he put down the cotton wad. "There. Anything else hurt?"

"My side." I wasn't about to tell him where else.

"Let's see. Open your shirt."

I pulled up my bloody shirt. Dark bruises were already forming around my torso. Mr. Hughes gently poked and prodded and I reacted to the pain.

"Well, they ain't broken, but that's a nasty bruise. It's gonna hurt for a while, that's all."

"Thanks Mr. Hughes. I thought..." I glanced over at the shotgun on the lawn.

"Thought I was gonna shoot you with rock salt?"

I nodded.

"I would have. But then I saw that you were hurt. It's the only way I can keep you damn kids out of my yard," he said.

"Sorry about that. It's just that going through the fields saves a lot of time walking to school."

"Tell you what. I'll let you cut through my fence, if you promise to use the driveway and keep off the lawn. And no more sneaking around. Deal?" he said, and offered me his hand.

"Deal," I said and we shook hands.

"Go on, now. Git."

"Thanks for fixing me up," I said, giving him back his ice pack.

"And don't let me catch you on my lawn again. Stick to the driveway or I won't hesitate to shoot you."

"Yes sir," I said, and limped away.

I walked down the block, still sore, but already feeling a little better. When I got home, my mom's car was gone, but I could hear the motor of the lawn mower in the back of the house. I figured Sean must be mowing the lawn, but I really didn't want to talk to him, so I let myself in the side door.

I'd had a really bad day and all I wanted to do was escape. I went upstairs, took off my school uniform and looked in the mirror. I was a mess. My face was a swollen wreck and my ribs were three shades of purple already. Mom was gonna flip.

I put on some play clothes, put on my space helmet and grabbed my flashlight from my nightstand drawer.

I went downstairs and into the basement and stopped dead in my tracks. In the utility room was a brand new, gleaming white, matching washer and dryer set. I had been with my mom when she picked them out a few weeks ago, but I had totally forgotten about them. The delivery men must have brought them today when I was at school.

The new machines were beautiful. They were so modern and

cool; the dryer actually *looked* like a spaceship! I inspected both machines from top to bottom. I opened the doors, played with the knobs. The dryer opening was so big, I could actually fit my helmet inside too!

I opened the dryer door, climbed in feet first, and got all the way inside, helmet and all. Then I turned on my flashlight, and with a smile on my cut and bruised face, I shut the door behind me. Unfortunately, unlike the old dryer, and unknown to me, this one locked.

Joemar held Captain Apollo's arms behind his back, as the Butcher landed blow after vicious blow to his face. Shondo held Lucinda on the sidelines, forcing her to watch.

"This is for destroying my brig!" the Butcher said, punching him in the midsection with all of his might. "And this is for rescuing the Empress!" He struck him full strength across his temple, opening a gash along his cheek and brow.

"Stop!" Lucinda screamed.

"And this is just because I hate you!" He shifted his weight, lifted his leg, and hit him with a roundhouse kick that nearly broke his nose.

"Let him go," the Butcher said. Joemar released him. He collapsed on the ground like a sack of potatoes.

He looked up at the Butcher and pleaded, "No more."

The Butcher smiled an evil grin and kicked him hard in the ribs. Again. And again. And again. He turned from the captain, started away, then turned suddenly and delivered one final kick to his face.

"He's all yours," the Butcher said to Shondo and walked away,

Joemar trailing close behind like a good little sycophant.

Lucinda helped hold Captain Apollo upright, supporting his weight with her shoulder as they staggered through the corridor of the vast ship toward the brig, Shondo directly behind them with a ray gun pointed at their backs.

"Shondo, you don't have to do this, you know," Captain Apollo said weakly. "Whatever the problem is, I'm sure we can work it out."

"I'm afraid it is too late for that, Captain," Shondo said. Then with genuine regret, added, "I'm sorry."

They stopped outside a large empty cell. Shondo moved ahead of them, still pointing the gun and pressed a series of buttons on a control panel on the wall outside. While he was entering codes, Captain Apollo took his weight off Lucinda's shoulders and made eye contact with her, nodding his head slightly, giving her a silent signal that he wasn't as badly hurt as he seemed. She nodded back, an almost imperceptible smile on her lips.

"You will find, Captain, it is not so easy to escape from this cell," Shondo said. "But thank you for pointing out the inherent design flaw in the system. It has been corrected."

"My pleasure," he replied sarcastically.

Shondo waved the gun, indicating the cell. Captain Apollo moved toward it, when Lucinda suddenly grasped her abdomen and doubled over in mock pain, moaning loudly.

"Ohhh!"

Shondo, momentarily surprised, shifted his focus to her, drawing his attention away and inadvertently forcing him to lower the muzzle of his weapon slightly. That split second was all the time Captain Apollo needed to grab Shondo's gun arm, push it away, and simultaneously punch him in the face. Lucinda grabbed the gun with both hands, attempting to wrestle it away.

A laser bolt shot out, hitting the ceiling and creating a blackened crater. She gained control of the weapon and wrestled it from his grip, as Captain Apollo quickly overpowered his former First Officer. He forced Shondo into the cell and punched the controls on the wall, instantly activating the force field.

"What was it you were saying about not being able to escape?" Captain Apollo said with wry amusement in his voice.

"I underestimated you, Captain, once again."

"Tell me one thing Shondo. Why?"

"Jealousy. No matter what I did, you were always better than I was. You have a natural ability and talent I could never hope to possess, no matter how hard I try. I came to resent you for that, so I turned my back on you. If I could never be better than you, then I would do everything in my power to destroy you."

"I feel sorry for you. And more than a little sad. You were like my brother. I hope that one day you can make peace with yourself. For what it's worth, I forgive you."

Captain Apollo and Lucinda turned to go.

"Captain," Shondo called after him. Captain Apollo turned back to face him. "There is a ship in hangar twelve. Brand-new. Experimental. The activation code is zero-four-one-one. Take it."

"Thank you Shondo."

"Good luck, sir."

Lucy sat on a chair at her kitchen table, waiting for the phone to ring. It had been nearly an hour since she watched Billy stagger away like a zombie in that horror movie *Night of the Living Dead* she saw at the drive-in last year with her cousin Samantha. He looked so beat up she wasn't sure he could even make it all the way home by himself. She hoped she did the right thing by letting him go off alone. What if he was really hurt bad and needed a doctor?

She still couldn't believe Butch had beaten him up so badly. The worst part was he would probably get away with it. Or, he would receive a slap on the wrist, like the three-day suspension he'd gotten for stabbing Billy with the pencil. Back in Texas, he would have been thrown out of school if he'd done that. They sure did things differently here.

She decided she was tired of waiting for Billy's call. He probably forgot. She opened the drawer by the phone, took out her mom's address book, and looked up the number for McBride. She picked up the phone and dialed the number. She let it ring about a dozen times before she gave up. No one home. Maybe Billy got home and his mom took him to the emergency room. She decided to wait a little bit longer and try again later.

Captain Apollo and Lucinda sneaked through the corridors of the *Black Widow* looking around corners and doing their best to avoid Mack the Black's troops. So far, so good. They moved cautiously down a long corridor and stopped outside a door marked *Hangar Bay 12*.

"This is it," Captain Apollo said. "You go ahead and take the ship. I'm going to get mine back."

"Do you think it's a good idea to split up?" she said.

"We'll have a better chance with two ships. And I've got a little surprise planned for them, but first I have to get to engineering."

Before they parted, she leaned in and kissed him on the lips.

"For luck," she said and exited through the door.

Captain Apollo held his weapon at the ready, making his way down to the engineering section of the ship, careful to avoid the enemy. He had a few close calls, but managed to get where he was going unmolested.

He opened the door marked Engineering and slipped inside. He was in luck; there was only one of Mack the Black's men monitoring the ship's engine control. His back was to the door and he hadn't heard the captain enter.

Captain Apollo sneaked up behind the man and knocked him out with a well-placed chop to the back of the neck. With the guard out of the way, Captain Apollo was free to carry out his sabotage.

Sean turned off the lawn mower and wheeled it into the garage. He took the green metal rake from its hook on the wall and returned to the yard, raking the cut grass into a pile.

He loved the smell of freshly cut grass and he loved the aromas of spring. Like the way the air smelled after a late afternoon rain shower. He had lost sight of how much he enjoyed the little things like that. Lately, it seemed he'd lost sight of a lot of things.

He'd been doing a lot of thinking in the last hour or so. He thought it was amazing how something as mundane as mowing the lawn could be so therapeutic. He had time to reflect on all the things that had happened recently.

Everything bad started when he began hanging out with Tim. Little by little, he had been influenced by him, thinking the older boy was so cool because he smoked cigarettes and grass. He had allowed himself to be seduced into trying both and ultimately, coerced into selling drugs.

He'd thought Tim was his friend. Only now, after it was too late, after he'd made a mess of his relationships and his life did he realize he was just being used. How could he have been so blind?

His parents were the first to see the truth. His mom had expressed her concerns months ago, recognizing the subtle changes in his behavior and pinpointing the source. In the end, even Ben and Jimmy saw Tim for what he really was: a leach and a vampire—nothing more than a lowly drug dealer and trying to turn Sean into one too.

And then there was Billy. More than anybody, he's the one who'd suffered the most. He'd done nothing wrong, and yet Sean had treated him like a pariah. The more he had expressed his concern for Sean's increasing erratic behavior, the angrier he'd become. Everything Billy had done, including following him the other night and confronting him about finding his stash, was done out of love.

Sean knew now that Billy told the truth, and in fact kept his promise to keep Sean's secrets; and how did he repay his loyalty? By rejecting him completely and beheading his beloved Snoopy—and then the final insult—breaking his heart by renouncing him as his brother. He had to find a way to repair the damage he'd caused. He only hoped it wasn't too late.

Captain Apollo wound his way through the maze of corridors until he was outside the cargo bay. Getting to his ship would be tricky. There were half a dozen troops guarding the entrance. He had to come up with some kind of diversion to get past them.

He surveyed the room with his eyes, looking for something he could use to distract them long enough for him to make his move.

Then he spotted it; a small sensor built into the ceiling. One bolt from his ray gun should activate the fire suppression system. He closed one eye, took careful aim, and fired.

Bulls-eye! The hold was instantly filled with multiple jets of white fog, obscuring everything. The troops guarding Captain Apollo's ship scrambled in six different directions.

In the confusion, he broke cover and ran to his ship, quickly boarding her and shutting the hatch. He entered the cockpit and activated the start-up sequence. He put his transceiver on his head and spoke into the mike.

"*Constellation* Fighter to zero-four-one-one, come in."

"I read you Captain," Lucinda's voice came back. "All systems go. Ready when you are."

"Punch it!"

The captain's fighter lifted off the cargo hold floor and hovered in place in front of the closed space doors. Several blasts from the ships laser cannons in rapid succession blew the doors away.

Seconds later the ship was outside the *Black Widow*.

Sean finished raking the cut grass and stuffed it into a large trash bag. After putting the bag in the trash can, he put away the rake and went into the house. He was hungry from his yard work and decided to raid the refrigerator looking for a snack. He settled on a piece of bundt cake and a glass of milk, taking it up to his room.

He was surprised Billy wasn't home yet. Maybe he went over a friend's house after he got out of detention. Too bad, he really wanted to apologize to him for being such a jerk lately. Ah well, he'd just have to do it when he got home later.

He turned on his stereo, put the headphones over his ears, and laid on his bed listening to the last album The Beatles had put out; *Abbey Road*. He considered it their best album ever, even better than *Sgt. Pepper*, if such a thing were possible. One of his favorite songs on the album, *Octopus's Garden*, was where they got the name for their band. Their final album, *Let It Be*, was due out in a few weeks and Max had promised him an advanced copy. He couldn't wait.

Captain Apollo's ship was rocked by a laser blast from an enemy fighter and he was getting a little light headed. He looked out the window and saw his oxygen venting out into space. That last hit must have ruptured the oh-two unit. Checking his instruments, he saw that the air was getting thinner, making it difficult to breathe. He'd decided he better go attach the reserve air tank.

He went to open the hatch and found that it was stuck. That's peculiar. He tried again. Nothing. He tried putting his back into it, but it just wouldn't open...

I pushed hard against the dryer door, but it wouldn't open. I tried pushing it open with my feet, but it just wouldn't budge. It was locked! Uh-oh.

"*Houston, we have a problem*," I said to myself.

I tried pounding my fists on the door. "Help! Help!"

I was starting to panic. The air was getting thinner. I was gasping for air and I was getting a headache. I started to think, *if I don't get out of here I'm going to die*.

Sean was listening to George Harrison singing about how the sun was coming and everything would be all right, when he heard the telephone ringing. He took off his headphones, went to his parent's bedroom, and picked up the receiver.

"Hello?"

"Hi. This is Lucy. Is Billy home?" She sounded panicked.

"No, he hasn't gotten home from school yet."

"Oh no."

"What do you mean, 'oh no'? What's wrong?"

"Butch beat him up pretty bad after school. I was afraid he wouldn't make it home."

"Where is he?"

"In the fields. Hurry!"

Sean hung up the phone and went back to his room to put his sneakers on. As he sat on his bed to tie them, he saw Billy's bloody school shirt stuffed into the trash can beside his desk.

My breathing was shallow; the air inside the dryer was almost completely gone. I was barely clinging to consciousness when I heard a bell. A phone was ringing somewhere and it was answered. Someone was home! I gathered up the last of my strength, and in one last-ditch effort, pounded on the door and screamed,

"HEEEEEEELP!!!"

Billy!

Sean heard his brother's cry for help and ran downstairs. He had to be in the dryer. Sean raced into the basement and threw open the dryer door. Billy was inside, unconscious. He pulled Billy out and laid him on his back and carefully removed the toy space helmet. Sean reeled at his brother's face; it was swollen, bruised, and cut and his lips were turning blue. He looked like he'd been in a car wreck. And he wasn't breathing!

"Billy! Noooooo!!!"

Sean did as he was taught in Boy Scouts and tilted Billy's head back, opened his mouth, and put his own mouth over his brother's, breathing into him. He breathed again. He lifted his mouth and started compressing his chest with his hands. He was crying hard.

"Come on, Billy! Don't do this!"

He leaned down and breathed into him a few more times, then repeated the compressions.

"Please Billy! You can't die! I didn't really mean it when I said I wished you were dead! I'm sorry I was mean to you! I'm sorry I ripped Snoopy's head off! I'm sorry for everything! Just please don't die! I can't live without you! Please! *I LOVE YOU!!!"*

Billy coughed. Then he coughed again. Then he took a deep breath.

"Billy?! Billy!!" Sean couldn't believe his eyes. He did it! He picked Billy up into his arms and held him close, hugging him and crying tears of joy.

At that same moment, thousands of miles away, after an agonizing week in space and against all odds, the crew of Apollo 13 splashed down somewhere in the middle of the Pacific Ocean. And the world breathed a collective sigh of relief. They were safe. They were home.

THIRTEEN

I woke up surrounded by my family.

"Where am I?" I said weakly.

"In the hospital. You stopped breathing," Mom said. "Sean saved your life."

"Hey Tiger," Sean said, stepping forward. "I got something for you." He handed me my Astronaut Snoopy doll; its head had been carefully sewn back on.

"Snoopy!"

"I fixed it myself."

"Thanks Sean," I said grinning up at him and hugging Snoopy. I looked over at my mom and asked, "When can I go home?"

"Tomorrow morning. They want to keep you overnight for observation. But don't worry, you won't be alone. You have a roommate."

The privacy curtain opened and Max Sherman, who had been hiding behind it, revealed the patient in the next bed. His head was wrapped in a gauze turban, but otherwise he looked okay.

"Matt!" I exclaimed. He was sitting up and smiling.

"Hi," he said. "Boy, you look like crap."

"Have you looked in a mirror lately?"

Dr. Washington came into the room. "Got room for one more visitor?"

"Sure," I said.

Sammy walked into the room. He stopped when he saw me and frowned. I must've looked pretty bad. "Hey Sammy," I said, and smiled.

"Hi Billy," he said and walked over to the bed.

"When he heard what happened he insisted I let him come visit you," Dr. Washington said.

"I'm glad you did," I told him.

We all visited for a while, and then Sammy's dad came over and did his doctor thing. He listened to my heart, looked into my eyes and down my throat, and seemed satisfied.

"How am I?" I said.

"You'll live," he said. "Now how about everyone clear out and let him rest. You can come back tomorrow."

"Thank you, James," Mom said.

"Bye Billy," Sammy said and left with his dad.

Mom leaned over to kiss me on the forehead. "Goodnight Sweetheart."

"Night Mom. Night Dad." I said.

"Goodnight Sport," Dad said.

"Night Tiger," Sean said. "Thanks for not dying on me."

"Thanks for saving my life."

"We'll see you in the morning," Mom said, and everyone left the room leaving Matt and me alone.

"Boy, Butch really did a number on your face."

"Is it that bad?" I said.

"Nah. It's an improvement."

"Shut up!" I said and threw my pillow at him. We both broke out in hysterics.

"Hey Billy?"

"Yeah?"

"I wish we were brothers."

"We are," I said and looked over at him and smiled.

Leo McBride sat back in his reclining black leather chair behind the desk in his modest office, waiting for his son. He hated having to discipline one of his boys, but as the father and head of the household, the responsibility fell to him. Katherine and he didn't believe in corporal punishment. He had spanked each of his sons once—only once—years ago and at different times. Nothing too severe, just enough so they felt it and would think twice before disobeying the rules to warrant another. The tactic seems to have worked; now all he had to do was threaten another spanking and the boys immediately got back in line. But not this time.

Although he was still very much a boy, Sean was growing up fast—too fast. This new generation was unlike anything he had seen before, and he didn't know what to do. This generation frightened him. He knew that every parent, from time in memoriam, felt that each new generation was somehow different and worse than the last. And while that may have been true to some extent, it was nothing compared to what was happening now. It seemed to him the entire world had gone collectively insane.

He hardly recognized Sean anymore. The loud clothes, the long hair, the attitude; he seemed like he was angry all the time, at everyone and everything. Gone was the respect he'd been taught, replaced with resentment of anyone older than he was. And now, on top of everything, he'd been arrested for dealing drugs.

There were, of course, extenuating circumstances. It seems that things may not be as bleak for Sean as they first seemed. And then there was the fact that he'd just saved Billy's life. Leo had just come to a decision when there was a knock on the door and Sean poked his head in.

"Come in," Leo said, in a stern voice. Sean sidled into the room and closed the door behind him. He stood in front of the desk, hands behind his back, looking nervous as he shifted his weight back and forth from foot to foot. Leo let the tension in the cramped room build, letting his son sweat it out until he was ready. Finally, Leo spoke:

"Do you have anything to say for yourself?"

"I know I screwed up and I'm sorry. I never meant to get involved in any of this stuff."

"But you did."

"Yes sir," Sean said, hanging his head in shame.

"What you did is inexcusable. I never dreamed a son of mine could get mixed up with drugs. This is the first time anyone in our family has ever been arrested, you know."

"Yes sir."

"I hope it will be the last."

"It will. I promise. I'm never going to go near that stuff again."

"Good. I know you're a good boy, Sean. You made a mistake, but you're still going to have to pay for it."

"I know."

"I talked to Detective Murphy about an hour ago." Sean jerked his head up with trepidation. "They arrested this 'Joker' guy. He confessed and corroborated your story that you'd only started a few days ago, and he threatened violence against Billy if you didn't agree to sell his drugs."

"He did?"

"Yes. Detective Murphy said they're willing to drop all the charges against you if you'll agree to testify against 'Joker' at trial. I already said you would cooperate."

"Does that mean I don't have to go to jail?" Sean said anxiously.

"That's exactly what that means."

Sean let out the breath he'd been holding, and it seemed as if the whole world just got brighter.

"It doesn't mean that there won't be consequences."

"No sir."

"So, I have decided..." Leo let it hang in the air for a moment; Sean chewed on his bottom lip. "You will be grounded for one month."

Sean deflated visibly.

"Do you think that's unfair?"

"No sir. It's just that my band is entered in the Battle of the Bands next month. We just got a new bass player and we really need to practice. The other guys were counting on me."

"Okay, how about this: I'll let you postpone your punishment until after the contest."

"Really?"

"Well, I don't want to punish your band mates, do I?"

"Thanks Dad! You're the best!"

"One more thing..."

Sean looked at his father apprehensively.

"After you finish your punishment, you and I will take a trip down the shore to that big boat shop in Mantoloking and pick out your new Boston Whaler."

Sean's jaw dropped. He must've heard wrong.

"What?"

"Sean, you saved Billy's life today. And I think spending a night in jail was probably worse punishment than anything I could dish out. Detective Murphy told me you tried to return the drugs, but that maniac threatened to hurt Billy if you didn't do what he wanted. So, in a way, you saved him twice. Under the circumstances, I'd say you deserved a reward."

Sean was speechless. He stood there, gawking at his father, his mouth opening and closing without being able to find the right words. Finally, he ran around the desk and threw himself at Leo, hugging him fiercely around the neck. "You're the best father in the whole world! I love you Dad!"

"Okay, okay," Leo said, awkwardly hugging back and patting his son on the back. He was uncomfortable with physical displays of affection.

Sean pulled out of the hug and grinned at his father, his eyes glistening with moisture. "Go get ready for bed," Leo said. "You have to get up early to pick up your brother from the hospital."

I was still a little sore from the beating I took, but it was mostly superficial. I would have some bruises for a while, but there was no head trauma. And I hadn't been unconscious from asphyxiation in the dryer long enough to cause any brain damage, which is what they were really afraid of, so I was getting ready to go home.

I didn't have anything to pack except my pajamas and the clothes I'd been wearing when I was brought in. My mom brought me my pajamas and a change of clothes last night. It was still early and my mom wasn't here yet, but I was ready to go. Matt was going home today too, but he was still asleep and I didn't want to wake him. He looked really peaceful when he was asleep. I debated whether I should tell him he snores. That was one of the reasons I was awake so early.

"Good morning," Dr. Washington said when he came into the room. I put my finger to my lips and tilted my head in Matt's direction. He nodded understanding and whispered, "What are you doing up already? It's not even seven o'clock yet."

Just then, Matt inhaled deeply and demonstrated a mighty snore. "I couldn't sleep."

"I see," he said, chuckling. He poked and prodded with his hands and felt my forehead. "How are you feeling today?"

"Okay I guess."

"Ready to go home?"

"Oh yeah."

"No more climbing in dryers, okay?"

"Yes sir," I reluctantly agreed.

"And try not to get into any more fights."

I looked down feeling a little ashamed and nodded. It wasn't really a fight. Mostly I just got beat up. "When is my mom coming to pick me up?"

"I told her nine o'clock. It takes a while to get all your discharge papers ready. I'll be back in a little while; I have to do my rounds now."

"Okay Doc, thanks."

A few minutes after Sammy's dad left the room, Matt stirred. He opened his eyes, yawned, and stretched. "What time is it?" he said sleepily.

"Almost seven. How's your head?"

"Hurts. But it's a lot better than yesterday."

"Do you want me to call the nurse or get you some aspirin or something?"

"Nah. I'll be okay. How are you doing? You look like a big bruise."

"A little sore. I guess I look worse than I feel."

A short while later an orderly came in to deliver our breakfast. Everything I'd heard about hospital food turned out to be true: rubbery eggs, cold toast, and oatmeal. Blech! The only thing palatable was the orange juice, but they only gave us a tiny glassful. After we ate, Matt got dressed and packed. Then we spent the next couple of hours watching Saturday morning cartoons.

Right before nine o'clock, my mom and Sean arrived.

"Good morning, Honey," Mom said, rushing to my side and kissing me. "How do you feel?"

"Fine," I said, trying to look around her so I could see *Scooby-Doo*.

"Hey Tiger," Sean said, sitting next to me on the bed and mussing my hair. "You about ready to blow this popsicle stand?"

"Do you know when my dad is coming to get me?" Matt asked.

"I talked to him earlier and he said he'd be here around nine. He should be here any minute."

As if on cue, Max came into the room carrying a paper shopping bag. "Good morning, boys."

"Hi Daddy."

"Morning, Mr. Sherman."

"I got you guys something," he said reaching into the bag. He pulled out two cast-iron Corgi Batmobiles, causing both of our faces to light up.

"Wow!" Matt said.

"Holy surprise, Batman!" I said.

I immediately started playing with my new toy. It had a retractable blade on the front grill, shot little plastic missiles from the three tubes on the trunk, and the orange plastic "fire" from the jet exhaust on the back moved in and out when the rear wheels turned.

"You like them?" Max asked.

"Yes!" we said simultaneously.

"Max, you shouldn't have," my mom said. "It's so extravagant."

She was right, too. I remember seeing it in the store and wanting one really badly, but my mom always said it was too expensive. They cost something like sixty bucks! But man, it was *so cool!* Corgi made the coolest toys. Besides the Batmobile, they made the Bat-boat, complete with a little trailer to pull behind the Batmobile; the Black Beauty from *Green Hornet*; James Bond's Aston Martin with machine guns in the front and a pull-up bullet proof rear window shield; *Chitty-Chitty-Bang-Bang*, with pull out wings; and even a Yellow Submarine from that Beatles cartoon movie.

"Oh, don't be silly," Max said. "Anything for my boys."

I smiled when he said *'my boys.'* I didn't know Max felt that way about me. It felt good. Like having an extra dad. Not that he could ever replace my own Dad. But it's comforting to know another adult had my back.

"You two get ready to leave," Mom said. "Max and I have to go downstairs and sign some papers, but we'll be right back. Sean, you stay here with the boys."

"Okay Mom," Sean said absently, already engrossed in the cartoon. He may be twelve, but nobody can resist the awesomeness of *Scooby-Doo*!

When Max and Mom left the room, Matt turned to Sean and said, "So, what did they do to Butch?"

"I hope they kick him out of school," I said.

"Nope," Sean said. "Him and Joey got a three-week suspension is all."

"What? You're kidding!" Matt said.

"Dad talked to Sister Joseph and she said since it's so close to the end of the school year, and because it didn't happen on school property and after hours, she wouldn't expel them. She wants to give them one more chance."

"How many chances is he gonna get?" Matt said, incredulously.

"That's what my dad said," Sean said. "He's really mad. So's your dad."

"Good," Matt said.

"Your dad said he might even sue the school, but I think Lucy's dad talked him out of it. He said he wanted to try something first."

"Like what?"

"I'm not sure. Hey, but guess what?"

"What?"

"Dad said I could buy my boat for saving your life."

"Wow, congratulations. I hope that means you're gonna be nicer to me now."

"We'll see," he said with a wink. And then he did something he hasn't done in a long time—he gave me an atomic skull-crushing noogie. Even though I was still sore all over, I laughed until my side ached. Sean was back.

We finally left the hospital around eleven o'clock. For some reason it takes *forever* to check out. Mom and Max were downstairs filling out forms and signing their lives away for over an hour. When they finally returned to the room, it took the nurse another half hour trying to find wheelchairs for Matt and me. They wouldn't let us walk out on our own; they made us each ride in a wheelchair like we were crippled or something. Max said it was for insurance reasons. They didn't want us to fall and break a leg on the way out and sue them. Yeah, like that would ever happen.

When we got to our cars, I don't know why, but I got a sudden impulse to hug Matt. Then I hugged Max. I guess I was just happy we were both okay. Especially Matt. For a couple days there, I didn't know if he would ever wake up. We all said goodbye and I told Matt I would call him later.

In the car, Sean continued being extra nice to me. He hadn't been this nice to me in so long that it made me wonder if something was up. Not that I'm complaining, I really liked it.

Mom had the radio tuned to WABC, the local New York pop station that all the kids listened to, when the DJ came on and said, *"Cousin Brucie here, and have I got a treat for you. Hot off the presses, it's the brand-new single from The Beatles! Yes cousins, you heard me right. No, they haven't gotten back together, but there's still one last record that hasn't come out yet. It's the title song from the soon to be released movie and album,* Let It Be! *Remember, you heard it here first on W-A-Beatles-C!"*

It started with just a piano and then the unmistakable voice of Paul McCartney started singing. It was a melancholy song that somehow seemed to tell the fans this was really the end and to just "let it be." It made me sad. When it finished playing, Mom shocked us both when she said, "That was a nice song."

"What?!" Sean and I said together and exchanged surprised expressions.

"I really liked it."

"You *do* know that was The Beatles, right?" Sean said, making sure we heard her correctly.

"Mm-hmm," she said. "Just don't tell your father." Sean and I looked at each other and laughed. Well, what do you know? Maybe there's hope for her yet.

"Who wants White Castle?" Mom said a few minutes later. Enthusiastic agreement erupted from the backseat. We both loved White Castle. It was a drive-in fast-food restaurant where you parked your car in a slip and they took your order through a little microphone/speaker box. When your food was ready, a uniformed waitress brought it out to your car on a tray and hooked it to your window. The hamburgers are *sooo* good, and they were so small you could eat like a million of them, plus they only cost fifteen cents each so you could have as many as you wanted. My mom ordered a sack of twelve for all of us and we gobbled them down with fries and a Coke. Mom had two and Sean and I had the rest. Hey, we're growing boys!

We got home a little before noon. I was still sore all over and feeling a little full from lunch, so I went right up to my room and laid down. Even though I was only in the hospital overnight, it felt good to be in my own bed again. I didn't sleep, but I closed my eyes and just rested; something I almost never do, mostly because I could never sit still that long.

I heard Sean come in and go over to his side of the room. He was being so quiet; I opened one eye to see what he was up to. Nothing. He was just sitting on his bed watching me. I closed my eye again, but I could still feel him watching me. I don't know why, but I don't like being watched or stared at. It makes me uncomfortable. I opened my eye again and he hadn't moved.

"Quit it," I said.

"What?"

"Quit watching me. It's creepy."

"Sorry. I guess I didn't realize how much you mean to me until I thought I lost you."

I sat up. I could tell he really meant it.

"I didn't tell on you."

"I know."

I went over and put my arm around him.

"I really screwed up," he said.

"It'll be okay. You'll see."

"I promise I will never do anything to hurt you ever again. I'm so ashamed of the way I've treated you lately. Can you ever forgive me?"

"There's nothing to forgive. We all say and do things we don't mean and wish we could take back. I know you didn't mean it. But I still want you to quit smoking. And that other stuff too." I couldn't bring myself to say it, as though naming it would bring down a curse.

"I will."

"Promise?"

"I promise."

"Thanks."

"How come no matter how bad I mess things up, no matter how mean I am to you, you still stick by my side?"

"'Cause you're my brother. And my hero."

"You're pretty incredible, you know that?"

"About time you noticed."

Captain Apollo jerry-rigged a patch for his ruptured oh-two unit, essentially putting a Band-aid on it and restoring cabin pressure. Then he resumed his attack on the hull of the *Black Widow.*

Lucinda flew alongside him in the prototype ship and joined in the fight.

"Lucinda! Concentrate fire on their propulsion unit. That should cause a chain reaction and destroy the ship."

"We won't be able to get close enough. One hit from their weapons..."

"I disabled their weapons and shields. Hit them with everything you've got. On my mark."

"Target locked."

"Now!"

Both ships released an unrelenting attack on the *Black Widow's* engines. Laser cannons, proton torpedoes, and disruptor beams hit the engines at once.

It started small, one explosion deep inside the ships bowels. Then another larger blast. Then another, and another, larger and larger, spreading throughout the entire vessel.

"Lucinda! Get clear, she's gonna blow!"

"On my way, Captain!"

Both ships veered off, getting clear, just as the *Black Widow* exploded into a billion particles.

"Good bye, Shondo," Captain Apollo said sotto voce.

BOOM!!!

A laser cannon hit the captain's ship.

"AHHHHHHHHHH!!!" a deranged voice shouted through the com speakers. It was Mack the Black! She had somehow escaped, coming at him in a small one-man fighter. "You're mine Captain!" she screamed.

Captain Apollo braced himself—he was out of weapons. He'd spent them all on his attack on the *Black Widow*. Mack the Black's ship took aim, and... exploded!

"You're all clear sir."

Shondo!

"It's about time!" Captain Apollo said, not even trying to hide his jubilation. "What took you so long?"

"My apologies, Captain. I was... preoccupied."

"Good to have you back, old friend."

"Thank you, sir."

* * * * *

"Report!" Captain Apollo ordered from his brand-new command chair.

"Science station ready," Mr. Shondo said, back at his post.

"Engineering ready," Lieutenant Sherman said.

"Helm ready," Empress Lucinda said.

"Very good," the captain said. "Take us out."

"Heading Captain?" Lucinda asked.

Captain Apollo thought for a moment, and with a twinkle in his eye said, "Second star to the right and straight on 'til morning."

"Aye sir," she said smiling.

The newly refit and fully upgraded U.S.S. *Constellation One* advanced gracefully out of space dock. Once it had cleared the last of her moorings, they accelerated to light speed and, in the blink of an eye, disappeared among the countless stars into the vast reaches of space, boldly going where no kids had gone before.

The previously vacant area of the McBride basement had been transformed into the United Galactic Fleet's starship *Constellation One*. And it was all Sean's idea. It took a lot to convince Dad to let us convert half the basement into a spaceship, but since Sean and I relentlessly reminded him that he'd saved my life and it would keep me out of the dryer, Dad finally agreed to help us build it.

We spent the next week constructing our new "child safe" play center. Dad removed the mechanical inner workings—the guts as I called them—from the old washer and dryer and brought the empty shells into the basement. He left the lid on the washer and the door on the dryer so my playmates and I could climb through the "hatches." Then we put the two empty shells on opposite ends and connected them with the empty cardboard boxes the new appliances came in. Finally, we hung black curtains around the sides to enclose everything, leaving enough room open at the top for light to get in.

Inside, Dad constructed a simple "bridge" using plywood and cardboard, loosely based on the bridge of the *Enterprise* in *Star Trek*. Next, we painted; Dad spray-painted everything white, and

Sean and I detailed it with red stripes and the words U.S.S. *Constellation One* stenciled in black in the center.

Inside we painted the bridge in bright reds and yellows. On the back wall, I painted a "view-screen," making a rectangle in red and painting the inside black. I got all the kids to help me add hundreds of "stars" by painting little white dots on the black screen. The finishing touch was when Dad donated his black leather office chair. After all, he said, a captain needs his chair. It was a small sacrifice to make to see his son happy. Besides, he told me it was time for a new one anyway.

It was about the nicest thing anyone had ever done for me. I had the coolest play set a kid could ever hope for, and Captain Apollo had a *real* starship.

Ahead warp factor ten!

FOURTEEN

Four weeks later...

Sean, Lucy, Matt, Max, and I all walked out of the Mount Clayton Cinema feeling a little sad. Max had taken us to see *Let It Be*, The Beatles last movie together. The album had officially come out last Friday, May 8th, but Max had some connections in the record business and was able to get his hands on an advance copy embossed with the words, PROMOTIONAL COPY: NOT FOR SALE on the front almost three weeks ago. He made a copy for himself on reel-to-reel tape and gave the vinyl original to Sean. That gave Matt and me plenty of time to prepare our own little surprise for tomorrow's Battle of the Bands.

"So, what did you think?" Max asked us outside the theater.

"I liked it," I said. "It was cool watching how they make a record."

"I liked the concert on the roof," Sean said.

"I know!" Matt said. "Can you imagine what it must've been like for those people on the streets, just walking around minding their own business and then the music starts and *wham!* A free Beatles concert!"

"'Til the cops came and made them stop," Lucy added.

"Just think," Max said, "that was probably the last time they'll ever play together live."

"I still can't believe they broke up," Sean said. "It was weird, watching them all together like that, knowing they're not even a group anymore."

"Do you think they'll ever get back together?" I asked hopefully.

"I hope so," Max said, "but I doubt it. You could see in the movie that they were having problems. And they filmed that well over a year ago."

"Really?" Sean said, surprised.

"Yes. In fact, they shot the movie before they recorded *Abbey Road*, so even though this was released almost a year later, technically *Abbey Road* was the last album they recorded together," Max explained.

"How come it took so long to come out?" I asked.

"There were disagreements between John and Paul over the producer of the soundtrack, plus I heard they were having trouble editing the film and they wanted to release the record and the movie at the same time."

"So what's gonna happen to them now?" Lucy said.

"They'll probably go off and do their own thing. Paul already has a solo album out."

"Yeah," Sean said. "It's called *McCartney*. I bought it last week.

It's really good."

"I thought you were still mad at Paul for quitting the Beatles," I teased.

"Hey, life goes on right? If I learned anything from you, it's how to forgive."

"What about the other three?" Lucy said.

"I'm sure they'll all start making solo records soon," Max said. "Even though they might not be making music together anymore, you can bet we haven't heard the last from The Beatles."

"I sure hope you're right," Lucy said.

"Don't worry. I wouldn't be surprised if their best is yet to come," Max reassured us. "Now, who wants pizza?"

The next morning, Rachael Anderson parked her old beat up Buick in the church parking lot/school playground at the bottom of the stairs leading up to the church. Father O'Malley had called her the day before and asked if she could come to the rectory today. He said he needed to speak to her about a personal matter and to please bring Butch along, as it concerns him too.

He'd probably done something wrong at school again. That kid was always getting into trouble. He had already been suspended twice in the last month, once for three days when the McBride boy accidentally sat on a pencil, and then again for three weeks for fighting with the same kid.

He swore up and down that the other boy started it and he was only defending himself. But according to the school, the McBride boy was beaten pretty badly and Butch was lucky the police hadn't gotten involved.

Whatever he did this time, she would have to give him a good beating when they got home. She had to knock some sense into him, the same way her mama had done to her when she was a girl—it was the only way to teach him a lesson.

This was the first time she had been here on a Saturday and she was surprised to see four other cars in the parking lot. She guessed there must be some kind of committee meeting. The church always had something going on, whether it was a bake sale, or a raffle, or a pancake breakfast to help raise money for the poor. *They should give some of that money to me*, she thought.

"Behave yourself inside or I'll beat your ass right there in front of the priest, do you understand me?" she warned Butch.

"Yes ma'am," he sheepishly replied.

They exited the car and walked together up the stairs to the rectory door. She tried to look her best today, but she'd accidentally over-slept and didn't have time to do her hair and makeup. She'd had a late night, and although she didn't realize it, her pores were leeching alcohol; she smelled like a distillery. They reached the front door and rang the bell.

Father Scott greeted her. His shoulder length hair and mustache surprised her; *if not for the collar*, she thought, *he could be mistaken for one of those new-age liberal college professors that she hated.* He gave her a warm smile and shook her hand with both of his, placing his left hand over the top of hers.

"Mrs. Anderson, welcome," he said. "We're so glad you could make it." He turned his attention to Butch and mussed his hair. "Hello young man."

"Hi," Butch said, pulling his head away.

"Please," Father Scott said, stepping aside, "come in."

The group intervention had been Frank Ross's idea. After Lucy had told him about the bruises and welts on Butch's back, he suspected his mother of child abuse. Of course, it was possible the boy received his wounds from a bicycle mishap, or perhaps a fight—Lucy told him how he was always bullying and picking fights with other children, especially her friend Billy—but he doubted it. If that were the case, his bruises would be all over his body and not confined to his back. It was especially suspicious that he had no marks on his face. But he didn't want to go off half-cocked and start accusing someone of something as serious as child abuse without any proof. That was when he decided to hire a private investigator.

For the past two weeks, Mike Holmes from the Holmes & Watson Detective Agency had been watching Rachael Anderson. He'd watched her every day, getting to know her daily routine. She rarely left the house except to go to Hal's Liquor Store, where he photographed her purchasing her daily fifth of vodka.

She didn't work, living off her ex-husband's alimony and child support payments and food stamps. He interviewed the downstairs neighbors, a sweet elderly couple in their seventies, who invited him in for tea and regaled him with stories of her constantly yelling the most profane words at "that poor boy," calling him every vile name in the book.

And the beatings! They could hear Butch's screams of agony and the snap of the belt as she whipped him, all the while begging her to stop. It was horrible how she treated him. When Mike asked why they never called the police, they said it wasn't any of their business how she raised her son, and they didn't want to get involved. They were from a generation that believed in "spare the rod and spoil the child."

When Mr. Holmes gave Frank his final report, he'd decided to go to a priest rather than the police. It wouldn't do Butch any good to be taken away from his mother by the state and placed in the foster care system. That was liable to do more harm than good and Butch's mother wouldn't get the help she needed sitting in jail.

Father O'Malley agreed with him.

At first, he'd thought the problem was just child abuse, but after the detective's report it was clear she was an alcoholic too. Frank was the one to suggest the idea of an intervention.

Back in Texas, one of his co-workers had a pretty severe drinking problem. When it started to interfere with his job performance, his friends got together and held one for him. It seemed to do the trick. He started to attend AA meetings regularly, and it had been over a year since he'd had a drink. Father O'Malley liked the idea and suggested they hold it at the rectory.

Frank made some phone calls to some of the parents in Lucy's class and explained the situation. They all agreed to attend.

In the rectory conference room was Frank's wife Karen, Leo and Katherine McBride, Max Sherman, psychiatrist Dr. David Grey, Fathers O'Malley, Patterson, and Scott, and Sisters Joseph and Immaculata. The children present were Sean and Billy McBride, Lucy Ross, and Matt Sherman.

Father Scott opened the door and escorted Rachael and Butch into the room. She scanned the faces and started backing up.

"What's going on here?" she said nervously.

"Hello Rachael," said an unfamiliar bearded man in a tailored suit. "I'm Dr. Grey. Won't you sit down?"

"What is this?" she said, backing further toward the door. Father Scott stood in front of the closed door, blocking her exit.

"Please," Father O'Malley said, pulling out a chair for her, "have a seat."

Rachael sat down looking frightened.

"Sean," Leo said to his son, "why don't you take the kids outside to play."

"Come on," he said and led them all from the room, Butch included.

"What was that all about back there?" Butch demanded as soon as we were outside. "What do they want with my mom?"

"They just want to help her," Lucy said.

"Help her do what?"

"Help her with her drinking problem," Sean said.

"She's fine," Butch said defensively. "She doesn't need any help."

"She needs treatment," Sean said. "The doctor says..."

"To hell with the doctor!" he yelled. "And to hell with all of you too! What do any of you know about it anyway?"

"We know she beats you," Lucy said.

Butch's mouth dropped open. He looked like he'd just been slapped in the face. He wheeled on me. "You told!" he screamed. "I'm gonna kill you!"

Butch started for me, but Sean stopped him, holding him back by his arms. "Let me go!" he shouted, struggling to break free. "Let me go, I'm gonna kill him!"

"I don't want to fight you, Butch," I said. "I want to help you."

"I don't need your help! I don't want your help!"

"Everybody needs help sometimes," Lucy said.

"We're just trying to be your friends," I said.

"I don't need any friends," he insisted defiantly.

"Everybody needs friends," Matt said.

Butch struggled to break free of Sean's grip on him. "Let me go!" he screamed. Sean released him. He stood there panting, looking like a caged animal. He looked directly at me, narrowed his eyed, gritted his teeth, and lunged at me.

I turned my body and moved out of the way, dodging his attack. "I told you, I don't want to fight you," I said.

"Hold still!" Butch said, lunging at me again. Again, I avoided the attack.

In the last month since Butch and Joey ambushed me in the fields, my dad and Sean had been giving me a crash course in defensive fighting. It was always best to avoid a fight, my dad said, but sometimes you had to defend yourself. I'd learned that the hard way. The very first lesson I learned was, "The best defense is not to be there." Butch swung at me again, and again I avoided his fist.

"Fight me!" Butch yelled in frustration. "Unless you're too chicken!"

I sighed, realizing this wouldn't end until I fought Butch, and reluctantly I raised my fists.

"Finally!" Butch said and we faced off. We circled each other, while Sean, Lucy, and Matt gathered around us and shouted their support for me.

We threw punches at each other, some landed, most missed. Butch seemed surprised by my new ability. He actually seemed a little scared at the force behind my blows that struck home. Even so, Butch continued to taunt me.

"Is that all you got? You hit like a girl."

I bided my time. I didn't want to hurt him.

"Come on faggot, hit me!" He was trying to bait me, but I was doing my best not to get angry. "What's the matter? Is mama's boy gonna cry? You're nothing but a no good... lousy... *nigger lover!*"

That did it! Now I had something to fight for! I had to defend my friend Sammy's honor. I waited for my next opening. A second later, Butch momentarily dropped his guard and I hit him with everything I had square in the face. Butch flew back, landing on his butt, blood gushing from both nostrils. The second lesson I learned was, "Always go for the nose."

"You broke my nose!" Butch cried, tears streaming down his face. I took off my T-shirt, knelt down beside him, and put the balled-up shirt to Butch's face.

"Here, put your head back." I tended to my wounded opponent, while Lucy went to the rectory for some ice.

"Sorry about that. I didn't mean to break it," I said, then offered him my hand in friendship. "Truce?"

Butch looked into my eyes. Even after all the torment he'd put me through, I was determined to show him nothing but kindness. He smiled at me, nodded his head, and shook my hand.

The Mount Clayton High School gymnasium was filled to capacity for the Fourth Annual Battle of the Bands. The competition was open to any band whose members were residents of Mount Clayton, seventeen or under, and currently enrolled in school. There were nine bands competing this year. Each band was required to perform three cover songs and one original. There were three judges, each a local professional musician, including Max Sherman and rock star Tommy James, who had international hit songs with *Crimson and Clover* and *Mony Mony* and lived in nearby Nutley, New Jersey.

It was four-thirty in the afternoon and there was only one band left to perform. Before the show started all the bands drew lots—Octopus's Garden got the last slot. In a way, that was good, because they got to see who they were up against.

Out of the eight bands that had already performed, three of them were downright terrible—sloppy, out of time, and off key. Two were comprised of grammar school kids who showed real promise, but weren't quite there yet. Maybe in another year or two of practice. The remaining three groups were all in high school and were really quite good. The best was a band called The Moon Dogs, four tenth graders from Pope John's High School. Everyone seemed to agree, they were the band to beat.

Octopus's Garden was almost finished setting up on stage. Each band had twenty minutes to set up in between acts. Because the drums took so long to set up and break down, it was decided all the bands would share a community drum kit, provided by Sam Ash Music store in Paramus.

John Grady, Tim's replacement on bass, was a year younger than the other three, but he was really good. Way better than Tim, in fact. It hadn't taken him long at all to fit in. They finished setting up, did a quick sound check, and signaled the Master of Ceremonies they were ready to begin.

A small, white haired man in a gold sequined jacket named Jimmy Ricky, apparently a minor celebrity about forty years earlier, took the stage and stood in front of the center microphone. The noisy crowd died down when he raised his arms so he could speak.

"Ladies and gentlemen," he said, carefully annunciating every word. "From Saint Anthony's Grammar School... please give a warm welcome to..." He paused to consult the index card in his hand. "Octopus's Garden!"

The stage lights came on and the audience cheered as they broke into a rocking version of *My Generation* by The Who. They were good and they knew it. The audience loved them, and let them know it. When they began their second song, *Eight Days A Week*, the girls all screamed like they were actually The Beatles up there performing. Jimmy's guitar playing was flawless. When the song ended, the crowd went wild. Sean pulled the boom mike set up for the drummer to his mouth.

"Thank you!" he said, and they screamed even louder. "For our next song, I'd like to bring out our two newest and youngest members. On piano, Matt Sherman! And my little brother and best friend, Billy McBride!"

Matt and I walked out on stage. Matt sat down at the Roland electric piano he borrowed from his dad, and I stood at center stage in front of the mike. Ben came over and adjusted it, lowering it to my height. I looked out at the audience and swallowed. I'd never sang by myself in front of so many people before. When I sang at the Waldorf, there were only a few dozen people there and I was with the whole Boy's Club choir.

Some people in the audience laughed, most applauded politely. When they were silent, Matt began playing. The song was brand new, but when he played the intro chords, everyone instantly recognized it from the radio and clapped in approval. Then I opened my mouth and started singing the new Beatles song, *Let It Be*.

My voice was beautiful, angelic, and completely unexpected. I even surprised myself. The audience responded in kind, applauding enthusiastically. Lucy and Butch, who were standing together in the front row, clapped hardest of all. By the time I got to the chorus, the entire audience was on their feet swaying to the music as though they were at a concert at Madison Square Garden. When we finished the song, the house erupted with wild, foot stomping, ear splitting applause.

I was beaming as I looked out over the crowd. I took a bow, and they just applauded louder. I heard Sean's voice booming over the loudspeaker, "Billy McBride! Let's hear it for my little brother!" I took one last bow and ran off into the wings with Matt.

"How about my little brother, huh?" Sean said, and the audience cheered again. "And don't forget Matt Sherman on keyboards! Not bad for a couple of second graders!" More applause. "Our last song is an original inspired by Billy. We hope you like it. One, two, three, four!"

The band broke out into a hard rocking jam that got everyone on their feet. They were all having the time of their lives. Sean leaned into the mike and sang:

I'm an Apollo Dreamer!
Thinkin' about tomorrow
I've got Apollo Dreams!
Rocketing to Mars
Apollo Dreams!
Dreamin' of the future
With my love among the stars!

The audience was completely theirs and by the time they finished the song, the entire auditorium was on their feet for a standing ovation. Sean came out from behind the drums and joined the other three. Sean waved Matt and me back on stage to join them, and the crowd erupted even louder as we came out and took a bow with the band. We all left the stage together while the audience was still applauding and we huddled backstage.

Mom and Dad were waiting for us in the wings.

"You boys were fantastic!" Mom gushed, completely overwhelmed by the audience reaction.

"I have to admit, I'm really impressed," Dad said. "Especially you, Matt. I had no idea you could play the piano like that."

"Thanks," he said. "It helps to have a musician for a Dad."

The lead singer for the Moon Dogs, a longhaired sixteen-year-old dressed in black leather, walked over to us.

"I just wanted to tell you guys you were really great," he said. "If we don't win, I hope it's you."

We all looked at each other, shocked, and thanked him, acknowledging that they were really good too. We wished each other good luck and he went back to rejoin his own band.

Lucy and Butch joined us backstage. Butch's nose was swollen and he was starting to show two black eyes. Fortunately, Dr. Grey had been there to straighten out his broken nose for him, saving them a trip to the emergency room.

The intervention was a great success, and Rachael agreed to go to Alcoholics Anonymous and to see Dr. Grey to stop the abuse. Butch hugged her and told her he loved her and they cried together. Dr. Grey said that was the first step to recovery.

Lucy walked up to me and gave me a huge hug and a kiss on

the cheek. "You were great!" she said. "I wish I could sing like that!"

"Thanks," I said, blushing.

"Yeah, McBride, I guess you're not a total loser after all," Butch joked, and gave me a friendly sock in the arm. I grinned back at my new friend.

M.C. Jimmy Ricky came back out onstage.

"I need all the bands back out on stage. The judges have decided and we're going to announce the winners."

The nine bands all walked out on stage, each in our own group, and stood behind Jimmy Ricky.

"Ladies and gentlemen, in third place, from Mount Clayton Junior High... The Lightning Bugs!" The audience politely applauded as four boys came forward and accepted a small trophy.

"In second place, from Pope John's High School... The Moon Dogs!" The crowd clapped enthusiastically for the band, stomping their feet and whistling as they took their award.

"And in first place... with a check for five-hundred dollars... from Saint Anthony's Grammar School... Octopus's Garden!" The room erupted in thunderous applause as all six of us came forward. Jimmy Ricky handed a three-foot tall trophy to Sean. He stepped up to the microphone.

"Thank you!" Sean said to more applause. "I want to thank all our parents for supporting us, especially Mr. and Mrs. Mason for letting us practice in their garage and for putting up with us even when we didn't always sound so good." He paused while the audience laughed. "But mostly, I want to thank my little brother, who showed me what it means to love someone unconditionally, even when I was being a total jerk. I love you Billy!"

The crowd went wild again, chanting, “Billy! Billy! Billy!” Sean handed me the trophy and gave me a bear hug. I grinned from ear to ear as Sean lifted me off the ground and put me up on his shoulders. I looked out at the crowd chanting my name and raised the trophy over my head in triumph.

This was the best day of my life!

AUTHOR'S NOTE:

This is a work of fiction. All of the major characters are made up. Because it plays against the historical backdrop of 1970, the reader may recognize certain actual events and pop culture references. It is my hope that none of these references has been misrepresented. There is no town of Mount Clayton in New Jersey.

Bullying runs rampant in our society. Unfortunately, very little has been done since the era in which this story is set. Only through education and tolerance can we prevent this epidemic from spreading. If you, or someone you know, has been a victim of bullying please contact

www.StopBullying.gov for more information.

About the Author:

Syd Gilmore grew up in New Jersey with an affinity for science fiction, monsters, and music, but it was his passion for movies that drove him to Hollywood where he enjoyed a successful career in the film industry. He went on to option several screenplays before finally settling on novel writing. He now lives in the country, free from the noise, smog, and traffic jams that plague Los Angeles.

Made in the USA
Columbia, SC
01 July 2017